T0288276

KEEFER STREET

KEEFER STREET

David Spaner

RONSDALE PRESS

KEEFER STREET
Copyright © 2024 David Spaner

RONSDALE PRESS
125A – 1030 Denman Street, Vancouver, B.C. Canada V6G 2M6
www.ronsdalepress.com

Book Design: John van der Woude, JVDW Designs
Cover Design: David Lester
Editor: Robyn So

Ronsdale Press wishes to thank the following for their support of its publishing program: the Canada Council for the Arts, the Government of Canada, the British Columbia Arts Council, and the Province of British Columbia through the British Columbia Book Publishing Tax Credit program.

Library and Archives Canada Cataloguing in Publication
Title: Keefer Street / David Spaner.
Names: Spaner, David, author.
Identifiers: Canadiana (print) 20240427238 | Canadiana (ebook)
20240427254 | ISBN 9781553807209 (softcover) | ISBN
9781553807216 (EPUB)
Subjects: LCGFT: Historical fiction. | LCGFT: Novels.
Classification: LCC PS8637.P348 K44 2024 | DDC C813/.6 — dc23

At Ronsdale Press we are committed to protecting the environment. To this end we are working with Canopy and printers to phase out our use of paper produced from ancient forests. This book is one step towards that goal.

Printed in Canada

For the Spaners.
Anne and Jack, Linda and Karen.

PROLOGUE

Stanley Park, Vancouver, summer 1932

T O ME, THE WORD SPAIN ISN'T SO MUCH A COUN-
try as it is an event that began in 1936 and ended in 1939.
Spain means the Spanish Civil War. But before I turn to
Spain in the 1930s or return to Spain fifty years later, there
is a day in Vancouver.

Every summer Sunday, our family ritual in the park begins with
the tree, a hollow cedar large enough to swallow a car. As my
father, Isaac, slowly backs the Chevrolet inside the tree, my sister, Rachel, and brother, Eddie, and I press against the windows
for a closer look. Then it's on to a sprawling meadow, alongside
a track-and-field oval, where my mother, Frieda, unfurls her
picnic blanket from Lithuania and we rest in the warmth eating brisket and blueberries.

My father takes a moment to remind us that such idyllic
moments are fleeting. "Russia," he shudders, "was no picnic.
And the boat ride over here. There's a storm and the boat's like
a *meshuggena* rocking chair. And my arms holding on to this
pole and little Sam's arms holding on to my leg." Before we

leave the oval, Eddie, Rachel, and I play with a ball and bat. My father watches his children for a few minutes, then rises restlessly from the picnic blanket and steps up to bat. He lunges at my slowest pitch and misses. My mother leans back on the blanket and laughs. My father steps away from our imaginary home plate, adjusts his fedora with a white feather, then tries again. This time he connects, bouncing a grounder to Rachel. He smiles and returns to the blanket.

After baseball, we pile back into the family car and wind our way out of Stanley Park. As we exit the park, my father points to the tallest building facing English Bay. "That," he says, "is the hotel Abe Goldstein named for his girl Sylvia."

As our plane descends into 1986 Madrid, I look out at the sprawling city. At night, the city from the sky above, black with scattered white lights, looks like the sky from the city below — islands of light. The woman in the next seat turns to me. "What," she says, "do your children think about what you're doing here?"

"Proud, I think."

ONE

THE MOMENT TO LEAP

Toronto, summer 1933

'M IN COACH LEAVING THE TRAIN STATION IN REGINA when I see dozens of bedraggled men and women suddenly appear on a slight slope as if undergrowth rising from the soft yellow brush. I twist in my seat to watch as they race down the hill to the train, then leap into boxcars. One by one they board the train this way. One man misses. Hands reach for him. The train rolls across his foot. The man's face lets out a torturous cry that I can't hear but can see, and I turn away from the window. I barely sleep during the four days from the West Coast to Toronto, much of my time spent staring out at endless prairie stubbled by towns where grain elevators seem to rise as tall as the budding skyscrapers back home in Vancouver.

The train trip east began with a shout through my bedroom wall. The rainy winter had been broken by the less rainy spring, and I was on my bed watching the rain race down the window when my mother shouted from the bathroom next to my room. "Jakie, when school's out, I think you should leave Vancouver, go to Bessie for the summer." She continued her thought standing at my bedroom door. "You could have a lot of fun with the boys. I think it would be good for you to get away from this for awhile. *Loyf un freyen zikh.* Run and be happy."

My father had stopped talking the day before, after telling my mother that the family was moving back to Fort Harold, the small town in the Cariboo region of B.C. where he'd spent his first decade in Canada. My father's clothing store was dying on Vancouver's Hastings Street; he hated the city, he wanted to go north. "Isaac, there's nothing for me or the children in that place," my mother said. "You'll go where I say," he demanded, and their voices were angry, and then there were no voices at all. Whenever my father was angry, he spoke with fury for a moment, then stopped speaking entirely. This time, he aimed the silence at Frieda and the children, too, as though we were all party to a familial conspiracy to undermine his astute intentions.

At Toronto's Union Station, my aunt Bessie's bulky arms engulf me as my cousin Max takes hold of my new second-hand suitcase, and we head to the streetcar that will take us to their home off of College Street. "Everyone's been looking forward to you," says Bessie, and I don't answer, feeling pressured to deliver exemplary companionship without indicting her brother, my father, Isaac. "And how is your father?" she asks. "Everyone's fine," I say quickly.

Bessie is in mourning. A year earlier, her husband, Nathaniel Gold, died as the family waited in anticipation for him to bring home his first brand-new car. Nate and Bessie had been farmers in Russia. In Canada, at first they operated a farm near Palermo, just south of Toronto, but they soon moved into the city, and Nate lost most of their savings playing the ponies. Nate had been doing better of late, having invested in a small hand-sewn hat factory, but returning home with his new Studebaker, a truck swerved head-on into his lane, driving his car's long steering rod into his heart.

When I arrive in Toronto, Bessie and her six children are living in a red brick semi-detached house, with a small living room filled with music and chatter and friends from across the neighbourhood. It's two storeys with an attic overlooking Grace Street. The previous summer, the Gold residence was a different semi-detached house on another of the Jewish streets off College. After Nate died, Bessie worked as a seamstress in a Spadina Avenue garment factory, and the older children quit school and found whatever work they could, with the eldest, Milton and Solly, providing most of the rent.

Milton manages a neighbourhood bakery and Solly is a recent middleweight champion of Buffalo. Like many Jewish boxers of the Depression era, he fights with a Star of David on his trunks. Bessie is frantic with worry on Solly's fight nights. Although she's urged him to quit fighting and refuses to watch him do it, being the uncritically supportive mother that she is, she sewed the star on Solly's trunks when he asked.

Bessie knew to bring my cousin Max to the train station to meet me, and he is the relative I become closest to. One month older than me, Max is a young man on the prowl, with shoulders in a permanent hunch and lips in a cynical curl, unable to remain in any one place for more than a few seconds. Being with Max is a quick way to learn Toronto, especially this Jewish neighbourhood. Its main streets are College and Spadina but its heart is bustling Kensington Market, with its pickle barrels and *schmatta* vendors and bagel bakeries. The next neighbourhood over is Italian.

One late July evening, after a day on the Canadian National Exhibition's rides and midway, even Max is immobilized from the humid heat. Drained, sprawled out on the living room floor watching the radio, I'm instantly wide awake when my cousin, Florence, passes my line of vision with a friend, Lena Horowitz, I'd not seen before. My eyes follow Lena across the room and out the front door. The following day, Max, his friend Rosey Goodman, and I stop by the City Dairy for ice cream just as Lena and Florence exit with cones. Florence rolls her eyes as they pass, Lena nods unenthused. I look down and walk quickly into the Dairy. "Let's go to Sunnyside Beach," Max says. "Do Florence and Lena ever go to that beach?" I say. "Who cares?" Max says.

The next few days, Lena, back from counselling at a summer camp near Pickering, is at the Gold house again and again. While I am thoroughly taken by her, I'm also certain she is unaware of my existence. In her presence, I am mute, but it is a blissful mutation, lost in smitten glances at her dark brown, waist-length hair, her large blue eyes, and blushed red lips. Slowly, I draw a biographical sketch of Lena Horowitz. Born in Toronto, a classmate of Florence at Harbord Collegiate high school, Romanian immigrant mother a seamstress on Spadina Avenue and father a butcher in Kensington Market. She likes swimming, art, and politics, and she is going to the ball game today at Christie Pits.

I've been planning to go to Christie Pits too, because my summer in Toronto is ending and this is my last chance to watch Rosey Goodman play baseball. Today he'll be in centre field for Harbord, the Jewish nine playing St. Peter's for the city championship. In the first half of the twentieth century, baseball is the Sport of Entry for young immigrants, especially in American cities but in Canada too. In the beginning, it was called the New York Game — North America's most popular sport which, once understood, could take on a kind of secular religiosity. Instead of ever studying scripture, each morning I absorb box scores with the studiousness of a Talmudic scholar. To me, it almost seems as though high holiday gatherings are timed to celebrate the World Series. In Vancouver, I played second base on the Strathcona school team and would walk across town to Athletic Park, where I witnessed the first night ball game played in Canada. Nothing, however, prepared me for Rosey. Max and I go with Rosey to shag balls at a schoolyard one day. When I begin this activity by smacking one to centre field, Rosey makes a spectacular catch, then throws a wire to home plate. I put down my bat, turn to Max and say, "Can I just stand here and watch him." I jog into the deep outfield, and Rosey steps to the plate and casually whacks 400-foot flies to my cousin and me. "Next spring," Rosey says walking home, "I'll go down to Florida, try out for the Dodgers."

Arriving early at Christie Pits, Max and I sit with the other supporters of Harbord on a steep slope down the first baseline. Milton and Solly soon show up, but no Florence, no Lena. Farther along the slope, short-sleeved St. Peter's fans pass beer and chant at the diamond in the pit below. Harbord is down 3 to 2 in the third when Rosey comes up with two out and a teammate on second. Between pitches, both slopes are ethereally still. Then Rosey swings, and it's as though the ball is a choreographer taking everyone on the field into its dance. The quiet shatters, and the players are in motion as I watch the ball arc towards left centre field, past an outstretched glove. I'm on my feet with the rest of the Harbord section as Rosey slides feet first through a dust cloud into third base. All of this activity takes just a few seconds, then both slopes again are quietly awaiting the next pitch. The lead flip-flops until the final inning. When Lena finally enters the Christie Pits ballpark, she stands at the bottom of the slope, with Florence, looking upward at the crowd, considering where to sit. As I silently plea for her to sit near me, a Harbord fly ball ends the game, 6 to 5 for St. Peter's. What happens next I miss because I'm fixed on Lena.

It begins with a wail. Everyone around me is on their feet and shouting. I look across the infield at St. Peter's slope and see that a giant swastika banner has been unfurled, shouts of "Heil Hitler" rising around it. Everyone on Harbord's slope has seen the newsreels from Germany and now we move en determined masse towards the St. Peter's slope. Fighting erupts all over the diamond and spreads through the park.

This hot summer evening the battle spills into the park's side streets. A couple of miles away, word of the baseball riot quickly reaches Spadina Avenue's crowded street corners and pool halls. The Spadina-College-Kensington Market area is a tough, working-class Jewish neighbourhood with plenty of young boxers and wrestlers as well as the Bluta Boys — Blood Boys — street gang. These tough, young Jews have lots of friends in the equally tough Italian neighbourhood next door. With news of the riot spreading, stake trucks arrive on Spadina to load up scrappy children of immigrants — Jews and some of their Italian neighbours. They break police lines to war with the swastika mob that's armed with baseball bats, blackjacks, rubber hoses, and knives, and draw reinforcements from its neighbourhoods too.

In the days that follow, I learn the riot was incited by the newly formed Swastika Club, which has spent the summer attacking Jews and other immigrants on Toronto beaches and initiating brawls at ball games. Next door, in Quebec, a fascist movement led by Hitler dress-alike Adrien Arcand is on the march, and there are brown shirts and white sheets across western Canada too. I would find out about this later. This night, after getting separated from my cousins in the chaos, I throw some bricks and fists then walk the eight blocks to the Gold residence. I finally unclench my fist to open the door.

"Jake, are you okay?" my beside-herself Aunt Bessie greets me, as her youngest children, Sally and Jerome, huddle frightened in the hallway. Milton is home from the war too. "Where are the other boys and Flo?" Bessie says.

"I don't know," I say, sighing my first words since the riot started. Then I fall into Bessie's warm welcoming arms, unclenching my other fist, the aches and anger jumbled into a matrix of confusion.

"This," Bessie says, "too shall pass."

My mother meets me at the Canadian Pacific train station on Vancouver's waterfront, and we make our way to the house on Keefer Street. As we walk, I fill her in on Bessie and the cousins and summer in Toronto. She stops walking, gives me a searching look, then walks and talks faster than before.

"Your father has gone back to Fort Harold."

"You're not going back there with him then."

"No," she says. "Eddie is looking for work here and Rachel wants to stay too. Do you want to stay?"

"Yes, I do," I say without hesitation.

TWO

THE RETURN

Madrid, fall 1986

HE SKY IS ON FIRE.

A tri-motored swastika bomber plunges towards Spanish soil. Overhead, a pursuit plane of the Spanish Republic turns away triumphantly. My eyes follow the bomber's fiery descent to the Spanish earth where vigilant lefty loyalists, with their daggers and rifles and pitchforks, stride ever onward in blazing scarlet and rust.

I proceed to the next poster.

My flight arrived from Canada last night, so I'm still feeling tired as I slowly move through the gallery's display of posters from the Spanish Civil War. In the next poster, an International Brigade volunteer declares, "*El Frente Popular de Madrid al Frente Popular del Mundo*" — the Popular Front of Madrid is the Popular Front of the World. The posters on these walls have the urgency of a new art of colours on fire, with graffiti-style script about invincible, burning will, fashioned for civil war. As I glance through prints for sale, I decide on a peasant raising a scythe and shouting, "*Libertad*," then I leave past other internationals crowded in the hallway, waiting their turn at the posters from our Spain.

The night before I had taken a window seat on a tour bus bringing international volunteers for Spain from Madrid's airport to a dinner downtown. It's the fiftieth anniversary of the Spanish Civil War, and in the past twenty-four hours more than 350 volunteers from nineteen countries returned for a reunion. Stopped at a traffic light, I looked through raindrops to see teens crowded around tables of fast food at a Burger Haven restaurant on the ground floor of a steel-and-glass office tower. Glass, rain, fast food — *I could be in Vancouver*, I told myself.

Sal Scarsone, a New Yorker seated next to me, had the World Series on his mind. "I'll bet New York's won the first game."

Across the aisle, Joan from Boston said, "What a terrible thought, Sal, but the first game isn't until tomorrow."

"Haven't cared about a baseball score in a long time," I said.

Across the street from the restaurant, our driver found one of the last spots in a parking lot filled with the reunion's buses. As I walked over to the restaurant, a cab darted past without slowing, narrowly averting me. I froze for an instant, the remorseless cabbie derisively shaking his fist at me. This was immediately followed, though, by another cab driver offering me the clenched-fist, half-cocked-arm salute of Republican Spain. When I got inside the cavernous restaurant, the Class Struggle of 1936 Reunion had begun. Near the doorway, I paused, until I saw a small Maple Leaf flag on a table, and I worked my way to these other veterans of Canada's contribution to Spain's International Brigades — the Mackenzie-Papineau Battalion. Mac-Paps for short.

I reached the Canadian table just in time to see Mac-Pap veteran Bob Mitchell cock a goatskin wine bag above his head. "I've never forgotten how to do this," he said, then spritzed the red wine on his chin instead of in his mouth.

"You've forgotten how to do this," said Tom Barkley, a veteran from suburban Toronto. We laughed.

At the next table, veterans of America's Abraham Lincoln Battalion were belting out a battle hymn: "There's a valley in Spain called Jarama...It's a place that we all know too well.... For 'tis there that we wasted our manhood... And most of our old age as well.... You will never be happy with strangers. They would not understand you as we." The singsong and conversations slowly quieted when master of ceremonies Josh Beren stood at the long head table, behind the banner proclaiming: ABRAHAM LINCOLN BRIGADE. A Lincoln captain in Spain, then a print shop–owner on Staten Island, Beren began the night's formal proceedings by introducing the mayor of Madrid's assistant.

"You are heroes," the mayor's assistant declared, then one by one we volunteers for Spain were summoned to the front to shake a hand and pin a medal on ourselves. Belated medals, with an outline of Spain, a wreath, a three-cornered star, reading *Homenaje A Cas Brigades Internacionales—Cincuentenario de las Brigadas Internationales, 1936–1986*.

The first veterans called up to the head table drew rousing ovations, but after the first few medals the din of conversation returned. I did not for an instant doubt the good intentions of the people doling out medals at the table, but receiving a medal in Spain was the last thing on my mind when I went halfway around the globe to get here in 1936. I had no doubt I would leave for Spain. It was an overwhelming feeling then, and now I was overcome at being in the same room as hundreds of men and women who did what I did fifty years ago. So I'd stopped hearing the voices at the head table. Instead, I was moved by the faces at these tables. The radiant faces of these nurses and soldiers who went to Spain too, my comrades in arms who, now, in this room, looked fully content to be back in a place that has given purpose and definition to their lives.

The man seated next to me nudged my arm. "I'm Peter Krawchuk," he said. "What's your name?"

"Jack Feldman."

"Did you fight in Spain?" he asked.

"Yes."

"Then," he said, holding up the medal strung around his neck, "why weren't you called up to get your medal?"

"I might have been. I wasn't paying real good attention."

"Then you should go up there now and see what gives."

I made my way to the head table. Upon reaching the front, I shook hands with the assistant to the mayor, who got the okay from Josh Beren, then fumbled with the box of medals and handed me mine. As I turned to leave, I saw an American man struggling, limping to get to the front, his slender torso weighted by a trench coat decorated with medallions and buttons and pins. He reached the table, exchanged words with Beren, who scanned the log. Beren shook his head at the American. "Not on it," he said. "But I fought in Spain. It's the one thing I never questioned. I..." said the distraught old man. "We don't have extras," said Beren. "Leave us your address. We'll mail you one." I handed the man my medal. "Take it," I said. The American put it around his neck. Startled by this give and take, Beren told me, "We'll mail *you* one."

After the dinner, I checked into the Hotel Convención. Before bed, I descended to the hotel bar, where Tom Barkley and his wife, Susan, sat with another Mac-Pap and a man at least thirty years younger. "I'm saying," Tom told me as I pulled up a chair, "that we would have won the war, hands down, if Mackenzie King and FDR and the rest of those bastards hadn't set up the blockade to keep arms from the Republic. Isn't that right, Jack?"

I told them that the day I left Spain, I was on a railway car in Perpignan, just across the border in France, where I could see stockpiles of weapons that had been sent to the Republicans from the Soviet Union and Mexico. "The blockade prevented them from reaching Republican troops."

"Jesus," said Henry Simmons, the other Mac-Pap at the table. "On the train to France, leaving Spain, you could hear the artillery in Barcelona. The fascists were attacking as we were leaving the country. That was hard to take. Then on the boat to England, we heard that Barcelona had fallen."

"You were repatriated. Had to leave Spain," said the younger man at the table, Jim Heathcott, an ex-U.S. Marine living in Valencia. A Vietnam War veteran, he met Lincoln Battalion veterans at a dinner in Madrid a year ago and volunteered to help organize this two-week reunion. "My father was in W-W-Two," Heathcott said. "He didn't talk about it much, but I knew which drawer he kept his medals in. He was a good man and I grew up believing soldiers were good men. So I went to war in Vietnam and lost everything I believed in. When I met Mel Fox in Madrid he restored my faith. What you guys did was the heroic act of the century."

Heathcott quaffed his beer and jerked from the table. "I'm going to bed. You boys should too. Long day." Dropping coins onto the table, Heathcott added, "Tomorrow morning, buses are taking people to see Civil War posters. I'm going with another group to Toledo. And later there's a big reception."

"I'm turning in too," Tom said.

"I'm bushed from that flight," said Henry. "What time is it back in Victoria?"

There were two entertainment options in my hotel room — I ignored the Spanish-language bible on the bedside table and turned on the chained-down television set. In bed, I glanced at the next day's reunion schedule, then channel surfed, passing nightly news broadcasts, stopping at John Garfield with Spanish subtitles in *The Fallen Sparrow*. I wondered if some programmer at this Madrid TV station purposely scheduled this movie — clearly about a member of the Abraham Lincoln Battalion — to coincide with this reunion of the volunteers for Spain. Probably a coincidence, I decided, but it's exactly what I wanted to watch and I'm soon fixed on this hotel TV screen.

John Garfield's character is back home in New York after fighting in Spain. He's determined to find the killer of his closest friend, Louie Lepetino, who'd helped him escape a Franco prison. "This isn't Spain," Maureen O'Hara says. "You're out of that world now." O'Hara is pleading with Garfield to acquiesce to Hugh Beaumont, an actor better known as Ward Cleaver, the father figure on *Leave It to Beaver*. This night on Spanish television, however, he is in a movie made long before he is Ward Cleaver, playing a German agent out to abscond with the International Brigade banner Garfield has brought home from Spain. "Please," O'Hara implores Garfield, "give it up."

"Maybe I can't tell it so you understand. It's mixed up and hard to tell," says Garfield. "There are some things you've got to do. It doesn't matter what you think about it or how afraid you are. You just have to do it. What else makes a man go up against a tank with only a rifle in his hands?"

America's father, Ward Cleaver, glowers at American rebel John Garfield, whose real life was devastated by the Hollywood blacklist.

"You," Garfield tells Cleaver, "should have been in Spain, sweetheart."

"Why?" says Ward.

THREE

BEYOND THE PALE

Vancouver, fall 1933

RACHEL IS FOURTEEN, I'M SEVENTEEN, AND EACH morning together we make our way to school through Strathcona, a neighbourhood that is a patchwork of neighbourhoods, its air spiced with latkes and pyrogies and provolone. To stay fit, I alternate running and walking each of the city blocks. When I run, Rachel tries to keep up, then falls back, then I wait for her and we walk and talk.

"Mom says I can go to Toronto next year like you did this summer," she says.

"I thought you wanted to go to Fort Harold."

"I decided not to, though I'd like to see Dad, wouldn't you?"

After she goes into the school through the "Girls' Entrance," I go shoot pool up on Hastings Street with my friend Art Posner. Skipping our grade 12 classes to play pool has become a regular pastime for Art and me this school year.

In Depression-era Vancouver, my mother is struggling to keep the family from fracturing any more than it has. Eddie is done with school but can't find work. The people I had watched hop rails on my train ride back to the West Coast all wound up in Vancouver it seems, some heading on to Vancouver Island or to the province's Interior, where for twenty cents a day they live at military-operated relief camps and work building roads and parks.

"I'm going to Vancouver Island to look for work," Eddie says at the dinner table.

"No, we'll get through this together — here," my mother says.

"You can't make the rent working as a seamstress," says Eddie, "and there's no work for me here. There's a relief camp on the island, building a park. Better than nothing."

"I would look in Vancouver, Jakie, I mean, Eddie."

"I haven't looked?" he says, exasperated.

"Look some more."

Two weeks later, Eddie leaves. For now, Rachel and I continue at school. Nights are spent around the radio in the house on Keefer Street, listening to Ed Wynn, the Goldbergs, Eddie Cantor. One evening, we're settling in to listen to George Burns and Gracie Allen when my mother pulls an envelope from her purse. "From Eddie," she says, unfolding a note.

"Finally," says Rachel. "Why didn't he write earlier?"

He's found work in a relief camp on Vancouver Island. There is a $5 bill in the envelope.

"I guess he didn't write sooner because he wanted to send something," my mother says. "Now, you two take the money and after school tomorrow go down to Woodward's and get something for yourself."

"Swell," Rachel shouts.

"But Mom," I say, "Eddie sent the money to you, not me."

"No," she says firmly.

And I don't argue. Twenty-two years earlier, there had been a quick romance, a sudden marriage, and Frieda was in a northern town with a near stranger. She left for the Canadian West with little more than the pieces of New York still found in the house in Strathcona — the satin chestnut pillow purchased on Grand Street, the kosher china, the woven red tablecloth her grandparents brought from Lithuania. Now, she has little beyond bare necessities to give to her children so, instead, she gives herself. She gives her pies, her uncritical support, her roof. It is a way of taking too, of finding satisfaction. So I don't argue.

After school the next day, Rachel and I walk to Woodward's department store, cutting through Chinatown, where shopkeepers cart produce onto the sidewalks, and exotic silks and opium are exchanged behind mystery storefronts. On to Hastings Street, with its handful of movie theatres and display windows left over from its brief era as a fashionable core of the city. There is another side to Hastings, its bars and hotels attracting gaunt men and women in tattered clothes, huddling against buildings or dancing a beggar's jig to keep feet warm through soles worn thin. Passing an alley, I glimpse a bonfire blazing from a rusted barrel encircled by roofless women and men.

Inside Woodward's department store, I browse the books and magazines and toy department, while Rachel looks at shoes. We meet in the cafeteria to sip Cokes.

"Jake, I think I should go to New York instead of Toronto. The way Mom talks about New York, it sounds so exciting. Broadway." Rachel was in her school's production of *The Desert Song* and is star-struck, with a consuming infatuation for Busby Berkeley musicals and Robert Taylor. After school, at least once a week, Rachel and her friend Polly Siegel walk to the Rex Theatre. They had planned to see *42nd Street* forty-two times, but protests from my mother and I kept it down to five. "Have you talked to Mom about New York?"

"Not yet, but she'll like it. The Pikes are in New York."

The $5 buys two sweaters and there is enough left over to get our mother a Burnt Almond chocolate bar, her favourite.

That evening, as we settle in to listen to Jack Benny and Mary Livingstone, Rachel broaches New York.

"I'll write your Auntie Miriam tomorrow," my mother says, no questions asked.

Before immigrating to Canada, Isaac lived in a Jewish village, a *shtetl*, in the Russian Empire's Pale of Settlement, surrounded by his sprawling family. Russian Jews were forbidden to live beyond the Pale. There were summer stays in the nearest city, Odessa, with more family members. Of these, only Isaac's younger cousin Sam, who travelled with him, and sister Bessie, who followed the next year, would also cross to North America.

After passing through the immigration station at Grosse-Île, on the St. Lawrence River, and before travelling west, Isaac deposited Sam with an acquaintance in Montreal and dipped down to visit a neighbour from the shtetl who was starting over in New York City. Isaac couldn't find his friend but he found Frieda Pike. He turned a corner onto Houston Street and saw Frieda walking briskly down the crowded sidewalk. She was walking ahead of Isaac, so he couldn't see her face, just her long dark hair falling straight to her knees. He followed, entered the tailor shop she entered. She stepped behind the counter, turned around, and finally, he saw her face. Strong, heavy-set, beautiful. He approached the counter and asked if she could stitch his broken belt.

Romance came quickly. Frieda and Isaac married, took the train to Montreal, then followed the track across the continent, selling men's clothing from the tent they would pitch along-side railway stations. Their travels stopped in Fort Harold, a town near the centre of British Columbia. A town "with a future," Isaac said. Eddie was born, then I was, then Rachel. Isaac worked nine hours a day, six days a week, to establish Feldman's Mens' Wear, from tent to awning in five years, only to sell it and move to Vancouver with Frieda.

The man born in a Russian village was more at home in Fort Harold than the woman born in Manhattan was. The move to Vancouver was a last-ditch compromise to preserve their marriage. While neither had thought much about Vancouver, it was somewhere between Fort Harold and New York and just maybe a place both could be comfortable with, particularly its Strathcona quarter. My mother found work as a seamstress at the Gastown Garment Company, my father opened a small Feldman's Mens' Wear.

I had to run to keep pace with my father's walks on the waterfront. In a white shirt buttoned tieless at the neck and a fedora with a white feather, he whistled the entire walk, one long melodious tune. I blow and huff and blow but not a sound. Following this daily walk, my father cuts home through an alley. This day, a man with one hand holding a bottle sits slumped on a backdoor step. "He was in the world war," my father says. As we return to the porch on Keefer Street, he reaches into his pocket. "Take this two-bits. You need a haircut."

Next afternoon, my pockets inside out, room upside down, I can't find the quarter. When Isaac gets home he rages when I confess that I've lost it. "I work for that gelt. Hard," he says, pulling the belt from his pants and chasing me barefoot into the rain. I shiver in the cold early dark for more than an hour, until my mother furtively slips me through the kitchen door to my warm upstairs room.

The romance over, my father felt like a stranger in Vancouver, bitterness and emptiness growing with the years, and it was all the fault of this New York woman who could never understand his cold, blunt northern life. In Fort Harold, he is back to his Russian roots. For my mother, the marriage had passed the breaking point and she was not at all sorry to see him go. She wasn't fully satisfied with Vancouver either, but at least it wasn't her husband's place, and it wasn't her parents' place, and it was a place she could live with.

My mother has never seriously considered moving back to New York, but she sees now that Rachel wants more, and how can she deny her daughter what she has denied herself. So she writes her family in New York that Rachel will be coming. Rachel finds after-school work at Sammy's Delicatessen, on tables and behind the counter, to save for her summer out east. Eddie works on the island, sending what he can. I'm finishing up high school.

At first, my mother doesn't say a thing, not wanting to worry us, but she's barely drawing rent and food money from the Gastown Garment Company. A week of potatoes and rice with milk finally moves her to speak. "I don't know how I'm going to pay the rent this month," she says louder than the living room radio. "Even with the money Eddie sent."

"I've saved twenty-seven dollars for New York. You can have that," Rachel says.

"No. That is your money. You worked for it. Miriam writes that they're so looking forward to your visit."

"She can go another time," I say, turning to Rachel. "Give Mom the money."

"I will, but don't talk to me that way, Jake," Rachel says. "I don't see you giving her anything."

"No, she has to go to New York," my mother says.

"Let her hop a train then," I say.

"I hate you, I hate you," Rachel yells, running from the room.

"Don't you ever talk to your sister that way, Jakie. You went out east. We paid for that. Rachel's entitled to use the money she's earned."

I grab my coat and boots, put them on outside the front door, and walk into the rainy night. Long strides, determined to walk forever. The rain pokes my face, flattens my curly hair, pastes my dungarees to my legs, soaks my hands red. My mother and sister are at the table when I step through the kitchen door, water dripping from my clothing, as though my entire body is crying.

"It's pouring," I say quietly.

"Looks like you were swimming in it," says my mother.

"I'm sorry," I say to Rachel. "I'm going to quit school and look for work."

"No," my mother shouts. "I've always told you, no. You've only got a couple of months to go to finish school."

"Look, you can refuse to take anything from us and we'll wind up in a one-room flat with nothing in the icebox," Rachel says.

"Or we can all pitch in," I say.

My mother gives her children an anguished look.

"I want you to get an education," she says softly.

"I read books," I say.

"Let's go to sleep," she says with resignation, "and we'll talk about it in the morning."

The next morning at the kitchen table, as my mother places a plate of fried matzo in front of me she speaks in the matter-of-fact tone that comes with no options.

"Don't quit school," she says, "until you've found a job."

Rachel and I walk to school. She enters through the Girls'
Entrance. I step towards the Boys, then turn into the rain to
look for work.

The relief camp is isolated. Unable to find a job in Vancouver,
I am glad to have work, any work. Doing road work for twenty
cents a day leaves little to send back home, but at least now I'm
not another expense for my mother. Second day on the job in
the B.C. interior's Okanagan region, I venture into Osoyoos, the
nearest town, and join some of the work crew at a hotel barroom.

"I've been doing this shit for a year," says Billy, from Castlegar.
"Got a wife and kid who are living on vouchers back home. It's
just hopeless."

"I didn't do hardly nothing today," says Lon, from Vancouver.
"First relief camp I was at I actually worked at tree planting.
Today, I moved wheelbarrows of dirt from one place to another,
as slowly as I can."

"Jimmy," says Billy, turning to the older man seated next to
him. "I don't know about this strike, Jimmy. What are we doing
that anybody gives a shit about anyhow?"

Jimmy Lowry is in his sixties, with salt-and-pepper whis-
kers, a face weathered by work and wander, union battles, and
prize fights. "Driftin' an' agitatin'," he says. Word around camp
is Jimmy was a Wobbly organizer in the States, arrested for
hobo-syndicalism in the clampdown of 1919. Whatever Jimmy
has done, he wears the sobriquet "working stiff" like a wizened
badge of honour.

"That is precisely why we should strike, Billy," says Jimmy,
his Scottish inflection's volume rising. "They don't care about

us or most of the work we do, and they like us residing here where they think they don't have to see our miserable mugs. We can sit up here and gripe all we like and nothing's going to change, but when we strike the camps and flood the city, they'll take plenty notice."

"But I got a wife and kid, Jimmy, and just want to get on with life without any nonsense," says Billy.

"Is what you did today getting on with life?"

"You're no spring chicken, Jimmy boy," says Lon. "A strike? What's in it for you?"

"No, I don't get paid to do this," Jimmy laughs. "I get something else out of it. When I was a youngster, a teacher told my class, 'If you're a conservative when you're young you got no heart, if you're a socialist when you're old you got no brain.' Thing is, he was an old conservative."

We laugh.

"Old socialists like me don't speak that way," Jimmy continues. "People like that teacher will tell you that the world is always this way, that way. But you've never been here before and you can make of the world what you will. Speak up. Speak alone, if need be. Speak together, if that's what it takes. But speak up."

The next morning, I push a wheelbarrow up a slope, through evergreens, turn from the soil I've just emptied to see Jimmy Lowry standing a few feet away, hands on hips. "You a city lad?"

"Yeah, Vancouver." I'm surprised that Jimmy has any interest in me because I'd been quiet at the barroom table. Didn't like the taste of beer, so slowly nursed one glass the entire evening while others tossed back mug upon mug. Even the one left me buzzy and I sat back, too much of a novice to participate, more inclined to observe the room's acquired gestures and loud voices, all of which made me like the beer even less.

"I could tell you're city the way you handle the work," says Jimmy, offering a toothy smile.

I shrug and begin down the slope. My hands have been worked into blisters and I don't relish hearing Jimmy's critique.

His smile fades. "Hey, I'm not running you down. You're a hard worker. That's the point — you're working too fast. Don't want to make the rest of us look slow, now do you?" I leave, in no mood to take instructions from Jimmy any more than orders from the military commandant overseeing the camp. Despite my obstinance, though, on just this third day at work I'm feeling as much disdain for the camp as anyone, including Jimmy.

Two weeks of moving dirt and I've barely saved $2. The barroom is nearly empty when I arrive after work. I don't like this place but can't think of anything else to do and its bleakness complements my own. I sit at a table by myself studying the beer glass, wondering if it might be more palatable were I to chug rather than sip. I press the mug to my lips, toss my head back, and as I pull the glass from my face, my eyes meet the eyes of Jimmy Lowry, who's standing at the table, watching me complete the gulp. Jimmy slides into a chair across from me. "Didn't mean nothin' by that city-boy crack. You're a good worker.... Notice you're also a mite slower worker the past few days."

"Wouldn't want to show anyone up," I say with a smile. "I've been thinking about what you said."

"When I was a lad in Glasgow, I went to work on the docks but a pugilist was all I wanted to be. I would have a few professional bouts all right. Well before that, however, there's a long strike on the docks. I'm fifteen, haven't thought about society and its troubles, certainly nothing about relations between the bosses and workers. The army came down on the picket line, and a strapping soldier, well over six feet tall, knocked down an old woman standing there in solidarity with us. I was no more than five foot five, but I was always in the gym boxing, so I belt him a good one. Knocked him cold." Jimmy shadow jabs, follows with a right cross, quaffs his drink, and leans inches from my face to deliver his punch line. "We get to court and the union lawyer asks the judge, 'Do you believe that wee lad,' and he points to me, 'could knock out this Goliath of a man?' And he points to the soldier. The judge tosses the whole thing out of court."

Jimmy lets out a laugh and I do too. We're joined by Billy and two others. Still haven't acquired a taste for beer, but this time the loudness and laughter don't seem so sad.

"Jimmy," says Billy, "you figure the camp will close down this week?"

"I expect so. The Relief Camp Workers' Union is collecting the strike votes, and any day now I expect word to shut it all down and head for Vancouver."

"Can't survive on twenty cents a day," I say.

"We'll go into that city until something is done," Jimmy says. "Cause a ruckus and see how it goes from there."

As we walk back to makeshift shacks near the work site, Jimmy tells me he's going up the mountain tomorrow. "Just like to get away at times. I'll wake you up at six in the morning if you'd like, and you can go up the mountain too."

We walk in the brisk Okanagan Sunday morning, silent at first, then responding to Jimmy's curiosity, I talk about family in Vancouver, summer in Toronto, train-hopping in Regina. As we walk, the cold darkness lifts and by the time we reach the foot of the mountain it's covered in a glistening, dewy blanket of sun.

"Anarchist Mountain," Jimmy proclaims. Formerly Larch Tree Hill, it was renamed Anarchist Mountain by Irish immigrant Richard G. Sidley, the area's customs officer and justice of the peace until he was stripped of the posts. "Surely, anyone who names a mountain Anarchist isn't going to hold those posts for long," says Jimmy. This stone anarchist is at the fringe of one of Canada's only deserts, and the Okanagan's usual pine and fir share this corner of the region with unexpected bouquets of cactus and sagebrush. We explore the mountain, emerging from sparse forest to find a small sloping field, dotted with turquoise brush, overlooking a valley of orchards. Jimmy seems to know the name of every bit of vegetation. Finding a soft perch in the blonde wheat grass, he pulls two books from his satchel. "Have you read this one?"

I accept Jimmy's battered copy of Theodore Dreiser's *Sister Carrie*, prop my head against a boulder, and begin to read. Slouched in the comfort of the sun, I'm immersed in written worlds as the spring day thaws.

A deer steps from the woods and we peer over the tops of our books, watching her share our solitude, arcing her neck to eat desert weeds. "I shot a deer once," Jimmy says quietly. "Shortly after I came to Canada, I was working up north and went hunting with some of the guys. Heard something and turned and shot. I walked over to the deer and its big, beautiful brown eyes looked up into my eyes as if to say, 'What did I ever do to you?' Never hunted again." I go back to my book, and the deer is joined by its fawn, seeming oblivious to our presence.

The air begins to chill and the sky darkens. Time to leave this tranquillity and head back to camp. I hold *Sister Carrie* out to Jimmy. "Keep it," he says. "Read it." By the time we reach the camp it is dark, but relief workers sit around a bonfire laughing and drinking.

When Billy catches a glimpse of us, he shouts out, "Jimmy, we're shutting it down tomorrow."

Jimmy joins the group and its talk about descending on the city. I stand at the edge of the group, in flickering shadows, watching, feeling excitement at what is brewing but also curious at some of the men's certainty about the future. I retreat to the shack and collapse onto the bunk, unmade from the morning's quick getaway. Read for a few minutes but my thoughts are on tomorrow.

FOUR

NO PASARAN

Madrid, fall 1986

T HE MADRID THEATRE IS FILLED WITH VOLUNTEERS from everywhere. They're feted by speaker upon speaker, who talk Civil War and current politics. And then a Spanish poet says it: "*No pasaran!*" He is referring to 1986 Nicaragua. To most in this audience, though, "No pasaran" (They shall not pass) were the words on the banners strung across Madrid streets fifty years ago when the city held against the combined force of Hitler and Mussolini and Franco. These words were spoken again the November 1938 day when departing volunteers paraded through Barcelona and shed tears to be going home before their war work was done. Now, in this ornate theatre — the Palacio de Exposiciones y Congresos — at first only a few voices repeat the poet's words, then his words rise slowly throughout the room until the entire audience is on its feet shouting "no pasaran" so loudly that I cannot even hear my own voice in the crescendo, but I'm shouting too.

The speeches resume, and as they wind down I slip out to meet up with other Mac-Paps in the lobby. We've been invited to the Canadian embassy this afternoon for crackers and wine.

"Have you seen Tom Barkley?" Bob Mitchell asks me.

"He was on the bus coming here. I'm sure he's around somewhere."

"That's Barkley. Always around when you don't need him," Henry Simmons pipes up.

"Look," says Bob, "we're supposed to be at the embassy in forty-five minutes. There's eight of us here now, and unless Tom shows up in the next five minutes I'm going to hail a couple cabs and leave without him."

Ten minutes later, I'm in the back seat of the second cab, pressed up against Henry, who is pressed against a reporter from Toronto, who is fidgeting with a tape recorder. He plans to capture Henry's memories for a magazine piece about the Canadian battalion.

Irene Blair is in the front seat. I met her two days ago when she sat next to me on the flight to Madrid. During the Civil War, Irene never left Canada but she was in a Spain support group that sent medical supplies and organized public meetings. The moment she heard about the reunion she knew she would come.

Two blocks later, the first cab veers to an abrupt stop. Bob Mitchell has sighted Tom and Susan Barkley on a sidewalk, and he bounds from the cab and calls to them to join us. Irene asks our cab driver to stop too. After a brief exchange with Bob, Tom moseys over to my open window, says there's no room in the other cab. So Tom and Susan find a way to squeeze into our already crowded taxi.

"Where were you, Barkley?" Henry snaps.

"Susan and I finally found some food we can eat. It was this schnitzel place and—"

"Just like the food in Scarborough," adds Susan.

Henry grunts, and the cab departs with a start, heaving our compacted bodies. "I was born in Demaine, Saskatchewan. My folks loved the land," Henry says into the reporter's recorder. "Grew up in Winnipeg."

"Can you two guys discuss Henry's childhood later on?" says Tom, squished on top of Irene's lap as our cab tails Bob's cab through twisting Madrid streets. "We're like bloody sardines in here, and Henry's voice is making me claustrophobic."

"Get out of the cab," Henry barks, shoving Susan's feet off his knees. "Stop the cab. How do you say 'stop the goddamn cab' in Spanish?"

The cab doesn't stop. "We can do the interview later," says the reporter, snapping off the recorder.

"You going to interview me too?" Tom says.

When the cabs finally stop, we slowly unpack ourselves onto a street. We slump along the sidewalk, all behind Bob Mitchell, a ringer for the aged Groucho Marx with turtle-neck, beret, and tilted shuffle. After four blocks of this, Tom stops.

"Where the hell are you leading us, Bob?"

"Should be just up here."

We walk another block, then huddle to examine Bob's scrap of paper with the address.

"It's got to be back there," Tom says, pointing at the five blocks we've already walked.

"I'm sure it's this way," says Bob, who starts in the direction he's been going. He quickly realizes no one is going to follow, so he falls in with everyone walking the other way, sulkily at the rear, a commander who's lost control of his battalion. By the time we reach the embassy, fifteen minutes late, Bob has again commandeered this ragtag parade, and when the elevator door opens it is he who shakes the ambassador's hand that reaches out to the battalion.

"Welcome," says the ambassador. Embassy staff usher our Canadian group into a plush suite, its tables piled with mini sandwiches and red wine. While half of us move on to the food, Bob has another objective. The Canadian government does not recognize the Mackenzie-Papineau Battalion as veterans and he is here to change that. "We were the first Canadians to fight the same enemy that Canada fought in the Second World War," Bob tells the ambassador he's cornered. "We should be recognized as such."

"Yes, you are fine Canadians," the ambassador assures Bob.

Nearby, Irene faces questions from the embassy's military attaché.

"Are you a Communist?" he asks her. "I understand that all of you people are Communist Party."

"Well—" Irene begins.

The attaché interrupts. "Don't you try and tell me that your friends sneaked their way into this country to fight for free enterprise."

"Well, no," Irene says.

Overhearing the exchange, a stringer for Canadian Press wire service turns to Tom. "Were you," she asks, "in the CP?"

"Thirty-nine years," Tom says with pride.

"Why did you quit?"

"I retired. Worked at Canadian Pacific for thirty-nine years. Got a pension out of it."

The reporter from Toronto gives Tom's answer a hearty laugh, then turns to the Canadian Press stringer. "How long," he says with a grin, "have you been with CP?"

Scanning a wall of Canadiana books, I'm approached by a Québécois woman.

"You are with the group, no?"

"Yes, I am with the group."

"I'm a communications officer for the embassy," she says, offering her hand. "I was living in Madrid with my husband, he's an architect from Montreal. So I came here and asked to be of service. Now, I am hired and I tell the Spanish media about Canada. I knew so little about what you did here then, but I am learning and what you did was magnificent. We spent last summer in Aragon, and whenever I mentioned I was Canadian the people remembered how valiantly you fought and how many of you fell."

She moves on, and I browse the bookcase, leaf through *Canada's Soldiers: The Military History of an Unmilitary People*. 401 pages. The Mac-Pap Battalion is relegated to a lone, brief footnote. That's all there is about Spain on a shelf of Canadians-at-war stories.

"Jesus, what the hell does Bob expect?"

The question turns me around and I see it belongs to Henry, his face inches away, staring at mine inquisitively. "Why does he think those Ottawa politicians are going to recognize us? They would have supported Franco back then. It was Ottawa politicians who passed their laws forbidding Canadians from fighting in foreign wars, from risking our own bloody necks." In one hand, Henry squeezes a slab of cheese between graham wafers. In the other, he holds one of the maple leaf lapel pins Bob doled out expeditiously before the elevator door opened to the embassy.

Meanwhile, Bob has again cornered the ambassador. "The Norwegian vets were recognized by their government as the first to fight the fascists. There's a monument in Denmark."

"Yes, you are fine Canadians," the ambassador assures Bob.

"Mr. Mitchell," says the military attaché, stepping between Bob and the ambassador. "Do you believe in our Canadian way of life?"

"I love Canada."

"Isn't it true that you came to Spain to establish red dictators?"

"We came to Spain to fight for democracy," Bob says.

"I know more about that than you might think," says the attaché.

This unanticipated verbal assault disconcerts Bob for a moment, but he's heard it all before.

"I believe in democracy," says Bob, "and we fought for democracy in Spain. And we should be recognized as the first to —"

The attaché steps back, takes a swig of his sangria. "Mitchell," he says, "are you now, or have you ever been, a member of the Communist Party?"

The ambassador spins away on his heel. He begins to walk off, believing he's escaped the attaché and Bob but comes face-to-face with Henry Simmons. "You are fine Canadians," the ambassador sputters, then zigzags around Henry.

"What you did in this country was splendid," the communications officer says as she returns to my side. I'd been standing apart from Bob and the attaché but listening in on their exchange. At first, I'd laughed at the attaché's are-you-now-or-have-you-ever-been question because it is something from another time and place that I have never heard an actual human being ask, and I believed it could, in 1986, only be said ironically. But the attaché continues berating Bob, and I stop laughing.

I trade pleasantries with the communications officer, then move closer to Bob and the attaché. When I reach them, the attaché is certain he has discombobulated Bob and is repeating with a self-satisfied smirk, "Are you now, or have you ever been, a member of the Communist Party?"

"Why?" I interject.

"Because," the attaché turns on me, "we don't want members of the Communist Party in Canada."

"Mikhail Gorbachev is a member of the Communist Party," I say. "He wouldn't have any trouble getting in, now would he?"

"You are a smartass," the attaché snarls at me, "and you are a subversive."

The attaché turns to Bob. "Mitchell, are you ashamed of being a Communist?" Although the attaché's attention is back on Bob, I am now irrevocably a part of these hostilities.

"Why don't you let him alone," I say.

"Feldman," the attaché says, "are you ashamed to be a Jew?"

"No. Not at all," I say. "Are you ashamed to be an asshole?"

Bob lets out a laugh.

There is a long moment of silence as the attaché searches for a smart retort but can't find one. Finally, he says: "No... uhm... not at all." He turns back to Bob — easier prey, he believes. But now Bob is laughing at him.

The attaché goes in search of another sangria. The communications officer tells me, "What you did was magnificent."

Wine and cheese is consumed with renewed civility for another hour, then the ambassador says he has a function to attend and so, unfortunately, it is time for his fine fellow Canadians to depart too.

Tom reaches for Susan's hand, takes a step towards the exit, stops, cocks his head back towards the attaché. "Military attaché," Tom says, "or CIA?"

The entourage piles into the elevator as the ambassador administers his final glad-handing.

"Have a nice stay," he repeats.

"Do you," the Toronto reporter asks the ambassador, "think the volunteers should be recognized by the Canadian government?"

"They're fine Canadians," the ambassador says as the elevator closes on his smiling face.

FIVE

JOAN THE BAPTIST

Vancouver, 1934–1935

M Y CHEST IS TIGHT, HEAD IS LIGHT AS I RACE UP the Japantown alleyway. After police on horseback ride into 1,000 of us at Ballantyne Pier, I'm on the run, darting past clapboard homes, their multi-colours blurring like a broken kaleidoscope. My eyes are watery from tear gas and soft rain sprinkles me. Welcome to Vancouver.

"In here, in here," a young Japanese man beckons, and four of us slip through his backyard fence and into his family's home. Hot tea never tasted so good. The four protesters invited into this house don't know one another, but each of us is shaken and exhilarated by the day's events. A grizzled, hollow-cheeked protester in his thirties says he saw a mounted cop trample a boy and his mother. "I threw a brick at him, and before it even landed a plainclothesman grabbed me, and then someone decked him and I ran."

"If they think," vows a freckly redhead in his mid-teens, "this is going to stop longshoremen, if they think this is going to stop any of us, they've got another fucking think coming."

I had marched on Ballantyne Pier with striking longshore-men and their supporters, including striking relief workers. Strikebreakers had been hired to replace the longshoremen. When we got to the pier, police launched their attack and the street battle went on for three hours.

It's revolutionary times and I'm a revolutionary.

After breaking camp in the Okanagan, I joined other relief workers from around the province and converged on the city, staging occupations at the Vancouver Museum and the Hudson's Bay department store and holding a series of flower tag–days. We stood on street corners with tin cans, a fundrais-ing protest for relief camp strikers. Those who gave received flowers in return. I got my picture in the *News-Herald*, at a flower protest alongside a young woman holding the banner: Homeless! No Work! No Relief! Help Us — Buy A Flower!

I finished *Sister Carrie* and read more Dreiser, other social-ist literature, spending hours browsing second-hand stores for books, as passionate about the left literati — Dos Passos, William Morris, Sinclair Lewis — and about becoming a writer myself as I had been by earlier discoveries of baseball, the mov-ies, and swing music. Once my interest in something is piqued, I am single-minded until the passion I think will never wane is replaced by another. My new political commitment, though, is different, *deeper*, than earlier interests I believe, and I attend every protest and the occasional meeting. Still not much of a joiner but now I'm interested in every kind of left politics. I see Emma Goldman speak when she comes through town, pull for the CCF's J.S. Woodsworth in this year's federal election, party with Communists like Alex Katz.

Eddie had come from the island and had found work at Ballantyne Pier, a short walk from the neighbourhood, but a week into his new job the longshoremen were locked out and the union went on strike. Eddie would be on a picket line all summer long.

"At least Rachel's got a job, *kaynahora*," my mother says. She's bouncing about the kitchen this Sunday morning, talking to Mrs. Finkel and baking *komishbrodt*, vexatious about her two sons. "Jakie goes into the woods and comes back in no time with nothing to show for it. Eddie gets a job on the docks and it lasts one week."

School is out for Rachel and she is checking the days to New York off her calendar, working full time for Sammy Swartz, who spends long days behind his delicatessen counter. He is a quiet man who lives alone above the deli he has operated through five years of waiting for his wife, grown son, and daughter-in-law to arrive from his old country. "Any day now," he would say.

Rachel is awkward with her sudden adult height. Her appearance is also altered by the latest movie magazine, drawing my mother's ire when she curls her hair like Joan Crawford and colours her full lips and round cheeks with a dollop of powder on her pug nose. She has also taken to lying on top of her sheets, legs falling from the foot of the bed, feet planted on the floor, eyes on the ceiling. "What are you looking at all the time?" I say glancing into her room one afternoon as I pass her open door.

"Right now I'm thinking about Robert Taylor. He's dreamy."

"Maybe you should put his picture up on the ceiling. What else do you think about?"

"Nothing in particular. I just like to think. You should try it sometime."

Despite my mother's concerns about Rachel getting all grown up too fast, she is mostly delighted with her daughter's development — her job, her travel plans. It's the boys that upset my mother, especially Eddie. "What is it with your brother?" she asks me, slamming the oven door on a blueberry pie. Eddie never fully returned home after his island work ended. For two months now, he disappears days at a time, then shows up at dinner, hurries away again, then reappears later that evening or the next morning or at any odd hour. "He's driving me *meshugga*," Frieda says. Rachel and I don't understand it either.

On a sweltering afternoon, I sit on our porch on Keefer watching the street. Art Posner is on the sidewalk down the block tossing a baseball with his kid brother, Joe. Younger children play on the street. Other neighbours watch from their porches. When the Feldman family left Fort Harold for Vancouver, we settled into the city's Jewish neighbourhood within the Strathcona neighbourhood. After we arrived, an internal westward diaspora began in the city, following a new community centre and congregation. Still, our Strathcona remains the closest thing to a Yiddish quarter west of Winnipeg. Strathcona has been the city's clearing house for immigrants since the nineteenth century, first from the British Isles, then came the Jewish, Italian, Japanese, Chinese, Black, Nordic, Ukrainian. Each staked out a portion of Strathcona, the Jewish section on Georgia and Keefer Streets with a delicatessen, a butcher shop, the first synagogue, and its residents walking pushcarts, working the waterfront, operating the second-hand shops, groceries, and tailor storefronts on the nearby main streets. Although each immigrant ethnicity has a particular street or streets where it predominates, there is a sprinkling of everyone, everywhere. At Passover, my mother hands me hampers of latkes and gefilte fish to deliver next door to Mrs. Gizzi and across the back lane to Mrs. Tabaka. At Christmas, Mrs. Gizzi sends over a pot of pasta in brodo, and on New Year's, we receive Mrs. Tabaka's fish cakes.

In the neighbourhood, there are rickety rooming houses and immaculate three-storied homes with stained-glass windows, pillared porches, and lush gardens. We live in a practical clapboard house between the Finkels and the Gizzis. Strathcona is a downtown neighbourhood with unlocked doors.

"I must pour the milk, drink it, and put the bottle back in the fridge by the time I count to one hundred," I instruct myself before pushing through our back door and into the kitchen to find Mrs. Finkel.

"Hello Jakie," Mrs. Finkel says casually as she fills a jar with sugar from the Feldman cupboard. My mother is at work. I nod to Mrs. Finkel, hurrying to the fridge, continuing the private numbers game I'm playing.

"Are you a hundred percent?" Mrs. Finkel says.

"Out of what?" I say, after quaffing the glass of milk.

"You don't look a hundred percent. You look like a Skinnay Ennis. I'll be making *komishbrodt*. You come over for some."

An hour later, when I walk into Mrs. Finkel's kitchen she is mixing batter, ashes floating into the bowl from the cigarette plugged into her mouth.

"You're getting ashes in the food."

"That's all right, Jakie," she says. "Take a couple pieces from the counter. I'm doing another batch."

I take Mrs. Finkel's pastry home, languish lazily in the heat munching it, leaning back in a wooden chair, a foot planted against the thick vertical post that runs from the porch to the roof's brim. At the end of the block, past the children in the street, I see Eddie, his face shaded by a fedora, jacket flung over his shoulder, sauntering along the sun-baked sidewalk. He crosses Keefer and is heading up the porch stairs and to the front door without acknowledging me.

"Hey, Eddie. Long time, no see."

Eddie pauses. "I'm taking a bath."

He has the look of a tired man after a restless sleep followed by the unaccustomed heat of early summer.

"You haven't been around for a few days," I say. "Something exciting going on in your life?"

"A bath would be real exciting about now," he says, reaching for the doorknob.

"I personally don't care what you do, Eddie, but Mom's worried. She doesn't let on to you how worried. Maybe you should talk with her."

"I've been having sex, every day, all over town, so I'm pooped. That's all I have to say," he says.

That evening, Eddie has disappeared again, and my mother is too restless to sit still for *The Eddie Cantor Show*, although the pop-eyed song-and-dance comedian's radio program is her favourite.

Unable to watch the radio, she finally blurts, "What's Eddie up to?"

"He won't talk to me. Believe me, I've tried," says Rachel.

"Me too," I say. "Maybe he leads a life of crime after dark."

"Eddie a *gonif*. Ha," my mother says.

From the little we do know, we try to piece together the life of Eddie. I say he does picket-line duty, but that doesn't take up much of his time, and he's not involved with any of the other political goings-on around the strike. Rachel says we know he's looking for another job, but he's already applied practically everywhere, and that's not the kind of thing you do after midnight.

"Well, most of his friends live in the neighbourhood," I note, "and whatever he's doing he's doing it somewhere else so..."

"I have got a sweetie known as Susie," Eddie Cantor is singing on the radio. "In the words of Shakespeare, she's a wow."

"I think," my mother suggests with deliberation, "that what Eddie needs is a girl."

"Don't you think that's his own business?" I say.

"Eddie is twenty-two years old," Rachel says. "He's, well, not particularly tall, but he is dark and you might say handsome. I don't know that he needs our help to —"

"Eddie," my mother concludes, "would settle down if he was with a nice girl. I'm going to speak with Rabbi Menkus."

Marcus Menkus was born on the Lower East Side of Manhattan. Although my mother and Menkus share New York and his synagogue is just around a couple corners, she only stops by for weddings, bar mitzvahs, and the occasional high holiday. Isaac and Frieda grew up in practising households, but he pretty much left his religion in Russia and she left most of hers in New York. Frieda did bring a Torah with her from New York, provided by her father, but in Fort Harold it came out of the closet on fewer holidays until, in Vancouver, it hardly comes out at all. But the rabbi knows his neighbours, religious or not, and makes it clear time after time that he is available for consultation. So my mother spends the next week's evenings at the synagogue, having discussions with the rabbi that are as opaque to me as Eddie's whereabouts. After a final session with Menkus, my mother bursts into the kitchen through the back door.

"This Sunday," she announces.

Sunday, at six o'clock, there is a knock on the front door. I open it to Ruth Solomon shuffling her feet, hoping no one would answer the door.

"I'm here to … I'm … Rabbi Menkus sent me."

My mother sweeps me aside to welcome Ruth. Her parents, farmers in Russia, homesteaded in Sonnenfeld, Saskatchewan, before the dust bowl blew them to the West Coast, where the neighbourhood is helping them resettle.

"Eddie will be here soon," my mother says brightly. "I told him to make sure to be here for dinner at six. I made *lokshen kugel*. He loves lokshen kugel."

Rachel sits on the staircase, elbows on knees, face resting in her hands, observing. I stand alongside the staircase.

"Ruth, have you had a good summer?" my mother says, directing the farmers' daughter to a worn, wine-coloured armchair in the living room.

"Yes, Mrs. Feldman," she says uneasily.

"Are you making lots of new friends in the city?"

"Some," says Ruth, forcing a smile.

My mother retreats to the kitchen. Rachel and I sit on the staircase watching Ruth dehydrate in the wine chair.

The front door is flung open. "Hi ya, Jake, Rachel," Eddie says, starting down the hallway to the kitchen, our eyes frozen wide on him. My mother emerges from the kitchen, smiles at Eddie, gestures towards Ruth. Eddie stops, glances at the living room, glowers at Ruth, then strides through the kitchen and out the back door. By the time my mother realizes Eddie is leaving, he has breezed past her and left.

Rachel and I huddle in the kitchen with a frantic Frieda. "Your brother got cold feet," she says in a trembling voice.

"I'll try to find him," I say, rushing out the back door. Rachel steps into the living room and gives Ruth a story about Eddie having to depart suddenly because of an emergency involving a close friend.

"He did know why I was here?" asks a shaken Ruth.

"Yeah, sure. He'll like you. We'll do it again," Rachel says unconvincingly.

Rachel walks Ruth to the door, then returns to the kitchen where my mother is beside herself.

"I hated having to make up a story to tell that poor girl. It was embarrassing," Rachel says. "What will you say to Rabbi Menkus?"

"Menkus, schmenkus," my mother says. "I have something to say to Eddie. Wait till I get my hands on that brother of yours."

The night before Rachel is to leave for New York, there is a knock on my bedroom window. My brother is calling me outside. Eddie and I walk down the street and into the park.

Eddie stops walking. "The reason," he says, pausing to take a deep breath, "the reason I couldn't go out with that girl is…"

Everything Eddie's been hiding from us pours out. Finally, he stops talking, his doleful face looking for some response, but I'm stunned speechless. I gather a bit of composure. "I don't care what anyone is. You should have told me about this before." I say this sombrely, but the absurdity of the situation strikes me and I sputter into laughter. And Eddie laughs too.

"I came tonight because I want to say goodbye to Rachel," he says. We walk quickly to the house. "Wait outside here," I say, then scamper up to Rachel's room where she's packing her suitcase. In a moment, the three of us are on the front porch and Eddie tells Rachel everything.

"Let Rachel and me tell Mom," I say. "She's really angry at you, Eddie. You made her feel lousy, and Ruth Solomon felt lousy, and Rachel had to lie. She told me she would never do that again for anyone."

Rachel nods, then returns with me to her room, where our mother is stuffing a blouse into the suitcase on the bed.

"That's yours," says Rachel. "Don't put it in my suitcase."

"That blouse happens to look gorgeous on you, Rachel. I don't need it."

"Okay," says a suddenly demure Rachel. "Mom, what do you think about intermarriage?"

"I don't think about it. *Hok mir nisht kayn chainik.* You planning to marry Robert Taylor?"

"How would you feel if I did?"

"We don't already have enough movie stars in the family? *That*, I probably wouldn't mind. *I* would marry Robert Taylor."

"No, seriously. How would you feel if my husband was from another background?"

"Your husband? Look, young lady, you're fifteen years old, so I don't have to think about that for awhile. What is this all about?" my mother says.

"What it's about, Mom," Rachel begins, then pauses, then accelerates, "is Eddie left the house like that the other day because he's been married for two months. That's why he didn't come home all those times, and his wife, Joan, is a Baptist, and she's from White Rock, and he loves her, and he didn't want to tell us because he thought we'd be hard on him... but I couldn't care less."

"Eddie met her at the West End confectionery, where she works," I say. "He was worried how the family might react to the marriage. She was nervous about her family too. Joan says

Eddie's the first Jew she's ever met. When she told her family our last name, her Mom said, 'What kind of a name is that?' And Joan didn't even know."

My mother is quiet, contemplative.

"You," I say, "always say people are people, there's good and bad in every neighbourhood."

She continues the silence for a long moment, then says, "Where's my Eddie?"

I nod towards the second-floor bedroom window. "Out there."

She starts downstairs where Eddie stands in shadows on the porch. Before he can move, they embrace.

"Eddie, *vos vilns du from my yunger yorn,*" she says, shaking her finger. "What do you want from my life? Come inside for something to eat."

My mother walks with Eddie to the kitchen, turns to him with a bemused smile and raised brow. "So...when do I meet Joan the Baptist?"

Rachel leaves for the other coast. Eddie and Joan, unable to find work in Vancouver, go to Fort Harold. I stay in the city and look for a job.

This morning, Mrs. Finkel comes by with a plate of her strudel. Later, I take a slice to our porch and lose myself this late summer afternoon in Upton Sinclair's *The Jungle.*

"Wanna go to the Towers, Feldman?"

"No," I say, before looking up to see who I'm speaking with.

"Let's shoot pool then."

Art Posner stands on the sidewalk at the foot of the yard, jerking his head for me to follow.

"I feel like reading."

"Come on. You've had your nose in a book on that porch all month. Let's pick up Leonard along the way."

Art and I collect Georgie Leonard and we make for Macey's Pool Hall on Hastings Street. Before quitting school, Art and I regularly skipped out of classes to spend an hour or two over a Macey's snooker table, play-acting that we were pool sharks. We weren't but we were adequate, at least by neighbourhood standards, and occasionally could luck a run of five or six or even seven balls. Georgie's pool play was far less than this.

"I feel hot today," Georgie announces as we're about to begin.

"Sure you do, Georgie," I say.

"I'll break," Art says, proceeding with the white-ball-on-red-ball crack that signals the start of the game. Art slouches nonchalantly, chalking a cue that doesn't need chalk as I take my turn leaning across the table, focused on delivering a difficult blue ball into a corner hole. I am about to tap the white cue ball when Georgie's doughy, mugging face appears at table level directly behind the blue ball I'm aiming at. My cue ball spins awry.

"Scratch," Georgie cries.

"Get your face the fuck away from my ball. I'll take the shot over."

"It was an asshole thing for Georgie to do," Art says, "but you don't get the shot over."

That sentiment becomes the consensus and we continue, Art slightly ahead of me, Georgie trailing.

"So, party at your house this weekend, Jake," Art says softly, as Georgie and his cue hunch over the table. The summer is winding down. I'd never hosted a neighbourhood party, and two weeks earlier Art suggested it was about time. I spoke with my mother and now the neighbourhood is coming Saturday night.

"Oh no you don't," Art shouts, lunging to grab the cue ball and place it against the edge of the table, where it was before Georgie nudged it a quarter-inch while Art and I looked away, contemplating Saturday.

"Georgie, you asshole," I say with a grimace, before he taps the little he can see of the top of the white ball, sending it into a pink ball, which rolls slowly into a distant pocket.

"Six points," Georgie says.

"Georgie," says Art, "you asshole."

"I need to be with my peers," says my mother, and she goes next door to Mrs. Finkel's just as the party is about to begin.

While most of the twenty or so who show up socialize over cold drinks in the backyard, a handful roll up the living room carpet and dance. The dancing pauses for next-door neighbour Sienna Gizzi's soulful rendition of "Brother, Can You Spare A Dime," then it is back to my record collection. There is Bing Crosby and Russ Columbo, but mostly I play the bands: Benny Goodman, Duke Ellington, the Dorseys. Goodman is tearing through "After You've Gone" when — between operating the turntable, pouring drinks, and keeping peepers away from Claire Gordon and Art Posner in my bedroom — I notice Maurice Hershkovitz knock against my mother's prize lamp. Hershowitz was a finalist in a city-wide dance marathon, so he's known in the neighbourhood as "Crazylegs." In full flight, I catch the falling lamp and nimbly re-place it on a table while Hershkovitz continues his fancy footwork to a rangy clarinet.

As the dancing heats up inside the house, Alex Katz is in a corner of the backyard detailing the Regina street war he just survived. I step forward to join the small group listening to him. The On-to-Ottawa Trek to protest relief camp conditions started out in Vancouver on June 3, 1935, intent on picking up thousands of protesters en route to Ottawa. It ended in Regina, though, on July 1, when soldiers on horseback attacked a public meeting, sending trekkers and their supporters to jail or to hospital. It was a six-hour street fight, with two dead and 100 injured, and Alex was in the thick of it. Now, in the Feldman backyard, Alex delivers his blow-by-blow account, then talks urgently about upcoming tag-day protests. "Details at the next Workers Circle meeting. Come."

Tall with a small winced face that uncoils into an earnest smile whenever anyone challenges the order of things, Alex has never been a close friend but has been friendly with me since elementary school. His parents, Esther and Harry, were arrested in Germany during the commotion that followed World War I, and upon their release came to Vancouver, where their house is home to the Jewish Workers Circle. Harry works on the waterfront, Esther is a shop steward at the Gastown Garment Company.

When the evening chills, the backyard empties and the living room turns into a crowded steam bath shaking to the Dorseys. I dance too. I do not know it at the time, but this is the last night I will dance with most of the people in this room. The rebellions I'm increasingly drawn to since returning from the relief camp will soon take me far beyond the neighbourhood.

One by one my partiers filter back into the neighbourhood until there is just Art and me on the front stoop.

"So what's going on with you and Claire?" I ask.

"She's sweet and all but I don't know what's going on, period. I only know that I'm not going to find decent work here."

"I won't either. Don't know, maybe I should go to Fort Harold."

"How are Eddie and Joan doing up there?"

"They live in Isaac's house and Eddie works in Isaac's store. In Eddie's letters, it's always 'I'm fine, Dad's fine, Joan's fine.' He always got along with the old man better than the rest of us, but I know he can't save anything on the money he's making, and he'd rather be in Vancouver."

"I'm thinking about heading out to Winnipeg," Art says. "Most of the family's there and maybe some work. You know I'd like to go to medical school, but for now that's not in the cards."

"Hey, maybe we can work on our pool game and travel across the country, be hustlers," I say.

Art laughs. We watch my mother's farewell to Mrs. Finkel on the next porch, and in a moment she is home.

"*Gott in himmel*, the noise you made tonight. I didn't come over because you're youngsters and have your fun, but what a racket." She walks through the doorway, then backs out. "My goodness, Jakie, it's like a hurricane's been here."

"Jake and I'll clean it up," Art says.

"You don't have to do that, Artie. It's after midnight," my mother says. "I'll do it in the morning."

"No. It's fine, Mrs. Feldman. We'll do it now."

"This Artie, he's a mensch," she says.

As Art collects bottles and glasses, I stack my record collection. "After You've Gone" is gone, I find, along with another Goodman record, a Russ Columbo, a Red Nichols, a Paul Robeson, and two Dorsey Brothers.

"Someone took my records," I shout. "My Goodman."

"Maybe they're in another room," Art says.

"No. They were all right here. Shit. Shit. Shit."

"We'll search the house for them," my mother suggests, upset with my language, but more concerned with my concerns. "They got to be here somewhere."

"They don't got to be anywhere," I shout.

"Don't blow your wig," says Art. "None of this is your mother's fault. We'll ask around about the records, okay."

My mother has begun sweeping the mess away.

"Mom, I'm sorry for—"

"It was nothing, Jake. We all say things without thinking. The records will turn up."

Art gently takes the broom from her hands and sweeps. I scrub the floor silently until it is clean.

SIX

IT'S YOU

Madrid, fall 1986

IT TAKES FOREVER TO GET OUT OF MADRID.

The tour bus crawls through morning traffic, past rows of motorbikes and compact cars, between tall office buildings and blocks of pale rising flats that appropriate post-war North America's suburban blandness, in discord with the city's architectural reminders of centuries of Roman, Gothic, and Moorish design.

It took forever to get into Madrid.

From July 1936 until March 1939, the city's rifles and fists fought back fascism, withstanding the first blitzkrieg, a German dress rehearsal for their saturation bombing of London. "No pasaran," had vowed the banner near the entrance to Madrid. "Fascism wishes to conquer Madrid. Madrid will be the tomb of fascism." Finally, the Germans and the Italians and Franco's homegrown fascists vanquished the villages around the city and marched into Madrid.

It seems this morning that the veterans are departing Madrid nearly as slowly as the fascists entered it. We are headed to Fuencarral cemetery for a commemoration of the

International Brigade members who died in Spain. Streets become narrow and buildings Spanish as the coach edges through outskirt villages. The Canadian group on my bus is small — Henry Simmons, the Toronto reporter, and Andy Tompkins, a Mac-Pap-turned-bargaining agent for Manitoba government workers. Other seats are filled by Lincolns, their friends and families. I pick up a loose copy of the *International Herald Tribune* from a bus seat to find a photograph of Josh Beren conferring with the mayor's assistant at the reunion's opening-night testimonial.

"I live in Los Angeles," a nurse in the seat behind me is telling the New York woman next to her. "I'm in a lovely apartment but I don't see anyone anymore. I walk along the beach, I drive, I watch television."

The biggest contingent of volunteers at this reunion comes from the U.S., largely New Yorkers. There are some, like the L.A. woman, who fought the good fight in New York, then sought the good life in California retirement. "I knew it was time to go to the West Coast," she says.

"I" — Henry is telling the Toronto reporter's tape recorder — "heard about Spain on the radio at the end of a day laying railway track in the British Columbia Interior. Decided then and there that that's my fight. So I went. I liked the idea of being part of an army pushing for the same ideals that got us beat up by cops in Canada. In Spain, we were armed and had a fighting chance."

"This is where you will find some of the finest shopping in the city," the tour guide explains as we crawl through Madrid suburbia. For two tours a month, ten months a year, the multilingual guide, from Portland, Oregon, stands at the front of a bus droning into a hand microphone. She has abandoned almost any vestige of tailoring her words for the particular tourist group's sensibility, instead offering the same sunny audio brochure whether guiding Americans for Republican Spain or Americans for Republican America.

"When I get back to Winnipeg, I say 'I'm going to Spain,' and my father says, 'You're nuttier than a fruitcake,'" Henry continues. "I say, 'Nope. I'm going.' This was before the International Brigades were formed, but I just knew I could figure a way into Spain, to help."

We slowly climb a road lined with parked tour buses and people, mostly elderly, making their way with deliberation towards the cemetery. I'm standing alongside the L.A. woman as we wait to exit the bus and begin our walk to the gravestones. "The anti-fascists buried here during the Civil War were dug up after Franco won," she notes. Now, this is venerated Republican burial ground where a stone memorial to the International Brigades was placed after Franco's death. When the last bus has emptied, the ceremony starts with a man who was in the Republican cabinet in 1939. Since I don't understand his language, I feel like I'm watching a Chaplin silent picture, the cabinet member's nuances and motions as moving as the words that are missed. An old woman in a black frock stands beside him sobbing silently. About ten feet in front of me, an American television crew chats and clatters, a cameraman ogling the young Spanish woman next to him who stares intently at the speaker, her right clenched fist cocked above her head the entire fifteen minutes he talks. About halfway through his eulogy to the volunteers killed in Spain, the young Spanish woman turns to the still-leering cameraman and snaps a few words that I cannot make out. She turns her eyes back to the speaker, and the cameraman looks down at the ground. "I presume she told him to piss off," the L.A. woman says. "I presume," I concur.

After the ceremony, the crowd begins its retreat to the buses, but Henry Simmons, Andy Tompkins, the L.A. woman, and I walk in the other direction to a large piece of stone engraved with the words VOLUNTAIRES DES BRIGADES INTERNATIONALES. I squat to touch the stone, stand with the others silently at this monument, then return to the bus. Since these buses resemble each other, some passengers have gotten onto the wrong ones, a confusion which exasperates our tour guide. This soon gets resolved though, and the guide seems to know to stop talking, and all is quiet on the bus as it advances into the city.

Back at the hotel, I step into the hotel lobby to find Tom and Susan Barkley hunkered over beers with the Toronto reporter. "This tour never sits still," Tom says with a groan. "They don't seem to realize we're pensioners," adds Susan. "Yeah," Tom says. "Back in Scarborough, I get up when I want. Here you're up at seven o'clock and they got you going all day."

Henry plops into a chair across from Tom. "I didn't see you at the cemetery, Barkley. How come?"

"Susan and I took a walk around the city, went for lunch — veal cutlets and potato dumplings — then we relaxed in the room. We needed a little time to ourselves."

I sit down next to Susan just as Jim Heathcott enters the bar and leans against a wall surveying the room.

"Do not like the food in this hotel," Susan says.

"Oh, quit your bellyaching," Henry says.

Heathcott approaches our table. "You boys know we're leaving for Valencia first thing tomorrow morning, so you've got to have your bags packed and outside your rooms before seven a.m."

"Jeez, Jimmy, you've got to slow things down," says Tom. "We're not youngsters anymore."

Heathcott strokes the goatee on his hard, narrow face as he gives our table a glare, a drill sergeant eyeing down the rest of his soldiers before turning on the lone insubordinate. "Look, Barkley," Heathcott says in a clipped, whispery voice, his neck tightening. He looks like he's about to explode but stops himself, relaxes his scowl, and smiles. "Maybe you've got a point there, Barkley. We'll see what we can do, but in the meantime there are buses to catch so we've got to have luggage out at seven a.m. I'll put your name on the wake-up list at the desk, Barkley. Anyone else want a call?"

"Yeah, put me on that too," I say.

Heathcott nods and abruptly walks off.

"Good guy," Tom says, raising his glass towards Heathcott's back as he departs the bar.

"Really?" I say.

Henry grunts and sneers, not so much at Heathcott or at Tom's tribute to Heathcott, but at Tom. "You're lucky he didn't clock you," Henry says. "You want to know what I think of this reunion — I'm enjoying all of it."

"Anyhow, did you hear what I said to that military attaché?" Tom says. "I said, 'Military attaché…or CIA?'"

"The CIA is American, Barkley, not Canadian," Henry says.

"Right, I know that but I thought it was a real good line," Tom says. Pleased with himself, the little man pauses to adjust his beret before continuing. "Bob Mitchell is convinced we can get recognition from the federal government. Don't get me wrong, I would like that too, but there is no way a Conservative government is going to give veteran benefits to the Mackenzie-Papineau Battalion. Their friends in the Canadian Legion wouldn't stand for it."

"The Conservatives are doing a pretty good job," Susan says.

"Baloney," Tom says, with the dispassion of someone who has argued this with Susan before. This time, though, it is embarrassing in front of old comrades, so he feigns anger. "BA-LON-EY!"

"I like what Bob Mitchell is doing," Henry says. "Someone needs to stick up for the Mac-Paps, for Christ's sake. That kind of stuff never used to matter to me, and I still don't care about the money but damned if we shouldn't be recognized as the first Canadians to go to war against the fascists."

"Bob told me he's going to speak about it before a parliamentary committee when we get back," the Toronto reporter contributes.

"I'm going to bed," Susan says, gathering herself from the table. "Come to bed soon, Tom."

"Sure I will," Tom says.

The reporter pulls his tape recorder from a knapsack and places it in front of Tom. "Where were we?" Tom says, clearing his throat.

"You just hopped a train in Northern Ontario."

Henry rises from the table. "I'm going to hit the hay," he says before walking out on Tom's memories. I leave too, walking past the clumps of volunteers that form and dissolve in the lobby from morning till night.

As I near my fourth-floor room, from behind me there is a soft voice calling my name. I turn to see Peter Krawchuk, a frail Mac-Pap who spends most of the reunion in his hotel room. "Jack," he says, "come over here, please. I have something you should see."

Although Peter was born and raised in Canada, he speaks with the slight accent of an immigrant who arrived long ago.

Brought to Canada as an infant, he was raised in Smokey Lake, Alberta, an insular Ukrainian farming community near Edmonton, and did not speak English until first grade. He's lived in Regina since the end of Spain's war. When I turn to face him in the hallway, it is the first time I have seen Peter's sunken cheeks and skeletal head without a fedora.

"Where's your hat?"

"Oh," Peter grins. "I know no one wears them anymore. I only wear it in case it rains."

"How are you enjoying the reunion?" I say.

"I only get out for one or two events a day," he says, "when I have the energy."

On the rumpled bedspread in his hotel room are books and papers Peter has been perusing for hours. He reaches his bony, age-marked hand purposefully into a pile of papers and pulls out a homemade book. He flips through its seventy-eight pages of handwritten observations, photographs, and clippings. "Look at this," he says, stopping at a clipping from the *Times of London*, 1927, quoting Churchill on fascism. "If I had been an Italian I am sure that I should have been wholeheartedly with you from start to finish in your triumphant struggle."

Voice rising, Peter says, "He supported Mussolini as early as 1926."

"Terrible, Peter. Is that what you wanted to show me?"

Peter shakes his head. The brittle hand goes back to turning pages quickly. It slows at photographs. He stops at a yellowing newspaper mugshot. "Nick!" he says. "After they shot the first of us in Estevan when we struck the mine, he jumped onto a truck and dared them to shoot him too. One RCMP raised his gun, methodically, and shot him through the heart. *Nick Nargan*." He says the name again, precisely, respecting each syllable.

Most of the snapshots are of men unrecognizable to me, but there is one of a big, blonde Lieutenant Hank Simmons in a crowded rowboat that will cross the Ebro River.

"Did you know Henry in Spain?" says Peter, as he turns to another page.

"No," I say, "but I did meet him in Vancouver many years later. You know he lives in Victoria now."

Peter shows me a crumbling Republican Army identity book resembling a passport, with a youthful headshot. *Petr Krawchuk*, it says. *Partido Politico–Antifascista.*

"Is this want you wanted to show me?" I say.

Peter's hand moves quicker now, then it stops. "This is what I want you to see."

It is a yellowed cracking photograph of a group of men milling outside their barracks, a factory near Ripoll, where the Mac-Paps were stationed while we waited to be repatriated to Canada. Some look away from the camera, but one smiles directly at the lens. He is slim with dark curly hair, not short or tall, unshaven, raised hand clenched into a small fist, wearing a navy blue beret and a khaki coat with a black rose pinned to the lapel.

"Jack... it's you."

SEVEN

THE WORLD HAS GONE MAD TODAY

Vancouver, winter 1935

I T IS A WICKED WIND THIS WINTER. SO FRIEDA BUN-
dles herself for her daily treks through slithery streets
between the garment factory and Keefer Street.

After a summer in Toronto and New York, Rachel is
home on Keefer, but her mind is on another street. Broadway.

On Broadway, Rachel had gone with Mom's sister Miriam
and her husband, Julius, to see *The Petrified Forest* and an Earl
Carroll musical comedy revue. Miriam also introduced Rachel
to *Anything Goes*, with Ethel Merman, featuring a title song
I would hear again. "I know, show business is your life, isn't
it, kid?" I say as Rachel goes into her living room–dance. My
gibes aside, I actually enjoy her home theatrics, although there
can be something irredeemably disruptive about Rachel and
her friend Polly transforming the house into a Busby Berkeley
set, with our narrow staircase playing the stairway to heaven,
the couch as "Shuffle Off to Buffalo" coach seats, and Rachel
and Polly's flapping legs as synchronized butterfly wings.

"I was going to listen to the hockey game in here," I say one Saturday, as Rachel and Polly prepare the living room for another extravaganza.

"No, we've got a show ready, and you and Mom watch," Rachel says.

"A show? I want to hear Foster Hewitt and the—"

"Leave the girls be, already," my mother says as she takes a front-row seat. "Your sister has so much talent, she's going to be a movie star. Just sit and watch and don't be such a *nudnick*."

So I forget the Maple Leafs versus Canadiens game tonight. Instead, I sit beside my mother, watching Rachel and Polly announce themselves—"Ginger and Ginger"—then prance before us in makeshift chorus costumes, their songs wrapped in the swell storyline of an RKO musical, with bits of the stage-craft Rachel observed in New York. My mother's smile just beams throughout. She claps wildly and I'm caught up in it all too, joining my mother in a standing ovation when Rachel and Polly's show closes with "Anything Goes"—"The world has gone mad today. And good's bad today... When most guys today, that women prize today, are just silly gigolos."

I consider joining Eddie and Joan, now living near Barkerville, mostly a ghost town but a half-century earlier the showpiece of Canada's Wild West. There is something appealing to me about heading to this northern B.C. town where I can imagine Canadian facsimiles of Buck Jones leaping from the rooftop of the local saloon, landing saddleback on a stallion, and with shouts of "Let's ride," galloping into a western movie serial. My fascination for these serials has faded, especially with my recent discovery of "progressive" literature, but I duly note that one Canadian leftist has a name straight out of the B-westerns my friends and I relished at Saturday matinees.

The Communist Party of Canada's Tim Buck could have ridden with Tom Mix or Buck Jones as Red Rider, the class-conscious cowboy, rescuing his neighbours' farms from a railroad baron's hired guns.

There is something appealing about a job, too, and my brother has found work in a gold quartz mine. Besides, Barkerville is in the same general direction as Fort Harold, and I haven't seen my father in two years. As much as I insist I am disinterested in him, I'm not. So, I write Eddie that I'll head north in the spring if I haven't found work in Vancouver.

"Vancouver's a cold, grey place," my mother says, barrelling through the back door with two bags of groceries. It's rainy and dark at 4 p.m.

"It's a beautiful city too," Rachel protests.

"Miriam just wrote asking me to come to New York and bring you with me," my mother tells Rachel.

"There's nothing stopping you from going to New York," I say.

"Maybe I will. Maybe someday," my mother says, taking bagels from a bag. "This is my home now. My family, my friends... But they don't know how to make bagels here. These are just bread. They don't have the recipe."

"I'll stick around here for the winter," I say.

While I devour lefty writings and attend street protests, meetings are another thing. Alex invites me to Workers Circle meetings, but I still feel uncomfortable at the notion of a meeting. When I used to pass by the Katz home on walks with my father, he would say in hushed tones, "Harry Katz is a Communist, a Communist with a capital C. They're all Communists in that house. Half the world already thinks half the *yiddelah* are Bolsheviks and *that* family has to go and be Bolsheviks. Makes it bad for everyone in the neighbourhood."

Not that the Katz's were the only Bolsheviks in the neighbourhood. And they were well-regarded by their neighbours. Harry's
mechanical skills were at the free disposal of Strathcona, and
Esther's great pot of *kreplach* was a highlight of community picnics in Oppenheimer Park.

In this neighbourhood, someone could be a liberal or social
democrat with a communist their next-door neighbour on one
side and someone with no politics at all on the other, but they
borrowed milk from each other, argued with each other, and
more often than not even liked each other. Everyone was in
Strathcona. And inside ethnic political organizations like the
Jewish Workers Circle, there was the intimacy that comes with
sharing an outsider's culture, a language too.

Despite my hesitancy to attend meetings, the day the
Workers Circle meets to discuss the upcoming relief camp
protests, I find myself imploring everyone I see to be there. A
couple of acquaintances I encounter on Keefer Street seem
interested for a moment, drawn along by my urgency. "Maybe
we'll go there," Fanny Gitten says. "But you sound like you
should really be there. Why are you walking in the opposite
direction?" I turn around and make for the meeting.

Ten minutes later I arrive to find the Katz place crowded
with a half-dozen people about my age, and a dozen more,
some old enough to be my parents or grandparents. Alex is
on his feet updating the trials of On-to-Ottawa trekkers taking
place in Regina courtrooms. Everyone listens intently as Alex
repeats, almost phrase for phrase, the account of the battle of
Regina he told at my party.

When Alex concludes, Harry Katz calls on Abigail Levey,
the Circle's delegate to meetings of SUPA — the Single Unemployed Protective Association — which has organized many of

the recent protests in the city. Five years older than me, with a rotund face and huge eyes, Abigail is a bridge between the generations and cultures in Strathcona. She is North American and Romanian — born into an orthodox family in Iaşi, arriving in Strathcona when she was ten, active in the Workers Circle since her early teens. An animated speaker with gesticulating hands, she is as committed as Harry and Esther, and the one the Circle's older generation entrusts to articulate its interests to the rest of Vancouver. A tin-can protest is one week away, she says. "We're going to force the issue until the politicians can't ignore the relief strikers anymore. The first time only eight people came out and they were arrested, the next time we had fifty, then a hundred, and now we're going to fan out across the city. I'm going to a SUPA organizing meeting this Saturday, and I want to be able to say how many tin-canners the Circle will deliver next week."

"I'm in," says Alex, raising his hand. "What's the plan? Are we going to be arrested?"

"I'm not sure what the police will do," Abigail says. "The more people who show up, the harder it is for them to arrest us. Who else is coming?"

My classmate Moe Shore is next, then other hands are raised. "Okay," says Abigail, writing a list. "That's Alex, Fred, Fern, Moe."

I raise my hand.

"What's your name?" Abigail says.

"Jake," I say. "Jake Feldman. I'll be there."

For the next few days, I'm consumed by the protest, impatient with anyone who isn't.

Art and Georgie are at the doorstep.

"Want to shoot pool?"

"Not today. Art, why don't you come to the tin-can protest?"

"I'll probably be in Winnipeg. And I'm no activist."

"You do that crap and you won't be able to get a job or go to a good university or anything like that," Georgie says. "They put you on a list."

"You're talking bullshit, Georgie," Art says. "I don't have a problem with what you're doing, Jake, but I just want to shoot a little pool. Come on, you aren't going to fix the relief camps today."

"It's not just those relief camps," I say. "We live in one big relief camp."

Early morning, it's dark out when I go to an office above a storefront and am dispatched, with an elderly man and a young woman, to Spencer's department store across from the waterfront train station on Hastings Street. We unveil a black and yellow banner: Relieve the Relief Campers. Workers Not Beggars. Passersby smile or sneer or avoid eye contact altogether. A young man in a suit in a hurry, with three more young men, drops a dime in the old man's tin can. "Now, don't you go spend that on alcohol," the young man grins, wagging an admonitory finger.

A clunky paddy wagon rolls to the curb in front of us. Two cops use their billy clubs to prod me into the back of the wagon, which is jammed with protesters. The siren wails and bodies bounce against the walls and each other as the paddy rumbles around sharp corners on bumpy pavement. We're deposited at the city jail, where scores are being booked, with more on the way. I'm placed in a cellblock with the old man arrested with me outside Spencer's. His grey stubble and calmness remind me of Jimmy Lowry, who I haven't seen since we broke camp in Osoyoos. I glance about for Jimmy. Not here. Drifting and agitating somewhere else, I suppose. The cellblock that the tin-canners have been crammed into is rife with revolutionary ardour and jailhouse rumour. "We'll all get a minimum five years for this," a scrubbed university student tells me with certitude.

I'd tossed the night away and not slept when Alex Katz visits after he's released in the morning. "Look at this, Jake," Alex beams, holding up a morning paper, banner headlined "Public outcry for tin-canners' release." Through cell door bars, he reads out loud: "Politicians, labour leaders, and church officials have called for the immediate release of 208 tin-canners arrested yesterday. 'Workers, not beggars,' was the tin-can protesters' message, and civic leaders have heeded their cry, calling for an end to 'deplorable' relief policies." Alex tells me the neighbourhood's star lawyer, Nathan Nemirovsky, is on the case and we should all be out today.

"Next time we'll have four hundred people. If they arrest us, we'll overflow the jails," Abigail Levey is telling a crowd here to cheer us on as I leave the lock-up. Abigail is enlisting volunteers for the next tin-can demonstration. A minister in the West End is planning an event in his church in support of the protesters.

Back on the streets I'm ebullient, but on Keefer Street I find my mother distraught, Mrs. Tabaka and Mrs. Finkel commiserating with her. They stop talking as soon as I enter the kitchen. Finally, Mrs. Finkel stands with hands on hips. "Don't you care about your mother? Always a commotion with you."

Adds Mrs. Tabaka, "Why do you worry her like this? Such *tsures*."

"He says he's going to save the world," says Mrs. Finkel, shaking her head.

Mrs. Tabaka looks puzzled. "You can't save the whole world."

"Not me. Lots of us," I say, smiling at my mother, who hasn't said a thing. "I'm okay," I tell her. "Are you okay?"

"I'm okay if you're okay," she sighs, "but you should go out east for a while. This place is nothing but trouble."

EIGHT

MORNING IN VALENCIA

Valencia, fall 1986

B OB MITCHELL IS KNOCKING ON MY DOOR, BUT by this time, 7 a.m., I have been up for two hours, placed my suitcase in the hallway, and am queuing for the hard roll, orange juice, and coffee provided guests in the hotel, another Holiday Inn by any other name. This time it's called Hotel Expo. After a few knocks, Bob leaves my door alone and continues on his wake-up rounds. After the continental breakfast, I fall into sleep on my tour bus seat as Henry Simmons's voice drones into the Toronto reporter's tape recorder behind me.

"We're in reserve when word comes the lines have broken across the Aragon Front," Henry is saying when I awaken an hour later. "The company commander says, 'We get our goddamn asses out of here.' That was the order."

The bus winds through Spanish hills, passing tumbleweed not unlike that in the Interior of British Columbia. We slow through villages and I smile back at waving children who, I know, are being told about the people on the bus by their finger-pointing parents and grandparents standing alongside them.

"I dreamed I saw Joe Hill last night." A roly-poly New Yorker begins to sing this song in a tuneless, nasal way. A couple other reunionists haltingly join in his attempt to rouse the bus in singalong, but they're unable to rescue the fading song. "Alive as you or me…"

There are things incongruous about old radicals at a formal reception in a palatial place. Shortly after arriving in Valencia, we blanket its glitzy city hall — beneath the chandelier drooping from an ornate ceiling, between expansive walls with intricate carvings and bold mustard-and-ketchup tapestry. Unlike this building, our entourage has no dress code. Some of us wear sports jackets or dresses, feeling self-conscious to be in such a place in dungarees. More dress casual, feeling self-conscious to be anywhere in a suit.

"Well, what do you think, Jack?" says Tom Barkley, approaching me with an endearing impudence twisted into his mouth.

"This is what we're here for, isn't it?" I say with a yawn, feeling depleted after a restless night and long bus ride.

"Don't know about you. I'm here for dinner," he says, motioning for me to follow him to tables crowded with sweet miniature egg buns filled with cheese or ham.

"Remember that guy I told, RCMP or CIA?" he says, taking his first bite. "I thought it was a real victory."

"Yeah, what about him?"

"I see that Mitchell has written a letter to the ambassador complaining about the guy," says Tom, stuffing buns into his jacket pockets.

"Tom, the Canadian ambassador was standing right next to the guy. He heard every word. Nothing seemed to phase him. He thought we were all perfectly wonderful."

Over the past few years, the death of some of the vocal veterans who had organized Mac-Pap alumni affairs has resulted in Bob Mitchell assuming a sort of unsolicited leadership. Tom jostles with his bag and pulls out a copy of Bob's letter. "Listen to this part, Jack. 'The man was intoxicated and did his utmost to ruin the reception. His rudeness should be addressed by the embassy, as it was most unfortunate and would reflect poorly on Canada's reputation abroad were it to continue in future....Military attaché aside, it was a marvellous evening and you were a most gracious host.'"

"It's a good letter," says Tom, "but so fucking earnest. Besides, I already nailed that guy with my one-liner. That Mitchell. He's on an ego trip. So he's the one who put together the Canadian part of this reunion. That's fine. But no one died and left him commissar. He's so desperate to get in front of cameras and talk to reporters and get recognition, for himself I mean. I never heard of the guy until he retired and made the Mac-Paps his hobby."

We move from the tables towards a lectern where resounding tributes have begun. We join a band of veterans, Bob included, standing attentively at the front.

"That wasn't much of a dinner," Tom whispers to me. "Let's go back for more."

I stay put but soon all I can see of Tom is a shrinking beret, bouncing jerkily through the crowd before it disappears altogether.

Morning in Valencia. Wake up tired, so I disregard the morning's tour schedule and make my own plans for the day. I heave soiled laundry down a chute, walk into an elevator, and come out on the wrong floor, into a mall adjoining the hotel. Past the showy specialty stores displaying Massimo Dutti fashions, Clavileño chocolates, and more.

"Jack!"

Jim Heathcott is calling me over to the mall bench where he's sitting with a sketchbook. As I approach, he closes the book, but before he does I catch a glimpse of a partial drawing of a striking Asian woman and, written in felt pen on the cover of the sketchbook, T.B. 1967. Heathcott looks up at me dolefully, grips the book tightly.

"Are you all right?" I say.

"I'm thinking of doing some travelling," he says.

"Where to?"

"North America," he says. "I miss the prairie sky. Vietnam, maybe."

"Why would you want to go back to Vietnam?" I say.

"Why would you want to go back to Spain? Unfinished business," Heathcott says. He stands, turns abruptly, walks away.

I step onto an escalator and exit the mall. I soon find myself walking through a one-stop tour of the world. It's a Disneyland facsimile filled with scale-model reproductions of architectural wonders, from the Golden Gate Bridge to the Colosseum. A Japanese tourist poses his family against the 25-foot replica of the Eiffel Tower. His son, unprompted, bends to tug at the tower's base, a photo opportunity to wow friends back home — mammoth child besieges the Parisian monument like King Kong on the Empire State Building. I pause at a mini-Leaning Tower of Pisa, then I'm past this little Italy and out of this world.

Back in the real world, I see a full-sized Bob Mitchell standing next to a tour bus parked at the hotel. "Jack, I've been looking for you," he calls to me. "You coming with us?"

"Not today," I say with a wave.

I rent a car and leave Valencia.

NINE

THE BOOK OF ISAAC

Fort Harold, winter 1936

STEP OFF THE TRAIN INTO WIND-BLOWN CIRCLES
of snow full of dark leaves and broken branches. It is thick
with winter when I come north, having left earlier than
anticipated, moved by the weariness of joblessness and curiosity about Isaac. Most of the day is grey, but some moments
the sun will break across the whiteness, and the slush and ice
are inviting through the plate-glass windows of my father's
store, Feldman's Mens' Wear. The sign with the misplaced
apostrophe runs across the cracked white plaster facade of the
storefront at Harold Street and Third Avenue. While no one
is getting rich off the men's wear, it feeds my father and the
smatterings of relatives who pass through this northern town.

"I wouldn't go there for too long," my mother insisted at the
station as she handed me a bag filled with meatloaf on rye
sandwiches, dill pickles, burnt almond chocolate, apples, and
bananas. The train was at first enjoyable, but as the 500-mile
ride was slowed by snowdrifts and fallen trees, day turned into
night and into day again, and the newspapers and magazines
were read, and I couldn't sleep, and wanted off long before

arriving in Fort Harold. As I drag my suitcase the two blocks from the station to the store, the cold pierces my coat and sweater and scarf. Warmth, I sigh, pushing open the wood-framed glass door, and cold white clumps fall from my clothing into the pool of melted snow on the tiles just inside the store.

"Hi, I'm Jake, Isaac's son," I say to a man in his late thirties standing behind a heavy brass cash register on the front counter.

"Ike's boy," the man shouts, shuffling across the store floor to a small office in which, through its window, I can see the top of my father's thinning head of hair.

"Ike," the man hollers as I pull at balls of snow stuck to the wool gloves that shield my hands, still raw-red with cold. He is in my father's office for maybe five minutes, but to me it seems much longer.

"Jake," the man calls, emerging from the office, standing at its door. "Come on over here. Ike wants to see you."

Inside the cramped office, my father is sitting on a swivel chair, with a green visor across his brow, in a well-pressed shirt buttoned tieless at the neck. The room is cluttered with papers, a steel safe tucked in one corner. "I'm doing the books," he says, almost smiling, pulling the glasses from his face. "Jakie, you need a job, is that why you're here?"

My father figures no one goes to Fort Harold just to visit him. They only go when the Depression makes even Fort Harold endurable, providing it comes with a job. Besides Eddie and Joan — eleven weeks — there had been my father's cousin Ira from Montreal — eight days — and my mother's brother Lou — seven weeks. It looked as though Lou, direct from Chicago's taxi wars, might actually stay a while, but on an outing in the woods he was mauled by a grizzly. He survived, but in New York.

"That's why my cousin Sam came," my father says, quickly casting a hand towards the man who greeted me at the entrance to the store. "You came for a job in the schmatta business, and you got your job, right Sam?"

"Yes, Isaac," Sam says, "but you find, after awhile, your attitude towards this place changes. At first, I didn't like it much, but now I hate it. You learn to hate it."

"But you bear with it," my father tells me. "Your brother couldn't bear it, and now he's down in a *fercuckta* coal mine someplace."

"Gold mine," I say. "Well, actually, I was on my way to see Eddie because he said I might get work there, but I thought being so close I might as well drop by. But I won't be staying long."

"We'll put you to work," my father says, placing the metal-rimmed spectacles back on his face.

My father does put me to work — sweeping floors, sorting clothing, moving boxes, and waiting on customers. I'm dressed in a grey wool suit he fronts me from an advance on wages. "This suit is very up to date," says Sam, as he watches me inspect myself in the mirror.

To Sam, "up to date" is the ultimate compliment, and he is convinced Feldman's Mens' Wear fashions are comparable to the best that Vancouver's stylish shops have to offer. But this store is a working-class outfit and does most of its business Saturdays, when the lumber workers from the surrounding mills, sober from Friday night, are looking for ways to spend their money not already lost in hotel bars. They purchase the leather boots, heavy gloves, and work shirts the store specializes in and, occasionally, an up-to-date suit or a fedora with a feather.

My father lives in a two-deck clapboard home at the other end of Harold Street. The house is tidy, surprising to me after seeing his cluttered office. He lives upstairs, Sam has the main floor bedroom, and I'm given the living room's springy couch. For entertainment, I cross the street to a park where the town ice rink is home to hockey from morning till it's too late to see the puck—rubber when Fort Harold's team plays other towns, often a wooden two-by-four or a "road apple" (a horse's frozen dung) when the boys and unemployed men wile away their days in pickup games. Shins padded by store catalogues and cracked sticks tenuously held together by sticky black tape. Once a week, I venture to the other side of downtown, eight blocks away, to slip into a movie at the Royal Theatre. It's a more rambunctious place than a Vancouver movie house. There are jeers and cheers and shrill whistles and widespread necking in the sprinkling of "loveseats" the theatre has provided by tearing out the armrest between two seats.

Chess becomes an obsession this winter, more than radio or books, watching hockey or catching a movie at the Royal. "This game is very good. It increases your brain power," Sam says, tapping his temple. Sam and I keep track of our matches, staging best-of-seven series, calculating how many moves it takes to win. "I can win this match in fifteen moves," I boast, and Sam shakes his head with a good-humoured grimace and beats me in twelve. "The two great thinkers," my father says when he finds Sam and me over a chessboard.

My father is as mysterious to me here, in the same house, as he was an endless train ride away. "Where does he go every night?" I ask Sam between chess moves one evening.

"He works on the books," says Sam, adding with a shrug: "Who knows? Who asks?"

"The Book of Isaac would be a whodunnit," I say.

"Who needs to be an open book?" says Sam.

Sam is a gentle soul who dreams of being a working musician and imagines New York and London stages as he plays concertos on a neighbour's modest piano. My father has been upset with Sam since an incident at the store a week after I arrived. I'm in the store's basement, sorting shoe boxes, when I hear my father shout and run up the long planked staircase. A customer has just informed my father that a "hobo" sauntered into the store, scooped up two work shirts, and walked out in full view of Sam. My father and this customer sprint from the store and catch up with the shirts a block away. After a brief tussle in the snow, the man breaks away, and my father returns to his store with the shirts and a bleeding nose. Dripping wet, he offers the loyal customer one of the retrieved shirts, then screams at Sam. "What in hell's name were you doing just standing there in a dream world while somebody walks off with my inventory. Nebbish idiot." Sam's head is down, his feet pacing on the spot, his body swaying from the blow of my father's words.' "He needed it more than we do," Sam mumbles.

So my father is losing patience with his transient worker relatives, and I am losing patience with Isaac and Fort Harold. Two weeks in, and I want out as badly as my father wants me out, but it is the mystery of Isaac that holds me here. He thrives on the place. He actually likes the weather and is liked by his customers. A couple times a week, brawny loggers challenge my father to an arm wrestle; he places his bull arm across a store counter and, after the grunts subside, inevitably emerges the victor. And despite the flood of the times in other places, here my father doesn't expect to contend with anti-Semitism. There is one occasion, though, when the foreman of a mill, a regular customer, comes into the store from the hotel bar.

"This is Friday night, huh, Ike. Don't Jews always give you a deal on Friday night?"

My father's smile instantly turns into a snarl. "You," he commands, "get the hell out of this store and don't come back."

The foreman comes back the following week, apologizes fervently, and remains a regular customer.

Despite my father's impatience with his visiting family, he interrupts Sam's and my chess match one evening. "Someone is breaking windows at the store," he says. During the past two nights, the window in the front door frame has been shattered by a rock. Nothing was stolen and no one tried to enter the store—just the rock and the window. "I spoke to Sergeant Donaldson, the Mountie, and he's going to hide in the office tonight and catch this lunatic. I said I would hide with him, and I want you to be there too."

That night the four of us crouch in my father's office, waiting for the rock. It doesn't come, but the following evening, minus the night watchmen, it comes again. "The sergeant tells me he can't spend every night at the store, but he'll come by once in a while," my father tells me. "But we're going to catch him. We'll take turns watching out. Tonight, Sam and me. Tomorrow, Sam and you. Then, you and me."

My father stops coming after another night, explaining this is the work of younger men. After a few nights, Sam and I drift through our days like sleepwalkers. Then one morning, my father's bellowing voice tears Sam and me from under our blankets on the office floor.

"What in God's name happened here last night? The window's broke."

Glass shards are scattered across the snow puddle at the front door frame.

"I'm sorry," I moan in exhaustion. "Just...couldn't keep... awake."

"Don't be a nebbish like Sam," says my father with a scowl.

That ends the night watch. The window-breaking also stops.

I bundle in sweater, scarf, coat, gloves to make the eight-block trek to the Royal, where Ken Maynard will conquer the west tonight. The town is black, except for a glow emanating from the bulbs on the stone street lamps imported from Vancouver. The weather bakes my eyes cold and the hard browning snow crunches under my boots. I hear a melodious Mozart symphony pouring from a neighbour's house and pull the earmuffs from my face. My ears, burning from cold, are flooded with music from Sam's chunky fingers. The melody shifts from symphonic sound to boogie-woogie Benny Goodman. The music dips and floats and moves me, swaying beneath a lamppost, the snow around me lit in the surrounding black. For a moment, the bleakness disappears.

I continue to my rendezvous with the Royal Theatre. There are few cars on the street and only an occasional body that emerges from the dark at the last instant to pass on the wooden sidewalk.

Arriving early for the show, I buy a ticket and slip from under the broken marquee, with half its bulbs burned out, around to the lane where one of the theatre's neighbours keeps a chicken coop. During my childhood in the town, before we moved down to Vancouver, Eddie and I came to the coop and marvelled at the chickens running wild. This backyard served as a sort of Fort Harold Public Zoo for children. Tonight there is just a single chicken, shivering in the cold near the dark entrance to the coop. I walk back up the lane towards the theatre. As I'm about to turn the corner onto the street, the back porch on my right is suddenly lit up. I glance instinctively and see my father with a woman who is fumbling through her purse. I pause a moment as she finds the key that opens the house and they disappear inside.

I proceed to soggy popcorn in a small brown bag, while my eyes dart past the kissing couple in the loveseat in front of me and settle on Ken Maynard's heroics.

After the movie, I return home through the night, hating the cold and the town. Fort Harold is Canada, circa 1936, and Vancouver is the anomaly. Fort Harold is the northern Wild West, filled with hard-working and hard-drinking vagabonds who don't ask questions or answer any either. There are rumours here of murderers, political refugees, and other wanted and unwanted men and women on the run.

In his way, Isaac is running too.

I watch the woman press her baby into my father's arms. "Take her so I can look at these shirts," she tells him. He holds the baby momentarily, then pinches her torso so that she cries and the woman pulls her away from him and leaves. "Better," my father turns to me, "to be rid of that than to sell a shirt."

"Why do you think your father doesn't want you around?" Sam says that evening between moves on the chessboard. Just then, my father walks into the room and flicks on the radio. "You know," he says, listening to the crackling radio. "This Ed Wynn on the radio is a yiddel."

"Georgie Leonard says Ed Wynn's a relative of his," I say. "Second cousin or something."

"And Georgie's mother is the queen of England," says my father.

"I hope the sawmill boys don't strike this summer," says Sam. "That mill owner Bert Williamson was in the store today. Really worried."

"I hope they do strike," I say.

"They're greedy," my father scoffs. "More money, more this, more that."

"Greedy?" My voice rises. "They built the sawmill. They produce its wealth."

"Greedy, greedy, greedy, greedy," says my father, piercing me through his thick lenses. "And I'm not asking for a song and dance from you, sonny boy. Talk that way in Russia if you want, but not in my house."

"Calm down," Sam suggests. "No reason to get all worked up over words."

"It's not just words," I say. "A lot of people can't find enough work to keep themselves eating and a few are wealthy without even working."

"You sound like a *farbrente* Bolshevik. Back in Russia, we had nothing," my father says. "We had pogroms."

"That," Sam interjects, "is a red herring, Isaac. We left Russia before the Bolsheviks took over."

My father's red face looks about to burst. "Russia's got nothing to do with the Bolsheviks," he shouts. "The Russians treated us like dirt before the Bolsheviks were born and they'll still treat us like that after every Bolshevik is dead and buried." He cracks a small smile, belatedly absorbing Sam's "red herring" reference. "How," he asks me, "is *mein* boy, the red herring?"

"Just tickled pink, I am," I say.

A few minutes later, my father moves on to the kitchen, and I tell Sam about the light on the back porch by the Royal Theatre.

"Of course, I know that. What he does in his life is his business," Sam says. "Isaac gives me work. I keep my nose clean. But Jake, I'm surprised it took you this long to find out. Everybody in this town knows. Why do you think your father doesn't want you here?"

Kitty Thomas bartends at the hotel between Isaac's house and store. She left a young marriage in her southern Interior hometown and worked in saloons and hotels from San Francisco to Dawson City before arriving in Fort Harold. My father and Kitty have become inseparable — after midnight. They are never seen together in daylight, though before I arrived, she often spent nights at his house.

"I don't care who he sleeps with," I tell Sam. "Believe me, Mom isn't up nights waiting for him, and I just don't care, so why...?"

"You're cramping his style," says Sam. "He doesn't want you to tell your mother. I don't know why. He just doesn't."

My father steps into the adjacent hallway, and we stop talking. He's wrapped himself in an overcoat and other winter garb, capped by a fedora with a white feather. "So Mr. Dreamer and Mr. Red Herring are still at the chessboard," he smirks, gripping the front doorknob.

"You should play chess sometime," I say. "It sharpens your mind."

"Don't you worry about my mind, sonny boy," he says. "The way you're going, you're going to be another Sam."

"You'll be glad to know," I say, "I'm leaving for Wells in the morning."

Wells is Barkerville's new twin town. If Fort Harold is remote, Barkerville is practically an apparition, its raised, plank sidewalks trailing past a dilapidated, boarded saloon, sheriff's office, mine registry. It was a boom town in the 1860s after Billy Barker struck gold but has long settled into memories of what might have been. The first rush of gold ran dry, but the town still drew itinerant pick-and-pan prospectors looking for their motherlode. Fred Wells's discovery of gold nearby initiated a minor renaissance in the area in the 1930s, attracting people to Wells, just west of Barkerville.

I find Joan and Eddie's house by inquiring at a café, where it seems everyone knows the town's happy couple. Joan greets me at their three-room clapboard house wrapped in hills on the edge of the new mining town.

"Eddie will be happy to see you."

"How is it here?" I wonder, loosening my boots as Joan pours coffee.

"We just rented this house, were over in Barkerville before. I'd like to get back to White Rock," she says, smiling at the mention of her hometown down by the U.S. border. "And Eddie misses the city. But we like this place too. We went for long walks along the trails in the woods and picked berries in the summer. Now we hike through the snow and curl up by the fireplace. It doesn't sound exciting, but it is, in a way."

"I guess anything seems nice after Fort Harold. Joan, I was just up there for a month, with the old man."

"Yes, we didn't like it there. It was too much."

"Any chance of work here?"

"You might get some. I'm not sure. Ask Eddie about that. We're five minutes from the mine and his shift just ended."

As Joan completes this sentence, Eddie walks through the front door and we embrace.

"Came in on the stagecoach this afternoon," I say.

"I know they call that thing you rode into town a stagecoach," Eddie says. "Don't know why. Are they trying to be cowboys? To me, it's just a little truck with seating."

"Any chance of getting work here?"

"I feel bad about this, Jake, because I wrote you that there would probably be something here, but they aren't hiring now. It's slow and there's a lot of guys wanting work. You should be able to get the odd shift, but I don't know if anything worthwhile will come of it."

"That's a shame," I say unconvincingly, having had enough of the north. "I'll head back to Vancouver in the morning."

"No, stay a few days," Eddie insists. "I'm taking you both out for dinner tonight."

Out for dinner means Wing's Cafe, the "Chinese Canadian Restaurant" with chop suey and hotcakes on the menu. The Chinese influx into the north is large enough to form, practically everywhere, tiny Chinatowns, and this café is in a five-storefront Asian strip, including a hand laundry and a general store. After taking the stagecoach into town in weather so cold it pinches faces, hot sweet-and-sour spareribs and chicken chow mein taste as fine as any meal in my memory.

"This here is Thirty Below, the chief cook and bottle washer," Eddie says, introducing Wing's proprietor to me.

"How'd you get that name?" I say.

"A lot of people have strange nicknames up here," Thirty Below says. There is the Ancient Maritimer, a grizzled Cape Breton Islander who paddled into the Cariboo looking for gold and now comes in from nowhere each spring to disappear each fall. There is Irish, once an actor on the Dublin stage, now a hotel bartender who one evening provided by heart an impromptu recitation of *Richard III* in its entirety. There is Johnny the Jew, who lives in a frozen book-lined shack outside town on the Willow River. Some say he was a professor or even a British MP who came to misfortune, maybe scandal, and now lives with his "friends" the birds. There is Big Trapper Sam, 4-foot-6, and Gabby Trapper Dan, a resident of Barkerville for fifteen years without speaking a word, though word is he's not mute.

"So," says Eddie, "how is the old man, really?"

"Can't say that I know," I say. "I don't think the old man knows how the old man is."

The rain as the train slows into Vancouver is welcome after a month in the snowy Interior. I was up north when a short-lived snowfall came and melted in Vancouver and the worst winter would offer the city was over. Discarding my toque and earmuffs for a fedora from Feldman's Mens' Wear, I walk Strathcona's rain-fresh sidewalks, and I turn into Keefer Street and home.

TEN

OLD FRIENDS

Valencia, fall 1986

RIVING ALONG THE COAST FROM VALENCIA, I leave the highway and proceed along a dirt road cordoned by olive groves. I pull up at the front yard of a whitewashed brick house, knock at the door. As a man's face tilts out from behind the door, "Victor," I say cautiously.

"My friend," Victor says, clasping my hands in his leathery ones.

"Lucia," he calls, and a slight, white-haired woman comes from a back room.

"This is Jake."

"This is Victor."

I was introduced to Victor Alba by Captain Phillip Shaw of the International Brigades. A journalist from Manchester, England, Shaw was charged with orienting incoming international volunteers at Tarazona de la Mancha, a village near the town of Albacete, the Brigades' main base. While we trained for civil war, the Spaniards at the base acted as liaisons between our brigade and the residents of Tarazona and Albacete, learning

English as they taught us survival Spanish and provided tours of the local menu.

"Victor," I said, reaching out my hand.

Seeing that he was scrutinizing my piecemeal uniform — britches too tight, shoes and shirt too large, a jumble of colour uncoordination — I said self-consciously, "Captain Shaw says I'll get a new uniform as soon as possible."

A day before, I'd crossed the border into Spain in the kind of shivering summer morning that turns blistering hot. The darkness was beginning to lift off the shadowy figures I'd shared the night with when our guide shouted, "We're in Spain." We stopped short, silent for a moment, then began to sing, in different languages, the same song.

"Arise ye prisoners of starvation..."

We sang louder than we will ever sing again, our tired bodies standing for our international anthem.

"A better world's in birth..."

The small sixteen-year-old in 1937, who looked even younger, is now a small sixty-six-year-old man, who looks older.

"Jake, I knew I would see you again," says Victor, leading me on a tour of his citrus field. We did not stay in touch following the Civil War, but before returning for the reunion, I wrote Albacete municipal hall asking about Victor Alba. I expected nothing in return and was surprised six weeks later to receive a letter from a town clerk who knew the Alba family. She sent me Victor's address, this farm north of Valencia. I contacted Victor and he sent back a friendly note with his phone number, which I called yesterday from Valencia.

"It's funny, hearing your English last night," he says.

"Your English was always better than my Spanish," I say. "Never had to learn that much Spanish in the Fifteenth Brigade." The basic Spanish I picked up fifty years ago is now mostly gone. The Fifteenth was the predominantly English-speaking international brigade, including Canada's Mackenzie-Papineau Battalion, America's Abraham Lincoln Battalion, the British Battalion, and the Irish Connelly Column.

My first day leave, I explored Albacete — down its long Lodares passageway and through its city squares and fairgrounds. Settling into a bar to write letters home, I was sitting on a high stool, under a low ceiling, beside two old men playing dominoes. I lost myself in writing and by the time I saw the time, I was almost due back at the base but had missed my ride with the supply truck that brought me. Frantically, I walked through town, coming upon Victor sitting with two friends in front of an adobe house. As I explained my predicament, he invited me inside the compact living room of this home — white-walled with stucco, mirrors draped in black bunting, dining table covered in thick handwoven wool, windows with wood shutters, heat from charcoal in an open metal pan sunk into the floor. In rapid-fire Spanish, Victor explained my situation to his mother, Gabriela. She bent her head, silver-streaked black hair falling around her face, listening with a perplexed expression. Then she offered me a reassuring glance and Victor instructions.

Following her directive, Victor and I walked hastily to a nearby Republican Army office in a small building. A robust man in a fresh-pressed uniform listened to our story, then motioned for us to wait in a nearby restaurant. We crossed the street to the smoky café and sat at a bare table. A single bulb hung from the ceiling, the walls papered with bullfight posters. Victor introduced me to the family at the next table — a middle-aged woman and man and their two children. "Canadiense!" the man said approvingly. I ordered beers for myself and Victor, which brought a laugh from the middle-aged couple, who saw the child in Victor, the cherubic neighbour they had known all of his sixteen years.

As Victor and I slowly sipped our drinks, we traded vocabulary. "Ceiling," I said, pointing to the knockdown texture above our heads. "Ceiling," he repeated, adding his Spanish translation: "Techo." As we talked, I noticed a reddish pink lump of healing flesh on Victor's left hand. "Techo," I said. Conscious that I have glimpsed his wound, Victor quickly pulled his hand back from the table. After a moment, though, he leaned forward and pointed to the pink mark. "Bullet," he said. "We keep Albacete from Franco. My brother and my friend die." Victor quaffed his beer. "Your ride now," he said, jerking from the table, acknowledging a young woman standing at the café's entrance and calling me to a food supply truck about to leave for the Tarazona base.

From that day forward, I spent my occasional days away from Tarazona with Victor's family in Albacete. Victor and I became friends and I was warmly welcomed by his parents and five sisters and brothers. While we often struggled to comprehend each other's words, I liked this family and they seemed to like this Canadiense.

Fifty years later, in body language and black-and-blue Spanish and English, Victor tells me that two of his sisters and his father died in the bloodshed that followed Franco's victory.

Victor left Albacete after the war and with Lucia raised four children on this farm. "They know about the Civil War but other things the important things," says Victor, explaining that his children left the farm for school and jobs in Valencia and Madrid. His mother died two years ago in the Albacete house where Jake had met her. "We wanted her to live here, with us, but she wouldn't leave Albacete."

Mostly Victor and I are quiet, resting under an olive tree in the perfect autumn, old friends.

"Did you see her again?" Victor says after a long silence.

"Just once."

The Alba family's wine and spicy hot cornmeal, cooked on an orange cylinder of butane gas, used to be a reprieve from the brigade base's olives and beans. Now, Victor, Lucia, and I eat rice and chicken and drink dessert wine, and as dusk comes goodbyes are exchanged.

"No pasaran," says Victor, giving me the Republic's clenched-fist salute with a hand still slightly marked with the old wound.

After returning the rented car, I find Mac-Pap Aaro Ononen in the Hotel Expo bar slapping his chest like Godzilla and grunting guttural epithets to the Toronto reporter. A broad barrel of a man, Aaro was a light-heavyweight contender in Finland.

"Imagine," Tom Barkley says, listening to Aaro tell his story, "him being light *anything*."

Aaro turned down an invitation to fight in Finland's Olympic trials, choosing to boycott the 1936 Games in Berlin and move to Canada. Upon his arrival in Montreal, though, the Spanish Civil War started. Having disembarked one ship in Canada, he got on board another and headed back to Europe — hiked four days to reach Republican territory, promptly turned around, re-entered enemy territory, where he spent the war and after with a band of Spanish mountain partisans whose language he didn't speak.

"We blow bridges and trains," Aaro bellows, slapping the table. He hasn't changed his white short-sleeved shirt since arriving in Madrid, and its odour and his oily stubbly face create a facsimile of his former guerrilla persona. "People… they hide us in barns," he roars into the face of the reporter seated beside him. Aaro returned to Finland to join the underground in World War II, and he would not immigrate to Canada again until the 1960s. The reporter knows Aaro has a story but he postpones the rigours of continuing the interview now and moves on to the table I share with Susan and Tom.

"Too much buses, too much meetings," Aaro groans, thumping his chest. Aaro has been drinking awhile and his outcries bring Bob Mitchell to his table. "Aaro," he says, "it's been a long day. I think it's time for bed."

"No bed," Aaro mutters. "No bed."

Bob gently tugs at Aaro's arm, urging him to come along nicely, but Aaro has never been one to follow niceties. Aaro did not come to Spain nicely in 1936, he did not blow bridges nicely and, damn it, this evening he is not going to bed nicely. He stands, raising fists, tensing his arms — now more girthy than muscular — and rages against Bob's paternalistic tone: "No bed, no bed, no bed."

Aaro now has the attention of everyone in the bar, and Henry Simmons stands to backup Bob. "Come on, Aaro, let's go to bed," says Henry, reviving the authoritative voice of his brief tenure as a Mac-Pap lieutenant.

"No bed," Aaro vows, lifting another beer mug to his lips.

"What's eating you, Aaro?" says Henry. To Aaro, Henry is a worthy adversary—a roughhousing defenceman in the Winnipeg

Junior Hockey League before Spain. So it takes but a moment for the two to square off, arms curled, knees bent, in classic bare-knuckle fisticuff poses worthy of John L. Sullivan.

"Break it up!" Jim Heathcott's commanding voice comes from the shadows of the bar where he has been drinking alone. The two old fighters freeze, still poised for battle. "Break it up, I said," demands Heathcott, stepping between the two. Henry drops his fists. Aaro grips his table and shakes, sending a half-full glass to the floor.

"Arrrgg," he says.

"Truer words were never spoken," I say.

"Me, Tarzan," Tom laughs.

Henry, deflated, walks from the bar, head down. Aaro, having at least defeated the table, carries himself out of the bar with drunken dignity.

"Those two are all right," Heathcott chuckles after they leave.

"Jack," says Bob, shaken by the confrontation, "Aaro's a good man. He's just not used to this hectic pace."

"What's Simmons's excuse?" Tom says.

"Everybody's tired. That's probably all there is to it," I say.

"Maybe we should get to bed then," Bob says.

Being back in Spain reminds us that we once ached to act and now seem incapable of it—elderly men and women who have been on the sidelines for so long, now touring old battlefronts and unmarked memorials of our war, being hosted at receptions or toasting each other in hotel bars. For a strong, physical man like Aaro, almost anything, even a barroom fight with Henry Simmons, seems preferable to an admission that his moment is past.

"I don't feel like going to bed," Tom says.

"Suit yourself then," says Bob, "but I'm done in. See you in the morning."

"I'm tired too," Susan says, and soon after Bob departs, the Barkleys do too.

I finish my beer and say goodnight, leaving Jim Heathcott alone in the bar, hunched over the table, settling in for the night.

ELEVEN

THEN THE RAINS CAME

Vancouver, spring 1936

VANCOUVER IS A GREAT CITY TO LIVE IN IF YOU like the month of October. It's October nine months of the year, with one or two months of summer, one or two months of winter. When the sky clears the morning after a downpour, there is a cool freshness — the neighbourhood washed clean, a floral perfume rising from its yards, soaked pebbles crackling to footsteps on the sidewalk's dark, watery sheen. Frieda did not go outside in the rain her first year in Vancouver. "I'll wait till the rain stops." Then the rains came, again, and like the rest of the family, my mother metamorphosed into the part-human, part-amphibian species unique to the city. Residents develop their own rain-survival techniques and rain barometers. I observe the splashing in puddles from my second-floor bedroom window to determine if rain gear is required, but I've become so accustomed to all of this that I seldom wear anything special or carry an umbrella. Visitors from dryer climes observe the strange ritual of people taking rain showers — necks protectively compressed into hunched upper bodies, eyes blinking like windshield wipers on scrunched faces. When a local version of Copenhagen's *Little Mermaid* statue is erected, instead of a fin it has legs, like the Aquamen and women that evolved with Vancouver's wet streets. There are people who bask in the rain.

"Liquid sunshine," Mrs. Finkel calls it.

"Do you think," Art says, "that maybe Vancouver is God's outhouse and whenever he has to piss…"

"At least," my father would say, "you don't have to shovel rain."

As spring turns to summer the rains come less often, but they never leave entirely, returning from out of the blue sky, an unpredictability always with the city, nourishing its spontaneity. There is the rare summer day when the rains are warmish, as if descended from a boiling cauldron that had blown its lid.

My mother's pot of flanken soup is boiling after I return unannounced from Fort Harold, coming through the back door and into the kitchen where she is so surprised to see me that she forgets about the soup on the stove. Rachel is happy, too, that I've returned from the north, and Mrs. Finkel is here, and the three edge me to the kitchen table for a heaping bowl of kasha and, when it cools, flanken soup.

"Eddie's fine, and Joan's pregnant, and Fort Harold's cold," I divulge through a mouthful.

"Joan's pregnant!" Rachel says. "How is she?"

"She's fine," I say, turning to my mother. "You're going to be a bubby."

"A bubby," she says testily. "I'm not that old. Do they get proper care up there?"

"They're fine. I was only there a day, but they actually seem to like the place."

"And your father?"

"The same. Always the same."

I thaw in the rain the next few days and start another job search. Again and again I'm told that these days the centre of neighbourhood activity is the Katz place. So I knock at the door. Alex isn't home, Esther Katz tells me. "And no, the revolution didn't begin while you were out of town," she says, laughing, then tells me of this week's Workers Circle meeting at this house to plan for a demonstration against the Nazi warship *Karlsbad*. It will be at Ballantyne Pier in a month.

"You know there's a ship from Nazi Germany coming to Vancouver," I say to my mother that evening. "Everyone should be there. You should be there."

"Don't make trouble, Jakie. There's bigger people than you who will stand up to them."

"There are no *bigger* people."

While I was up north, the Katz family acquired a new lustre, respectability even, as a conduit for the neighbourhood to express the anguish that's been building over events in Europe. So when I arrive early for the meeting at the Katz place, securing a chair in the living room, it seems the entire neighbourhood is there. The living room is jam-packed, with more in the kitchen and on the front porch.

Abigail Levey sits in the middle of the room detailing the scenario. On the day of the protest, there are plans for the Nazi crew to parade from the waterfront to a downtown civic reception at Bear Hall, behind Christ Church Cathedral.

"You mean," says an astonished Sammy the deli-man, "the mayor is going to welcome these *antisemitten*?"

"Yes," says Abigail, "we just saw the official schedule today. I can't emphasize enough how important a statement we'll be making at this protest. It is time for Vancouver to stand up and be counted — to say Nazis are not welcome here no matter what any Canadian politician says."

Voices speak over voices. "*Shtey oyf*," Georgie Leonard's father, Abe, seated next to me, says barely audibly. "Time for us to stand up."

The room quiets as Abigail outlines the protest — the Workers Circle will join other protesters to confront the ship at Ballantyne Pier, at a Board of Trade luncheon, and again at Bear Hall. "They will get a warm reception," says Alex, rising to his feet to list the organizations — left, labour, ethnic — in the broad coalition protesting the *Karlsbad*.

I'm seated across the room from Alex, watching him speak, when she walks through my line of vision. My eyes are fixed on her as she removes her green trench coat, and her hair, darkened by the drizzle, falls below her waist. Every seat taken, Lena Horowitz sits on the arm of a couch and, for the first time since I caught sight of her, I exhale.

My mother's pot of flanken soup is simmering as she leans against the kitchen sink, her attention on the letter Rachel has received from my father. (At least dictated by my father. Written and mailed by Kitty.) Rachel is reading it to our mother and me: "Dear Rachel. Happy birthday. Here is five dollars to spend on whatever you want to get or save it for a rainy day."

"That's every damn day around here," I say.

"I understand," Rachel continues reading, "you were the star in your school play. That's a real feather in your cap. It seems we have a coming actress in the family. Some day I'll see you perform. Yours truly. Father."

I'm pleased our father is showing an interest — any interest — in one of his children. Rachel is less impressed. "He didn't even mention you, Mom," she says indignantly. "It's like you don't exist anymore, or never did."

"At least," I say, "he sent the five dollars. That was nice of him."

"*Nice?* What else has he sent?" my mother says.

I drift from their conversation, instead anticipating who might be at this evening's meeting at the Katz place.

⁘

I was absorbed with Lena at last week's meeting but anxious that my words would come out babble if I said anything to her. Now, I rise from a bench, just inside the doorway to the crowded Katz living room and turn to exit the house the moment Lena enters. "'Scuse me," I say, performing a nimble sidestep to avoid colliding with her.

"You don't have to do that," she says, believing I have risen to offer her my seat.

"No. I was just…"

I was just getting up to go for a quick cigarette before the meeting, the Katz family having decreed that smoking be done on the porch. When Abigail Levey calls things to order, I butt my cigarette and return to the living room to happily discover seating space alongside Lena on the bench.

"More than twenty groups were represented at the Anti-Nazi Coalition meeting I attended last night," Abigail is saying. "We will organize this city, neighbourhood by neighbourhood, block by block, to fight fascism. We need people in our neighbourhood to hand out leaflets and put up posters, to talk to the newspapers, to paint banners and placards, to be marshals, to link up with other communities."

Swept along by the enthusiasm of the room, I'm about to volunteer to help write a leaflet, but instead, uncertain of my writing, my hand shoots up with several others offering to distribute leaflets. Then my attention shifts to Lena, sitting upright alongside my sloping posture, hair draping the back of her green blouse, staring intently at the discussion underway, unmindful of me.

"Why don't the leaflets," she suggests, "have the same design as the larger posters. That way they'll reinforce each other in people's minds."

"Smart idea, Lena," says Abigail, her thick fingers dancing as she speaks. "Will you work on that?"

"Yes, I can design the poster."

"Great. Let's talk about that later."

When the meeting dissolves an hour later, I muster the nerve to approach Lena. "Are you in touch with Florence in Tor—"

"I don't have time right now," says Lena, spinning to speak with Abigail.

"Jake," Alex calls out, coming at me from across the room. "I want to talk with you about something that's in the works. It's something that needs a bit of privacy."

When I return to Keefer Street after the meeting, Sam is sitting at the kitchen table, blowing on a bowl of my mother's flanken soup.

"*Sam.* So you finally escaped Fort Isaac," I say.

"*Essen*," my mother tells me, placing another bowl on the table. "I'm not hungry."

"If I stayed at that job and in that house," Sam says, "I'd have ulcers and bleeding piles."

"Not to mention," I say, "all the things you'd get from being around my father."

Sam has a way of showing up without advance notice. Since leaving Montreal two years ago, Sam dropped into Bessie's in Toronto, Isaac's in Fort Harold, and the homes of untold relatives I'd not heard of in towns that don't exist on the globe my mother gave me a birthday ago. Sam will stay on the Keefer Street couch for a couple of days until he finds a room, then he'll pursue a job and his music.

"Eat," Freida says.

"I'm still not hungry," I say.

"How about a game of chess, Jake?" Sam says.

"Not tonight. I'm tired," I say, departing to my room with other thoughts in mind. There is the rally, and there is Lena, and she stays with me until I slump asleep.

I'm lying in bed contemplating the morning's raindrop dance on the bedroom window when Rachel and Polly pass my open door.

Rachel pauses. "I want to go to the rally," she tells me.

"Me too," adds Polly.

On the way to meet Alex, I encounter Georgie Leonard in front of Sammy's deli.

"Let's shoot pool some day, Feldman."

While I was in Fort Harold, Art Posner took to the rails, last reported in Winnipeg, and I haven't looked at a cue ball since returning home.

"Don't have time these days, Georgie. Working on the anti-Nazi rally. You're going to be there aren't you?"

"You know what?" Georgie says.

"Not personally," I say.

"I've got my future to think about."

"But Georgie, even your father was at the last meeting."

The little delicatessen is bursting at lunchtime, customers bunched at its counter and tables. "Great place for privacy, Alex," I say, wiping crumbs from the small table where he's seated. It's crowded with a mustard jar, ketchup bottle, and bowl of dill pickles.

"We can talk here, Jake," he says, "It's so noisy no one else will hear a word we say to each other." Alex rises from the table to collect his chopped liver and bagel from Rachel, who's working behind the counter. "You want anything, Jake?" he says.

"Potato knish," I say, handing him a couple of coins.

While Alex fetches lunch for us I sit reading his morning paper's sports page.

"I've never seen the neighbourhood so ready to do something about anything," I say when Alex returns.

"Yeah, everyone feels the same way the Workers Circle feels about this ship. And there's talk...and I want to see if you're interested...in upping the ante a little."

"How do you mean?" I say, biting into a crusty knish stuffed with spicy mashed potato.

"The plan now is to meet the ship at the dock and listen to a few speeches, and everybody'll feel good, or bad, or whatever, and then go home. Some of our Circle people and some of the Italian comrades and guys in the unemployed union are saying that's just not good enough. We need to do something more dramatic that gets everyone's attention."

Alex stops explaining and examines my face for a response.

"I'm interested," I say. "What gives?"

"We go to the big rally at the dock," Alex says quietly, his breathy mouth inches away, "but then break away on our own to confront the Nazis on that ship and again when they meet with the mayor at Bear Hall. Make it very hard for the mayor to have a civil meeting with Nazis."

Other customers are oblivious to the intrigue between Alex and me, including an unkempt man who approaches our table, takes the ketchup bottle, and pours it into the glass of water Sammy has given him. He mixes this Depression Special with a knife, selects a dill from the bowl, and steps back against the wall, eating his lunch alongside framed black-and-white photographs of David Oppenheimer, who left Bavaria to become the second mayor of Vancouver; Mary Livingstone, who left Strathcona to team with Jack Benny on radio and in life; David Belasco, who left Victoria to adapt *Madame Butterfly* for Broadway; and young Nathaniel Nemirovsky, who will leave Vancouver to become, Sam is convinced, the first prime minister from the neighbourhood.

"We got to know how many people we've got before we can decide to go ahead with it," Alex says. "Would you do this?"

"Sure I would." I sit back, suddenly stirred by the notion. "But what exactly are we doing and how many of us are there? I'm not running onto that ship with just your mom, your dad, and you."

"The pieces are coming together. I'll keep you posted."

Abigail Levey huddles in a corner with Esther and Harry Katz and Hy Fried. Tension pervades the Katz place, and at first I think it is all mine, something to do with my preoccupation with Lena, who is standing at the dining table taking her poster art out from a folder. Abigail starts the meeting with a report on the growing interest in the protest in other neighbourhoods.

"Downtown, West End, you name it," she says. Abigail calls on Lena, who steps up to the front with her poster — a charcoal sketch of a man, woman, and child with shovels and rifles slung over their shoulders, facing the world with impassioned eyes, marching under the fiery script "STOP THE NAZIS. Lives Are In Your Hands."

When she holds it up for all to see, I consider the poster's Soviet realism, Canadian style, and its artistry having come from the dazzling left hand of Lena Horowitz, I concur with Levey's assessment: "Terrific. I'll take it to the Coalition meeting for approval this week. And we'll have two weeks to cover the city with it."

Abigail's tone turns terse. "I have a matter to air," she says. Hy Fried, a founding member of Vancouver's Workers Circle branch, stands beside her as she sits forward, fingers locked tightly, eyes burrowing the faces in the living room. "We don't think," she says, "a militant confrontation is called for at this time. The Coalition's anti-fascist stand has more support than ever before, and such militancy will only alienate the public from a cause seen as just by liberals and clergy and practically everyone. If anyone has any thoughts about doing something unapproved by the Coalition, they should talk to us first. We have everything under control."

"Who's *we*?" I blurt.

Abigail's fingers squeeze her chair and she shoots me a glare that says she has identified one of the conspirators. "*We* are the Anti-Nazi Coalition leadership. We are the ones who were politically engaged long before there was any talk of a warship docking in Vancouver. And we have a lot at stake in this protest. We want it to be successful because we are in this struggle for the long haul."

There is a long moment of silence, finally interrupted by Alex. "Jake's got a point. There are a lot of people in this room who are as committed as you, Abby, who feel that listening to speech after speech at the dock isn't enough. As long as no one disrupts that part of the protest—the Coalition's part—what other people want to do after that is, frankly, none of your business."

Half the crowded room is on its feet wagging fingers and fists. "Don't you ever speak to Abigail in that tone," Hy Fried shouts at Alex, whose father, Harry adds, "We must have a unified demonstration. You know that, Alex."

Calmer now, Fried adds, "This kind of militancy alienates the people, but fighting among ourselves is unproductive. Let's all settle down and discuss this quietly."

"This is bullshit," Alex booms. "Do whatever it takes to stop the Nazis." Some applaud; others call out, "No...no."

"Militancy," says Fried, all flustered again, "sets back the progressive cause."

"Revolution," Lena snaps, "is militancy, carried out by a lot of people, at the same time, in the same place."

The waterfront is decorated with banners: Relief Camp Workers Against Fascism, One Big Union, Finnish Organization of Canada, International Typographical Union, Red International, Communist Party, Chinese Unemployed Association, Anti-Nazi Coalition, Mayday Committee, Pacific Coast Fishermen's Union, Co-operative Commonwealth Federation, Ukrainian Anti-fascist League, Waterfront Workers Association, Order of Sleeping Car Porters, Hotel and Restaurant Employees Union, Jewish Workers Circle.

The sun is broiling the dock and its thousands of protesters. I stand with the Workers Circle contingent. One by one, speakers step onto a makeshift stage beside the *Karlsbad* and rail at the Nazi warship, decrying Hitler and Mussolini and Franco's week-old fascist revolt in Spain. I spot Lena circulating by herself, watching the stage, stopping to chat with Rachel, who has pried herself from the Rex Theatre to be here along with Polly Siegel, Ruth Solomon, and Georgie Leonard's father too.

When it's Abigail Levey's time to speak, she thunders from the stage: "We must all stand for humanity and against fascism. We must work to destroy Nazi Germany and defeat the rise of Franco in Spain." We cheer Abigail's call to arms, but it isn't a call to actual arms, and many watching her know that something more is brewing in this crowd. Before Abigail leaves the stage, she hastily introduces Luigi Mundello of the Italian Workers Youth. "The Anti-Nazi Coalition's rally has now concluded," Abigail says. "We are not responsible for anything else that occurs as of this time."

Mundello's appearance on stage is the Coalition's concession to its militant faction, which had threatened to withdraw organizational support for the rally unless permitted a speaker. A swarthy, muscular man in his early twenties, wearing black trousers and a baggy white shirt with rolled-up sleeves, Mundello, before uttering a word, turns his back to the crowd, places his hands on hips, and stares down the ominous ship in Vancouver's harbour, German sailors slouched over its starboard side to get their first look at a Canadian protest. Mundello slowly raises a clenched fist, his back still facing the demonstrators, their fists now also rising into the *Karlsbad* sailors' faces. Then Mundello abruptly turns to face the anti-Nazi crowd, spitting into the megaphone: "We aren't going to talk to fascism, we aren't going to shout at fascism, we are going to smash fascism."

"We are going to smash fascism," the crowd repeats, meekly at first, then "Smash fascism!" rises louder and louder, again and again. It is the signal.

"Let's go," says Alex Katz, grabbing at my sleeve as loudspeakers on the *Karlsbad* start playing the Nazi ode "Horst Wessel" to drown out the chanting demonstrators. Most everyone's eyes are on Mundello when I break for the gangplank with about ten other protesters. A barrel-bodied relief striker, Billy Sweeney, cold-cocks the German guard at the foot of the ship's ramp. We quickly reach the ship, shove aside another guard, and make a dash for a massive Nazi flag at the bow.

At first, few sailors are aware we are on board, but by the time I'm near the flag, the squeals of shunted guards have alerted the entire ship. Standing between us and the flagpole is a pack of aroused sailors. We throw fists at the Nazis and I slip through to the flagpole. According to plan, whoever reaches the pole first will climb for the flag while the others hold off the *Karlsbad*'s crew. I had no idea that would be me but now I scale the pole, glancing down at the dock and its thousands of anti-fascist protesters, each of whom is fixated on the bedlam on the ship. Pulling a lighter from my pocket, I reach for the swastika flag billowing over Vancouver Harbour. Meanwhile, others from the large protest try to join us on board and a donnybrook erupts on the gangplank. Some of these protesters break through the *Karlsbad* sailors on this plank and sprint towards the flagpole.

While I fumble with the lighter, a sailor's hand grapples with my boot. I drive my foot onto his hand and reach out the lighter as far as my arm can stretch. Another hand grabs my leg and I tumble onto the deck. "Smash fascism!" the rally crowd is howling as I'm kicked in the head, the ribs, the mouth. As I'm about to pass out, I see Art Posner on board and try to shout his name. Our eyes catch for an instant, I force a bleeding smile, then I'm gone.

When I come to, I'm being dragged from the ship by two cops — groggily I take in the sailors' jeers, the demonstrators' cheers. I'm booked into the city jail on the edge of Japantown, my face smeared with caked blood, shirt shredded. Also in the cell are Warren Hutchins, a gawky eighteen-year-old arrested at the protest, and two prisoners who've been there a while. One lays silently on a lower bunk as, above him, the other rolls from his upper berth to examine his new cellmates. "What are you in for?" he says.

"The *Karlsbad* rally," says Warren.

"I would have been there if I wasn't here," the prisoner says affably. "What's the latest from Spain, boys?"

Spain is the word of the day in the world's headlines, union halls, campuses, and apparently, even jail cells. A week before, Francisco Franco and his fascist generals, backed by Hitler and Mussolini, had overthrown the elected leftist Popular Front Republican government. Franco installed himself as dictator, but Spain spontaneously rose up against his rule, prompting a worldwide outpouring of support for this Republican resistance.

"It goes well," I say. "I understand most of the country has been taken back."

"They got me for breaking and entering," says the prisoner, "and if the Spanish Republic is winning I'll be smiling in the can." The prisoner is a skilled carpenter out of work for most of the Depression, he says. Hutchins is a dentist's son from the

West Side, unnerved by his first arrest. "I'll bet Nat Nemirovsky is on the case right now," I assure him. "We'll be out soon.... I'm sure. I think."

The cell door opens. Hutchins and I are whisked through the downtown lock-up and deposited in an alley. "Freedom," I shout to myself in the dark, stenching lane, finally feeling exultant about the *Karlsbad* boarding. We walk briskly around to the front of the jail where fifty noisy supporters including Alex Katz are chanting "Free the *Karlsbad* three," scaled down from what had started as "Free the *Karlsbad* eleven." With the release of Hutchins and me, this becomes, fleetingly, "Free the *Karlsbad* one," then the last of the arrested, Billy Sweeney, appears and the crowd moves along to Strathcona's Ukrainian Hall, which has been rented by the Coalition for an after-rally anti-fascist bash.

Alex updates me on the arrests as we walk the five blocks to the hall. Released fifteen minutes before me, he learned that police boarded the ship and arrested eleven anti-*Karlsbad* demonstrators. After our arrests, the crew sang the "Horst Wessel" as they marched up Burrard Street to a reception at Bear Hall, where they were met by more protesters. A woman with the Anti-Nazi Coalition was dragged away by police when she began to speak through a megaphone from the cathedral stairs next door to the hall. There were scuffles and more were arrested, taken to a jail on the outskirts of the city. "Nemirovsky says the ones arrested at Bear Hall will be out soon too. He says the charges won't stick," says Alex, as Art Posner catches up with us and throws an arm around my shoulder, and we stride the last block to the hall. "I thought you were in Winnipeg," I say. "And I thought you just wanted to shoot a little pool."

The crowd outside the Ukrainian Hall's entrance parts as the eleven of us stride triumphantly into the sticky warmth inside. "All eleven have now been released and they've just entered the hall," Luigi Mundello says excitedly from the stage. This wooden box of a hall is filled with 400 perspiring partisans shouting and applauding. Abigail Levey slaps my back and kisses my blood-splotched cheek. "You did good, Jake."

"But I thought you thought we would alienate the masses."

"In retrospect, it was terrific," she smiles, before pecking Alex Katz's cheek too.

A political jug band takes the stage and soon the sweat is flying. In mid-dance, Rachel catches my eye and leaves the floor to toss her arms around her brother. "My hero," she sighs melodramatically.

"What happened to Robert Taylor?"

"He never fought the Nazis and got their flag, not even in the movies."

"Hey, what happened with that swastika flag anyhow? I passed out before..."

"The sailors couldn't save it," she laughs. "It burned."

Taking hold of a bottled beer, I meander the sweltering hall, its long tables crammed with voices calling up battles to come, then I stop. I've come upon Lena sitting alone sipping coffee, in light summer dress, tanned skin oiled by the heat, a white flower pinned to her hair.

"Great job," a nameless face from the demonstration tells me.

"Thanks."

"You still got blood on your mouth," he says.

"Yeah, well, I better wash it off then," I say, and turn to look at Lena, who is speaking to Alex Katz. I lean against a wall and consider how best to approach her. Now she is alone again, but to me there may as well be a moat around her. Unapproachable. While I consider this, the Movement Minstrels, a band featuring the voice of my neighbour Sienna Gizzi, breaks from its dance repertoire to perform "The Internationale." Voices join in and fill the room, but I mouthe along to the song, another anthem with lyrics I do not know. Then more dancing. Rachel flies into the hands of Crazylegs Hershkovitz and others stop dancing and form a circle around the two to watch.

"Pretty good, aren't they?" says a voice over my shoulder. I turn to face Lena. I'm silent for a few seconds, then blurt, "What did you think of the rally?"

Lena puckers her face. "It was good…until the action on the ship. That was great."

"That wasn't such a big deal," I say demurely. The moment this is out of my mouth I realize that I must sound silly because everyone in this hall, including me, thinks it was a big deal.

"Well, I thought it was great," Lena shrugs, turning to greet Abigail.

They are absorbed with each other while I stand alongside them fidgeting.

"Well, I've got to go," I say, and the two jerk their heads goodbye without a pause in their conversation.

As I make for the exit, Georgie Leonard's father, Abe, calls out to me. "Hey, Jake. Are you all right?"

"Great," I say, raising my hands in partial surrender. "Everything's great."

"You took quite a beating, I heard. *Gezunterheyt.*"

"I'm fine," I sigh, walking into the breathless summer night.

TWELVE

FELLOW TRAVELLERS

Gandesa, fall 1986

"LET HENRY SIMMONS HAVE THE MICROPHONE," BOB Mitchell shouts from the rear of the bus en route to Barcelona. "Henry, get up there and talk."

We are approaching the Ebro River, so the tour guide's microphone disappears into Henry's large calloused hands as he painstakingly details his memories of the International Brigade's last big victory.

"The Ebro offensive. I'm in command of thirty-odd men. Part of a huge Republican force. We cross the river in rowboats at night. Surprise the fascists. Take thousands of prisoners."

The mostly New Yorkers on the bus listen politely to Henry's recollections. "A few months later, we're in retreat across the Ebro River. A half-hour after I cross the river, fascists bomb the bridge, and Mac-Paps who hadn't gotten over have to swim across—the ones who can swim."

Henry falls silent when the tour bus crosses the bridge over the Ebro. A bellowing baritone from the back of the bus fills the silence. "Those were the days, my friend," he booms. All is silent for a few seconds, then he sings the next line: "I thought they'd never end." In a moment, practically the entire bus has joined in the singing of the Mary Hopkin hit single. "We'd live the life we choose/We'd fight and never lose/For we were young and sure to have our way." The rollicking singalong continues as the bus rolls along twisting roads through rust-red hillsides.

All is quiet again by the time we pull onto another battle site, Gandesa, joining other busloads in its town square where locals who remember are paying homage to the International Brigades. Afterwards, I join a long line of famished reunionists waiting outside a restaurant. When I am finally seated, it's at a long table with seven fellow travellers, including a tall woman from Miami saying how moved she was by the town-square ceremony.

"What," she turns to the Toronto reporter seated beside her, "did you think of it?"

"It *was* moving," he says, raising an arm to capture the server's attention.

"I don't get a chance to speak to many young people here," says the Miami woman's husband, a stocky Lincoln veteran. "Why did you come?"

"I'm a reporter."

"It must get boring," the Lincoln tells him, "being around old people all the time."

"No, I'm barely aware of the concept of age anymore," says the Toronto reporter, in his mid-thirties, about my son's age. "After a couple of days here, I had a better understanding of older people than I ever did back home. I've learned that ideals and aspirations don't have an expiry date. And people your age talk about their children to their friends the way people my age talk about their parents to their friends."

"You mean, bragging about them eighty percent of the time and feeling neglected the other twenty?" says the woman from Miami.

When you're young most everyone you like is alive — the musicians you listen to, the movie stars you watch, the athletes you pull for, your friends and family. One by one, they begin to disappear from your life. Slowly at first. So at this table, I say, "For a very long time, the *older generation*, to me, meant my mother and her friends. Then, before I knew it, they were gone. Seemed to happen overnight. So one day, without realizing it was happening, our parents' generation was almost entirely gone and we were the old ones. I mean, the young men and women who volunteered for Spain are now the old men and women."

"And one day, without our children realizing it is happening, the volunteers for Spain will all be gone and our children will be the old ones," says a smallish woman with sharp features and shoulder-length brown hair.

"In other words," says the Lincoln, turning to the Toronto reporter, "you're next."

The server arrives and points out the names of soups and rices, eggs and fish, on the stained paper menus. That doesn't work well at our table, so he points to appetizing-looking dishes on the next table over.

After we order, introductions fall like dominoes around the table. "I'm Rebecca Ornstein, New York," the woman with shoulder-length brown hair tells the table.

"Joan O'Donnell, from Boston," says the woman next to her.

Sadie Savransky, the tall woman of Miami by way of Milwaukee and New York introduces herself and her husband Barney, the stocky Lincoln; then it's the Toronto reporter; and Helga and her niece, Olga, from Germany.

"Jack Feldman," I say, "from Vancouver."

"Vancouver? I just flew out of Seattle," Rebecca says from across the table. "Had to see my daughter there before I left for Spain."

I look at Rebecca just as she looks at me, and our eyes lock. She smiles. I smile.

"I met the doctor from Canada — Bethune — in Spain," Helga says. "I was a nurse."

"I'm not taking it anymore," shouts one of the touring Americans at a neighbouring table. The entire restaurant freezes. He shoves the table, dishes rattle, and a plate hits the floor. "I don't need this shit," he yells, neck flushed. "Art, calm down, calm down," says another man at his table, but Art overturns his plastic chair and bolts the restaurant. The object of Art's outrage remains seated at the table he shoved. She stoops slightly, then lifts her grey head, cringing. The other man at the table, ex-Lincoln commander Mel Fox, scampers out the door in search of Art. It takes a few seconds for the room's silence to ebb, a few voices at first, but within a couple of minutes it's back to full volume. Through a slit of window between the restaurant's yellow drapes, I see the two men in the street — Mel talks calmly to Art, who is waving his arms and mouthing lividly. The woman they left at the table, Art's wife, Selma, huddles close with another woman, Mel's wife, Hildy.

"I'll bet they're married," Sadie says.

"They are," Joan says.

"Who knows what gives?" says Sadie. "But I'm *with* her."

Barney glances at Sadie, then addresses the table.

"Anyone heard who's winning the Series?"

"I don't follow baseball anymore," I say.

"I still do," says Barney. "Baseball and going to the movies was pretty much it for me when I was a kid. I mean, a Brooklyn boy didn't go fishing on the weekend with Uncle Lou and you didn't go hunting with Uncle Ira. We had the Dodgers and we were baseball crazy." Barney scanned the single *International Herald Tribune* sports page he found in his hotel lobby this morning but was unable to find scores from the two-day-old World Series.

"Boston's ahead two games to none," says Joan. "I think they should be playing the third game about now. One of the Lincolns on our bus gets phone reports from his son."

"So," says Rebecca, examining the reporter as she stabs an olive. "I've children about your age."

"So what do they think about all this?" he says. "About Spain?"

"They're not politically active. They have their own lives, but they're supportive."

"Not a lot of activism in the States since the early 1970s, is there?" the reporter says. "It's about the only country I can think of that doesn't even have a socialist party."

"You should say nominally socialist," says Sadie. "This government of Spain is not my idea of socialism."

"Listen, the Cold War was billed in America as a war against the Russians, but it was really a war against other Americans, an excuse to wipe out the domestic left," Rebecca says. "The blacklists and the witch hunts."

"They won that war," Sadie says, "for awhile."

"Were you in that war?" the reporter asks Sadie.

She nods.

"Sadie," Barney says proudly, "helped to organize the garment workers in Milwaukee and went to Spain with the American Hospital Unit. She was a—"

"I've always been active," she says.

"Even in the 1950s?" the Toronto reporter says.

"Even in the 1980s," she says. "Don't fool yourself. There are still plenty of progressives in America."

"And our actions have never been dictated by twerps like Joe McCarthy," says Rebecca.

"Where were your medical units located during the Civil War?" the reporter asks.

"We followed the battlefront," Sadie says.

"Hospitals in caves, convents, schools, tents," Rebecca says. "I was a nurse too. In Villa Paz, Romeral, other places."

Barney leans in towards the German women, quietly talks Yiddish to their German, languages that can read similar but can sound planets apart.

Rebecca turns to me. "You have children, Jake?"

"Yes, three." Her brown eyes search mine for more about them. "They're supportive of me and the idea of this reunion too, I think," I say, "but it's hard for them to know what Spain was to us."

"Yes," Rebecca says. "When I learned about the reunion I had to go."

"I had to go — then, I mean," I say. "You know, I love to read history but military history leaves me cold, and the idea of being a soldier never ever entered my mind, but when Spain happened I had to go."

Art returns to the restaurant with Mel Fox and sits down sulkily at the neighbouring table while avoiding his wife's eyes.

"What do you do in Boston?" Sadie asks Joan.

"I leave Boston," she says with a laugh. "I'm a retired public defender and I travel as much as I can. At home, I'm involved with a group trying to clean up the harbour."

"I went down to an AIDS hospice in Greenwich Village and volunteered," Rebecca says. "So I go in once a week, change dressings, empty bedpans. It's sad but uplifting too. They're really fighting. Everybody there is."

"It is uplifting," Olga says.

"Good thing Mel Fox was at that table. He can handle anything," says Sadie, nodding towards the gangly Lincoln wolfing seafood with Selma, Art, and Hildy, the frenzied interlude having subsided. It is befitting that the last commander of the Abraham Lincoln Battalion physically resembles the actual Abe. Mel has a natural-born dignity that made him a battalion captain in Spain at twenty-one, then a fighter pilot in World War II, then a target of McCarthyism. When the blacklists came he was unceremoniously expunged from the military, became a television repairman in a beach town in L.A.'s South Bay.

"I interviewed Mel Fox," says the Toronto reporter.

"Mel's gone Hollywood," Rebecca says. His earthy reminiscences in a recent documentary about the House Committee on Un-American Activities drew so much acclaim that he now has an agent. "He just played Bruce Dern's father in a TV pilot."

"Mel told me his favourite movie about your movement of the thirties is *The Way We Were*," the reporter says.

"You know, Barbra Streisand's uncle died in Spain," Rebecca says. "He was in the Abraham Lincoln Battalion."

"I didn't know that," I say.

"Well, he wasn't Barbra Streisand's uncle yet," she says. "She was born a few years later. He was Joe Streisand, from New York."

"Have any of you seen any of the movies about Spain, like *Blockade*?" the reporter says.

"All of them," Sadie says.

"*Fallen Sparrow* with John Garfield was on television the night we arrived," I say, "but I was so exhausted after everything that I fell asleep during it."

"After the war, in New York, I was on my way home from work one day, and the bus passes a theatre with *For Whom the Bell Tolls*," says Sadie. "Got off at the next stop. So I sit in this nearly empty movie house watching Gary Cooper as an American fighting in Spain. He was later a friendly witness before HUAC, so you may as well have had Ronald Reagan play a Lincoln. But Ingrid Bergman was wonderful, my favourite actress, and the only one in the cast with decent politics."

"My daughter Susan," says Rebecca, "she married Lewis Chernick, the grandson of David A. Chernick, the movie producer. Lewis is a producer, too, and I always tell him 'Make a movie that stands for something.' I visit them in L.A. and they bring me to these affairs, and Lewis likes to introduce me as my-mother-in-law-the-Bolshevik."

"So, tell us, Rebecca, who have you met?" Sadie asks.

"Oh, they don't impress me.... One time Warren Beatty gives me this look and says, 'I know about the blacklist. I know what you people went through.'"

"So now he wants to put us through his movies," Sadie says. "We haven't suffered enough?"

"I like his movies," says Barney.

"There's this revival theatre in Vancouver called the Ridge that shows old Hollywood movies and foreign films," I say. "Abbott and Costello and Fellini."

"I would go there," says Rebecca.

"I met Julius Epstein there," I say. "He wrote *Casablanca* and was in Vancouver to introduce a screening of it at that theatre. And it just so happened that in the middle of the movie, he walked into the bathroom and stood at the urinal next to the one I was standing at. So I asked him something I've always wondered about — 'Was Rick Blaine, of Rick's Café, a member of the Abraham Lincoln Battalion?' He kind of frowned and shook his head no, but sometimes someone writes something that can only mean one thing to other people, and they might not even know that themselves."

"Yes. Rick in *Casablanca* was a New Yorker who fought in Spain," says Rebecca, "and he was a Lincoln."

"I met Sylvia Sidney at a function in Los Angeles — at the beach — when I took a train out to the coast right after Spain," Barney says. "Now there was a progressive."

"I love Sylvia Sidney," I say.

"She was from the neighbourhood," he says.

"What neighbourhood?" I say.

"All our neighbourhoods," says Barney.

"I know what you mean," I say.

"Did you see *Daniel*?" the reporter asks

"More dreck," says Sadie.

"I liked it," Joan says, shaking her head in disagreement. "The Rosenbergs' funeral stretched for blocks through Brooklyn. I went down from Boston for it."

Other tables have emptied. Now, we rise from our table to leave too.

"I was there, too, and at Paul Robeson's funeral," Sadie says, bowing her head.

"Loved him," says Barney. "Our two daughters were with us after his show in Peekskill. Right-wing mob stoned us, rocked our bus. The kids were so scared."

"I was there," Rebecca says.

"He sang at the U.S.-Canadian border near Vancouver," I say. "Thousands of people came from both sides. I heard him sing live once. Never saw him."

THIRTEEN

IT MUST BE LOVE

Vancouver, summer 1936

RACHEL IS ON THE PHONE FROM LENA'S PLACE. "Why don't you come over to Lena's," she says, "and we can go to the movie from here."

As soon as Rachel says this to me, I am on my way, quickly walking the few blocks there.

Rachel opens the door of Lena's second-floor flat. Lena, wearing a flannel bedgown, is at a white oval kitchen table sipping coffee. "Want a cup?" she says.

It is a sparse room, with a small bookshelf, a couch, a vase of roses at the centre of the kitchen table, a large radio against a wall, and a poster on another wall.

"Here's why I called you over, Jake," says Rachel, pointing to the poster titled "The Battle of Christie Pits." Before relocating to Vancouver, Lena designed it for a Toronto commemoration of Christie Pits. It's a dramatic collage of photographs, headlines, and her own sketch from that riotous day.

"I thought you'd want to see this," Rachel says.

"Very powerful," I say.

"Thank you," says Lena.

"Lena just got a letter from Florence," Rachel tells me. Lena and Rachel met during my sister's summer out east, their acquaintance renewed when Lena found work at Sammy's deli.

"Oh yeah. How is everyone in Toronto?" I say.

"All right," Lena says, slapping her coffee mug on the table in front of me. "Flo is working at Milton's bakery and at his stall in the Ex. She says her mom's fine, Sally's being a little nudnick, and Max went down to Florida with his friend Rosey Goodman, who wanted to try to make it as a baseball player. Max came home, but Rosey, who Flo was seeing, has a contract with some team in the States."

"Yeah," I say with sudden animation. "Rosey got signed to the New York Giants and he's on one of their farm teams."

Lena gives me a bemused look, mystified by my reference to baseball's labyrinthian minor league system. "How would you know that?" she says.

"I read the *Sporting News*."

"We should go," Rachel says. She and I have been planning to go to a matinee today, a movie version of *The Petrified Forest*, one of the plays she saw in New York.

But I don't want to leave—I'm enjoying Lena's proximity and the closest thing we've had to a conversation.

"The movie starts in forty-five minutes and I've got a couple of stops along the way," Rachel says. "Sure you don't want to come, Lena? That brochure you're designing can wait. You need a break from important political work."

Lena is preparing, with Abigail Levey, a brochure on organizing against the right in Canada that will be distributed at a West Coast socialist conference hosted in Seattle by the Washington Commonwealth Federation. "Can't come," she says, and moments later Rachel and I are in the aging Ford she purchased from Polly's father on an accommodating payment plan. The movie is about to start by the time Rachel and I scale the thick red broadloom that flows over the Orpheum Theatre's wide stairways. As we approach the top of the second flight, my heart jumps. Lena is standing there, arms folded across her chest, waiting for us.

"I do need a break," she says.

The Orpheum is a motion picture palace, built when some movie houses were constructed with the care given an opera house — plush carpets, multi-tiered balconies, intricate wall carvings, chandelier dangling from a domed muralled ceiling. It is a multi-purpose venue featuring real-life vaudevillians as well as the latest Hollywood pictures. Rachel danced here, with Polly, in a Saturday afternoon amateur contest won by a clown juggling dinner plates. Now an usher with a flashlight directs us to seats in the front row. I make sure I'm sitting alongside Lena, and once the movie begins I slip a glance at her and see Bette Davis and Humphrey Bogart flickering across her face. Lena, however, is immersed in the black-and-white action.

After the movie, Rachel drives through downtown and is about to release Lena at her Georgia Street flat, when I blurt, "Do you want to go for a drive, Lena?"

"Uh...I guess."

I turn to Rachel. "Could I borrow your car...please?"

Rachel smiles curiously, nods approval. "I'll call you tomorrow, Lena, after your drive," says Rachel as she disembarks at Keefer Street.

I move to the driver's seat and it's onto Hastings Street, past our neighbourhood, past Vancouver. As I pull up in suburban Burnaby and begin to turn back home, I notice fresh green paint on a no-frills diner's window. "Cloverleaf Restaurant — Famous for Fine Foods."

"Want to go in there?" I say.

"Sure," says Lena. "I could use some *fine* dining."

After hamburgers and a chocolate shake, we head back towards the neighbourhood but veer north on the narrow bridge that crosses to the North Shore, then travel a twisting seashore drive to a wilderness park with a lighthouse. Sitting on a boulder overlooking the ocean, Lena says: "This is wonderful. Lake Ontario just doesn't cut it."

"It doesn't have the ripples," I say, staring out at the setting sun's glittering swath through the sea.

"It doesn't have the rocks," says Lena, "and it doesn't have the mountains."

"That mountain," I say, "is an island."

As we drive back through the city towards the string of beaches out by the university, I glance for the first time at the gas gauge. "We might run out of gas," I say. Lena's considerable brows furrow suspiciously. "No," I say. "The gauge, it really is nearly empty."

"I'll buy some gas," Lena says, pointing to a service station.

"I'll pay," I say.

"Forget it," she says. "I'm working."

We get gas and drive to the beach. When we get out of the car, it's getting dark along the beach shore lined on one side by wooded hillsides and steep sand walls, and on the other by waters crested with small foamy whitecaps breaking across barnacle-studded rock. We walk silently from rock to rock, log to log, shoes not touching the damp sand. With Art and Georgie, I used to stroll these beaches and, always unsuccessfully, try to climb to the top of the sand walls. Lena and I stop at a clearing with an almost vertical, towering wall of compacted sand. This wall teasingly makes ascension seem possible with its slight gradation and occasional branch to reach for. So I run at the wall, driving my hands into the wet sand, surging almost two-thirds of the way to the top before tumbling back to its base. I land intact at Lena's feet, and she laughs. We continue our walk on the rocks, through the evening ocean chill, back to the car.

"This reminds me of a place out east," says Lena. "I used to go there, just walk and walk. Haven't done this in a long time."

Driving Lena home, I am nervous, wanting to say something or make some gesture that affirms our bond. After the car stops in front of her flat, we turn to each other.

"I've got to go," she says and exits quickly.

The next morning, blissfully, I do practically nothing, sprawled lazily in bed, then browse magazines on the porch. Early afternoon I walk to the boxy rooming house where Lena lives. She opens her flat to me and introduces a thin, triangular-headed man drinking coffee at her kitchen table. "This is Pat. He's a very old friend from Toronto."

"You don't look very old, Pat."

Pat gives me an inexpressive half-smile, then turns his pallid face to Lena. "So Bernice has gone to Montreal. She couldn't stay any longer, trying somewhere else, just for a change."

Lena nods agreeably, and they talk about Toronto and Bernice and other friends for fifteen minutes while I fidget, then rise to leave.

"Where are you going?" Lena says as I reach for the doorknob.

"I've got to get going," I say with a wince and slip out the doorway.

"What's wrong?" she says, following me into the hallway, her face unconsciously mimicking my anxious expression.

"I don't know. Got to go," I say, halfway down the stairs. "I can't talk now."

"Jake," she says quietly from the top of the stairs. "Come back later."

"I'm going to a party tonight," I say.

"Come afterwards."

Swing music on the turntable at Claire Gordon's place. Don't feel like dancing, but I'm in flight, greeting everyone without talking with anyone. "Hi, Claire, how are ya?" "Art." "Sophie."

"Jake," Art says, "I got a couple of beers. Let's go out back."

"No. Not staying here long. Got someplace else to be."

"You're all flushed. It must be *some* someplace."

Just before midnight, she opens her door. I sit on a small chair by the window overlooking Georgia Street. Lena retreats to the coffee pot on the stove. "Okay," she says, handing me a coffee mug. With a deep cigarette exhale, she plops into a wooden kitchen chair at the table. "How," she says, "are you?"

"Pretty good, I think."

"How do you feel?"

"How do I feel?" I rise from the chair, clenching my fists, determined to sound self-aware. "I feel…"

"Huh?" she says.

"I feel that so much everyday conversation is phoney. I mean, people ask how you are, not because they care but so you'll like them. Everyone is telling you how to think, so you have to go through a ton of B.S. to find out who you really are."

Completing this thought, I unclench my fists, drop down on the couch, hoping to have sounded insightful.

Lena shrugs her face. "Okay. But clearly, something is bothering you? How do you feel?"

"How," I ask Lena, "do you feel?"

At that we sit, silent, sipping coffee.

"Do you want more coffee?" Lena says, finally breaking the silence as she withdraws to the kitchen. When she returns to me, Lena sits on the floor, in her red flannel gown, arms wrapped around her knees, hair about her face and down her back, eyes inspecting my angst. The silent night continues for more than an hour.

Finally, I say, "It's been nice thinking with you."

Lena laughs and slips towards me, taking my hand, and dropping her head on to my lap. I softly stroke her silky hair and we sit until morning breaks.

A day passes. Then the phone rings on Keefer Street.

"Jake, I want to talk to you. Do you want to talk?"

I scoop Lena up in Rachel's car and we drive to Little Mountain, raggedy parkland said to have been the site of ancient volcanic eruptions. It was in actuality the pitted quarry that had provided the stones that paved much of the city. Lena and I sit facing each other on slightly damp, sloping park lawn, surrounded by fir trees.

"Jake, I've been thinking about you and I. Would you like to spend more time together?" Lena looks quizzically at me, lights a cigarette, awaits a response.

Yes, I want to, but this is a question I've never been asked and in my bewilderment say, "I don't know."

She turns her mouth away from my face and lets out a shot of smoke. Silent, again. We watch the downtown skyline, sun glinting from the art deco rooftop of its signature skyscraper, the Marine Building.

"Jake, what do you think of Morris Hershkovitz?"

"Crazylegs? I don't know. He can dance."

"Rachel's wondering whether to continue seeing Morris. Do you know him very well?"

"Not that well. I didn't know Rachel and he—"

"Well, Rachel talks to me."

More silence and we kiss and our fingers entwine and we hold hands to the car and to spaghetti at a small café near Strathcona. Afterwards, at Lena's flat, she stirs coffee to classical music on CBC radio. I ask if she minds if I switch stations to *The Burns and Allen Show*.

"Do you want to go to bed," Lena states pointedly, after another cup of coffee and fifteen minutes of comedy radio, "or do you want to listen to Burns and Allen?"

We move to the bedroom, onto her floor mattress covered in red quilt, and embrace, hands pouring through hair, mouths melting into each other, one body dissolving into another, relinquishing self-consciousness. Then, Lena says "Jake, let's just hold each other this time."

"Sure."

I move my head onto a pillow, pulling her close. Lena wraps her arms around me. We cling in silence, eyes lost in each other's eyes.

"Jake, you're pretty wonderful."

"You seem like a different person," Sam says after I crumble before his chessboard assault, amiably losing a second game in a row. "It must be love."

Now that Lena and I are mutually smitten I do feel different, but I am surprised that someone else would notice this. Sam rises from the table, and I ask where he's going, and he blushes and grunts and says nothing as he heads to the bathroom. He sleeps in a rooming house a block away but usually appears on time for dinner, staying afterward for a radio show or chess. After this day's two matches, I sprawl on the couch absorbed in a *Life* magazine spread about the war I've been preoccupied with since the *Karlsbad* left town.

"I'm going to go to Spain," I say aloud to no one in particular.

"You're meshugga," my mother says, looking up at me fearfully from her ironing board across the room. Sam raises an eye from the evening paper.

"No. People are volunteering to go to Spain. They need all the help they can get. Luigi Mundello's going over."

"Help here, if you're such a Samaritan," my mother says.

"There's a revolution in Spain," I say.

"*Revolution, schmevolution*, you've got to have the dollar," she says. "Bigger people than you will take care of Spain."

"There are none," I say deliberately, voice rising. "No bigger people. People *are* people."

"Don't be an open book and reveal your whole life," Sam admonishes me. "Keep some things to yourself. Take Rachel, she says everything about herself. She tells people if she's going to the bathroom."

Our relatives go to Isaac to be employed, to Frieda to be unemployed. Sam and I had been this year's unemployables, but Sam became a piano-playing bartender at a downtown hotel, working there one month before he would tell anyone he had the job. I've just found part-time work in a Red Top taxicab. I had been fascinated with stories of my mother's itinerant brother Lou, who spent some time in Vancouver convalescing from his grisly experience in Fort Harold. During a short stay in Chicago, Lou drove for the Checker Taxi Company at the height of the city's territorial cab wars, and he was a veteran of a fare-fight shootout between rival drivers that left one cabbie dead and others wounded. After his visit to B.C., he moved back to his hometown, New York, drove Yellow, no longer keeping a revolver in the glove compartment. Still, there was a taxi war in Manhattan, too, over access to hotel cab stands, with slit tires and shattered windshields.

When I'm not in a taxicab, I'm with Lena. She introduces me to the ristretto she learned to drink in Toronto, and I introduce her to the Marx Brothers (seeing *A Night at the Opera*) I met at the movies in Vancouver. She likes books and magazines as much as I do, and we spend hours discussing what we've read together. We both like the *New Masses*, *Canadian Forum*, and the *New Yorker*.

I take an evening off work to see Major Bowes' radio amateurs. It's a travelling showcase of recent winners of the popular radio talent contest *Major Bowes Amateur Hour*. I know it's one of the few radio programs Lena listens to, so I've bought a couple of twenty-five-cent tickets and we're back at the Orpheum. We sit happily through a yodeller, a "xylophone wizard," impressionist Vivian Barlow, and a couple of fair musical acts. Then, magic happens.

"This is what I've been waiting for," Lena whispers. The Hoboken Four takes the stage and their slim young vocalist begins to sing. "Some day when I'm awfully low...I will feel a glow just thinking of you." Lena and I take each other's hands, and there is dead silence in the room as the voice continues. "With each word your tenderness grows, tearing my fear apart." When he finishes there is a roar of applause along with a teenage scream or two. "Who was that?" I say. "Frank somebody," says Lena.

The week after the Bowes show, Lena and I go to a community hall to hear another kind of music. At the Orpheum, I didn't cross paths with anyone I knew, but I seem to know everyone at this hall where the neighbourhood's Movement Minstrels are opening for a Yiddish sing-song ensemble from Toronto.

At this concert, we run into Art Posner and Claire Gordon. Claire's excited that she's just been accepted into the University of British Columbia to study school teaching. Art says he's going to Winnipeg next week to visit his mother's family there. "We should shoot pool before I leave," he says.

"I have to tell you," Claire says. "You two are the worst pool players in the world."

I laugh, say, "Sounds like you've never seen Georgie Leonard play."

I turn to Lena, but she's gone.

"She's up there," says Art, pointing towards a near-empty balcony.

I look up, see Lena standing by herself on the balcony. I wave at her, but she doesn't see.

I go up the stairs to be with Lena. "Why did you leave like that?" I say.

"Didn't feel included," she says. "Don't feel very sociable."

We stand together silently for a song or two then I make my way downstairs. By now I've learned a few lyrics from "The

Internationale" and am able to partake somewhat when the evening ends with a rousing rendition. By this time, Lena has left.

The next morning I phone Lena. There's no answer, but as soon as I hang up the phone it rings.

It's Lena. "I'm in Crescent Beach with Abigail Levey, visiting friends of hers. Going to spend the night at their place. Why don't you come down? It's beautiful."

"I'm driving cab today."

"Why don't you just get in your cab and drive it here?"

"Can't."

Waiting in my cab outside a downtown nightclub, I corral a man too imbibed to drive and endure the odours and the ravings across town. Drop him off, wipe away his vomit, and I'm driving alone on the Burrard Bridge in the rain when the cab seizes. Miserable at midnight, sitting in the dark on the bridge, I try unsuccessfully to comfort myself. "I'll soon be in a warm bed, and this, too, shall pass." A passing Yellow Cab stops and takes me to the Red Top office.

I have told Lena I'll be over after work and am about to book off when I'm offered another car to complete my shift. Tired and wet and anxious to see Lena, I decline at first, but I want to derive something from this unfortunate evening and know that the train station sometimes produces a late-night fare. After several weeks on the job, I've gotten into the habit of ending my shift at the station, but this night there is no one, it seems, on the last train from the other coast. So I've resolved to call it a workday when a robust man, no more than

KEEFER STREET · 133

twenty years old, tears open my cab door. "Take me to Shelt," he demands in a soft Scottish brogue.

"What?"

"Take me to Shelt."

"You mean Sechelt," I say, referring to a town just up the coast. "You'll have to wait till morning to get there by steamer."

"Then take me to a hotel. Nothing fancy."

As we motor toward a low-rent hotel, he says, "I met the most beautiful girl in the world, but... she's got rotting yellow teeth." He contorts his body so that his bulky index finger can pry open his mouth to show me the whereabouts of this woman's stained molars.

"She lives in Sechelt?"

"Shelt it is," he continues as we wheel over neon reflections across wet pavement. "Nice town you've got here. Big. Never been anywhere before, except to the French seaside for a ruggers championship. That's where I met her. Wouldn't pay me no mind until the last day before she left. Told me she lived in Shelt."

To get rid of the lout, no doubt, I tell myself. *She never dreamed he'd actually follow her all the way to Canada.*

"Have you written her?" I ask him.

"I wrote her a letter."

"Did she write back?"

"Up all night. Every night. Couldn't think of nothing but her."

"Did she write back?"

"No. I didn't send the letter I wrote. I had no address to send it to. But someone in Shelt will tell me where she is, or I'll be ringing some bleeding necks." The passenger's ham-sized hands go into a phantom stranglehold, as he heaves backward and forward, rattling the front seat like it's about to come off its moorings. He slumps back, softly says, "Back home I'm up all night, every night, can't think of nothing but her. My folks said I have to come to her. She's the most beautiful girl in the world except…she's got rotting yellow teeth right back here."

"Dental school," I say.

"What?"

"Have you considered working with teeth?" I say.

"Are you being smart?" he says.

"Probably."

As he continues on about her teeth and Shelt and chokeholds, I tune out, fantasizing about depositing him on the doorstep of a sleazy politician and telling him this is Shelt, and the man in that house knows where she is. Instead, I proceed to the Reco Hotel.

"I got kicked out of Calgary," he says. "Got drunk at the station and missed my train and hit a pink man."

"Pinkerton?"

"That's it. They told me, 'Get back on the train or go to jail,'" he recalls, adding softly, "Do you know where I can get drunk and fight?"

I recount my woeful evening in the Red Top taxicab at Lena's flat after work.

Lena swallows a mouthful of hot coffee. "Jake," she says, "I don't want to see you anymore."

I didn't see this coming and rapidly retrace the evening in my mind — after leaving the Reco Hotel, I drove to Lena's, she opened the door, flicked her wrist towards the couch, said "Coffee?" That's when I told her about tonight's encounter with the fare.

"What's wrong?" I say.

"I feel very vulnerable right now," she says brusquely. "I don't think you understand that at all."

"But Lena," I begin.

"I think you think you're in love with me," she says sharply. "But it's just some idea of me. You don't know me. We don't really talk. It's probably easier for you to talk with some certifiable passenger who you'll never see again."

"Can't we talk about it?" I say.

"That's what I thought we were doing," Lena says. She pours another coffee.

"I know this is my fault. I haven't told you, shown you, what I think of you."

"That's fine. But how do you feel, Jake? Look, I don't want to see you anymore."

"But Lena."

"I am of course aware that you have certain admirable qualities," she says.

"Sounds like you're head over heels," I say.

"I like the way you can be funny and frank at the same time about some things. *But*. But you won't talk about your feelings. I've waited for you to come around on this, and I finally realized that isn't going to happen because you don't even know what they are. When I'm with you, I usually have to infer things from what you don't say."

"Well, how do *you* feel, Lena? You say more about me than you say about yourself."

"I," she says, "don't trust you enough to talk about my feelings with you. Look, I'm not going to argue with you about this."

"If I don't agree with every word you say, I'm arguing."

"I'd like you to leave."

I walk quickly across the flat, sag at the door. "But Lena, this doesn't change my feelings towards you."

"Whatever those are."

"I really care for you and wouldn't do anything to hurt you."

"Jake," Lena says, "you're not capable of hurting me."

The three blocks walked to Keefer Street are a blur. I pull bedsheets over my face, shuddering, awake for the night. The next afternoon, Sam hauls me from bed for a chess game I don't want to play but lose expeditiously. Afterwards, I look for respite at the Rex — ballerina (Ginger)-meets-hoofer (Fred), ballerina-and-hoofer-are-swept-off-their-feet, ballerina-dumps-hoofer, ballerina-and-hoofer-rekindle-their-romance, ballerina-and-hoofer-dance-into-the-sunset. Maudlin plot, I might have thought yesterday, but how their feet float, and in my plight today the fine romance and Gershwin lyrics offer answers. Funny how everything seemed more black and white when the movies were black and white. Usually, I don't observe others in a movie audience, but today at the Rex I see the ones who are alone and wonder how many have come to *Shall We Dance* for a two-hour refuge from a broken heart?

The internal chatter persists after the movie as I drive to the beach and stride along the shoreline, recalling each misstep I took with Lena. Maybe Lena decided to break up two evenings earlier when we went to the hall to see the Toronto ensemble. Lena and I struggled to find words for each other that night, but we often do. We are more in sync discussing a book than we are talking about emotions. "How do you feel?" Lena was the first to ask me that. Not so easy to answer, I figured, but I liked that someone cared enough to ask. Now that she's gone life seems over, or never really started, at such a young age, heart under attack.

Not wanting to encounter anyone on Keefer Street, I quietly slip through the back door and into the house, but my mother knows who is in her kitchen even though she is in the living room. "Jakie," she casually calls through the wall, "Artie came by. And Lena phoned you." I grab the phone on the kitchen wall and call Sammy's deli.

"You want Lena?" Sammy's nasal voice shouts over the deli din. "You want to wait a minute." Almost five minutes later Lena says hello.

"Lena, it's Jake."

"Jake," she says, breathless. "Sorry I kept you waiting. It's busy here. How are you?"

"Not great," I say.

"I can understand," Lena says, "if you don't want to see me after last night. But I've thought about it and I'd like to talk with you. Do you want to meet?"

I hear her exhalation of cigarette smoke.

"I guess so," I say, feigning reserve but smiling broadly into the phone.

"When?" she says.

"How about today?"

"Jake, are you breathing? It sounds like you're holding your breath."

It's my turn to exhale.

FOURTEEN

THE BLACK ROSE

Barcelona, fall 1986

A THICK TANGLE OF DARK PONYTAIL BUMPS AGAINST me as a young woman steps back from the Diego Velázquez print she is examining. "Excuse me," she says, and I continue browsing prints in the small Barcelona gallery. Two hours later, as I begin the block-long walk from the subway to the Hotel Condor I glance in a pasteleria window and see this woman again — in a coordinated black purple blue orange outfit — at the counter making a purchase. A few minutes later, I press the hotel elevator button to the third floor and as the door closes she steps in. She presses the third-floor button too and bites into a custard-filled doughnut miniature. When the elevator opens, we walk out to the left and down a long hallway, stopping at the doors of our rooms next to each other.

"Excuse me," I say. "You and I collided earlier at a gallery just off the Ramblas."

"I remember," she says, as though she didn't recognize me from the gallery until this instant. "What a coincidence running into you again. Another American staying next door."

"Canadian."

"Really. You look like you're from New York."

"No. But I've been travelling with New Yorkers since I've been here. I'm here for a reunion."

"Of who?"

"People who fought the fascists in the Spanish Civil War. Fifty years ago."

"First I heard of it. I'm just here for a few days before going on to Florence. Enrolled in art school there. I'm from D.C."

"B.C. I'm from Vancouver, B.C."

She inserts the room key, begins to open the door, says, "Want to go for a drink later?"

"Sure," I say, surprised by the offer.

"Just come by. I'll be here tonight."

In my room, I wonder how she could be drawn to Spain without knowing about the Civil War. This country *is* the Civil War.

The legend is wrapped in black. Like *Ed Sullivan*-induced zealots at the altar of a pop icon — Elvis, say, or the Beatles — the reunionists inside this Barcelona union hall have abandoned all composure in the presence of this frail old woman. I stand alongside Peter Krawchuk and Tom Barkley as Bob Mitchell grapples with Lincoln veterans and members of the German Thaelmann Battalion and the Latin American Espanol Battalion for foot space close to her. These volunteers for Spain fall over each other as they manoeuvre for a look, an autograph, a photograph of this woman about to turn ninety, seated stooped over a long folding table. Bob hands me his camera and steps behind her to squeeze into the photo frame he signals me to snap. She has been brought here to pay, and to receive, homage, so she tilts over the photographs, books, posters, and paper scraps that are shoved in front of her, and she slowly signs a name that exudes the passion of Spain's Civil War.

"La Pasionaria," I hear a suddenly reverential Tom tell the Toronto reporter, "is one of the great orators of this century."

Rebecca Ornstein overhears Tom, too, as she approaches me. "She was the best public speaker I've ever seen," says Rebecca. "How have you been?"

"Pretty good," I say. "I'm okay. I'm enjoying the reunion. You?"

"Lunch with you and the others in Gandesa was one of the high points." She smiles. "*Full of surprises*. You said you live in Vancouver. My daughter lives in Seattle and when I was visiting her once, we drove up to Vancouver for a couple of days. I liked it. Such a beautiful setting. We stayed at a hotel across from a beach. The Sylvia."

"I'm not far from the ocean," I say. "I've been to your city too. I always wanted to see New York but didn't get around to it until a couple of years ago. I went to Caffe Reggio in Greenwich Village. Broadway shows. MoMA. Macy's department store."

"Macy's department store?"

"I like exploring department stores. What can I say? It's a habit I picked up as a kid."

Rebecca laughs. "I find that this reunion is like revisiting your whole life," she says.

"That's true for me too. Maybe it's because Spain stayed with us so vividly no matter what else was going on in our lives as the years went by."

"That's a good point. Everything about Spain fifty years ago is still so vivid to me. I still remember very well every nurse, doctor, patient I became close to."

"The taste of cold Gazpacho soup," I say. "The voice of La Pasionaria."

A young woman prepares La Pasionaria's departure. "Back up, back away," she tells the crowd. "She's old, she's old." But they are all old, these veterans, and they continue to advance towards her through the throng surrounding the table, and instead of rising to leave, La Pasionaria continues to sign her name. Bob is beaming as he leaves the fray after collecting three autographs. "Hey, aren't you fellows going to get in there," he says to Peter and me. At the table, pushes turn to shoves and elbows between a wire service photographer and a television cameraman vying for space. The scuffling is brief, and union security moves the crowd back, but Tom has slipped through the lines and is crawling on top of the twenty-foot-long wood table to reach La Pasionaria. She presses on, not missing a stroke, not stopping because this room's clamour is the answer to an invitation she proffered some fifty years ago.

I'd seen the Spanish Republic's La Pasionaria once before. October 28, 1938. It was an undisciplined parade, the international volunteers' farewell march through Barcelona. The internationals stopped often, some briefly disappearing into the massive crowd lining the parade route to say goodbye to someone they recognized. Spanish women and men darted into our parade, too, to embrace a departing soldier or nurse; children ran alongside us or climbed lampposts to watch, seemed like a million flowers floated onto us from rooftops. Canadians marched behind the Mac-Pap banner. I was quietly lost in the emotion of the day when a familiar hand reached to me from the crowd. It offered me a black rose. I reached for the rose and our hands touched. The hand was gone as suddenly as it appeared.

The crowd's roar only quieted when the parade ended and La Pasionaria took to a balcony overlooking the street. "Comrades of the International Brigades," she began, "political reasons, reasons of state, the good of that same cause for which you offered your blood with limitless generosity send some of you back to your countries and some to forced exile." I clenched the black rose in my left fist as the passionate voice wafted above the multitude listening intently to every word. As I listened, I took a good long look at the volunteers around me in this street — our bodies bowed from weariness, our resolve unflinching. "You can go with pride," La Pasionaria continued. "You are history. You are legend. You are the heroic example of the solidarity and the universality of democracy.... We will not forget you; and when the olive tree of peace puts forth its leaves, entwined with the laurels of the Spanish Republic's victory — return! Return to our side for here you will find a homeland. All will have the affection and gratitude of the Spanish people who today and tomorrow will shout with enthusiasm — Long live the heroes of the International Brigades!"

"Did you get her autograph too?" Rebecca asks as we depart the union hall.

"No. I'm not big on autographs. But I was happy to be there."

As we make our way to the reunion's inevitable buses, a garage door opens in front of Rebecca and me, and the limousine La Pasionaria is in passes inches from us. I watch it stop at a light. A half-block from the hall where she was revered minutes ago, La Pasionaria is now, to passersby on a crosswalk, another passenger in another car waiting for a light. It turns green, and I step behind Rebecca onto a bus bound for hotels.

There are parts of Barcelona that would make a visitor from the Middle Ages feel postmodern. Inside the new post-Franco Barcelona is an ancient city of meandering brick streets and cobblestone plazas. But the Barcelona of this tour bus is generic enough that it seems the driver is circling the same buildings we passed fifteen minutes ago. "Didn't we pass this block before?" I say to Rebecca, in the window seat beside me. "Maybe the bus driver's lost," she says. The notion makes an impression across the aisle on a tired New Jersey woman.

"The bus driver is lost," she repeats resoundingly.

"He's not," the tour guide says.

"Yes, he is," the Jersey woman says. "He's driving in circles."

"He is not lost," the guide bellows. "He has driven in this city for many, many years."

"Well," the New Jersey woman mutters, "someone said he was lost." She is the target of other passengers' glares, and I'm embarrassed, although no one else, including the New Jersey woman, blames my aside for her outburst. I forget about this when a minor collision stops us for five minutes in the traffic's diesel cloud and throbbing horns. Our impatient driver finally backs the bus until it's touching a parked wooden camper, then lurches forward onto a wide sidewalk, honks pedestrians from his way, and passes the traffic bottleneck before returning to the street.

"This driver's not so bad," the New Jersey woman says.

"This place is like a morgue," says Rebecca, looking out at the city's fleeting images. "More like visiting a ghost town than visiting a country. So many friends who decided to come to Spain the day I decided to come, but they never came home."

The morning that would change her life, Rebecca was rushing to class at Brooklyn Jewish Hospital. "Another nursing student, Sarah Weintraub, stopped me in a hallway. She was excited about the meeting that evening of the Spanish Medical Aid Committee. 'I'm going there,' Sarah said. 'Why don't we both go?'"

Before they left that meeting at the New School in Greenwich Village, both had signed on for Spain. Rebecca and Sarah soon completed their nursing studies, worked briefly at the hospital, then sailed for Spain. Seven doctors and nurses from that Brooklyn hospital went to Spain. Sixty-six Lincolns left from Brownsville, Rebecca's neighbourhood in Brooklyn. Only twenty-five of them came home. Sarah lost her leg when a fascist fighter bombed a hospital tent. Her boyfriend, Joe Streisand, died at Jarama. Rebecca was among the last of the volunteers to leave Spain.

The driver pulls to a stop in front of Rebecca's hotel. "No one at that meeting had to convince me to go," she says. "I was overjoyed at the prospect of joining the Spanish people's fight."

"You don't have to explain to me how you felt. I know," I say.

As she starts to leave the bus, she turns to me. "Glad to hear you've been doing pretty good," she says.

"I'd like to hear how you've been doing," I say. "How about dinner at an actual restaurant?"

"Sure," Rebecca says. "I've had enough food at receptions to last me a lifetime."

"Yes, I do appreciate the receptions," I say, "but rubber chicken is rubber chicken whether it's served to legionnaires or Mac-Paps."

Back at my hotel, passing through the lobby, I stop where Peter Krawchuk and Andy Tompkins sit with two Lincolns. "Have you seen that reporter from Toronto?" I say. "He's been after me for an interview and I said I'd set up a time with him." As they shake their heads, I pluck an *International Herald Tribune* from a coffee table and plop onto a couch. "Anything about the Series in that rag?" asks a Lincoln, who's irritated to learn the sports section is the one page missing from the newspaper. "New York's up two games to nothing last I heard," Andy shouts from the other couch.

I continue my search for the reporter, through the hotel coffee shop to the bar where Jim Heathcott, alone, is standing with a drink and his sketchbook. I glance at the picture he's drawing of an elderly face on fire.

"You can draw," I say.

"I paint," he says. "Probably not very good at it. But I paint."

"Have you seen that reporter from Toronto?" I say.

"No," says Jim, "but I'm sure he's out interviewing one of you Canadian heroes who singlehandedly could have saved the Republic if it weren't for fucking Roosevelt, and your Mackenzie King too."

"I guess that means he could be talking to any one of us."

The artist opens the hotel door next to mine. "Why don't we just stay here and have a drink and watch TV," she says. "I'm tired and there's drinks and stuff in the cabinet." So Susan Costantini and I crunch potato chips and sip beer and soda water while the set flickers images of Spanish-speaking Montgomery Clift and John Wayne driving cattle and men to an infectious movie score in *Red River*.

"So," she says, "you're here for a reunion about a war?"

"There was a civil war in Spain in the 1930s, and people from around the world came to help stop the fascists who were trying to take over the country. General Franco's fascists were supported by the dictators in Germany and Italy. The Spanish people found support everywhere. In Canada, for instance, it was illegal to come here but we came anyway and now we're back for this reunion."

"My dad was in the war too. Just a boy then. He's from Italy. After the war, his family moved to Brazil."

Probably another fascist hiding in South America, I'm thinking.

"I moved with my parents to D.C. when I was really young."

"The war in Spain wasn't the Second World War, exactly, although it was its beginning," I say, eyes on cattle stampeding across the TV screen. "It was a civil war. And it was a revolution. In Barcelona, factories and buses, hotels, and restaurants were taken over by workers and run without bosses."

"Really," she says. "This all happened when you were here fifty years ago?"

We're talking revolution in Spain while on TV, Montgomery Clift is overthrowing his father figure, John Wayne.

"Tomorrow, I'm going to Gaudi's park," she says.

"That's supposed to be really something."

"Would you like to come?"

Back in my room, *Red River* ends with a portending fist fight between the generations. I watch this fight thinking that it reflects what actually happened between the acting generations of the 1950s—Hollywood's one-dimensional John Waynes versus its methody Montgomery Clifts. I click off the television.

Gaudi's Park Güell is above the city, like ruins that invoke no place except dreamlands on a child's bookshelf. Antoni Gaudi was at the forefront of the architectural revolution that paralleled upheavals in literature, painting, sculpture, the streets. He remains an apt architect laureate for a city known for anarchy, his free fantasy realistic yet demanding the impossible or, at least, the unlikely. Gaudí's hand has helped to make the city as unpredictable as a walk in his park. Turn a Barcelona street corner from a staid block of new offices, and Gaudí will be there, swiping senses with a building of vibrantly coloured, swirling stone. It may be a home with seaweed iron-work, brilliant porcelain mosaics, and crooked chimney pots. Or an apartment edifice, as magic as beach stone beaten into shape by the ocean, its balconies bulging with metallic Lone Ranger masks. Or an unfinished cathedral, its twisted, dispro-portionate spires towering above the secular city.

The artist, outfitted as gaudy as Gaudí, and myself, in a colourless sport shirt and beige slacks, wander Park Güell, exploring the woods that share this mountain with the archi-tect's visual amusement park. We promenade through the columns slanting like trees in a tropical hurricane, down the dragon stairway, past the gingerbread cottage, and out the gate, to the subway downtown.

At a spacious plaza, I twist my fork through a plate of paella, picking at the seafood and chicken hesitatingly, while the artist devours.

"Why did you come to Spain?"

"Because," she pauses. "It's beautiful and it's exciting and the people and the art. It's wonderful. You remind me of some hip older people I know in D.C. Were you bohemian when you were younger?"

Before I can answer, a young man leans forward from the adjacent dining table. "Excuse me," he says. "I can't help won-dering...are you with the Civil War group?" He is a Cambridge student, a Brahmin from West Bengal, touring Europe with a train pass before resuming classes. When I tell him I am with the reunion, he says excitedly, "I've read about the Spanish Civil War and know the Republican military forces were like nothing that's come before or since. Everyone on the left had their own army in this fight — Communists and social democrats, Trotskyists and anarchists. I'm very interested in anarchism and Barcelona. I've got this book." He reaches into his knapsack and pulls out an Orwell book I'm familiar with. "Just let me find this one part." He reads us a short passage from *Homage to Catalonia* about a time when the Civil War became a revolution and subservient roles and moneyed classes seemed to vanish in Barcelona. "There was much in it that I did not understand," he reads with conviction, "in some ways I did not even like it but I recognized it immediately as a state of affairs worth fighting for."

Susan gives the excerpt a broad smile. The Cambridge student closes the book. "Some of it is difficult to understand," he says. "I'm thinking of travelling to interview the anarchist Federica Montseny for my thesis. She lives in France now." He motions towards a black banner with an encircled white *A* hanging from a nearby table spread with books and pamphlets. A young woman seated behind the table wears a *London Calling* T-shirt with its *A* also encircled.

"It's odd," the Cambridge student says, "that those punk rockers selling books at that table are the new anarchists of a country that had the massive movement that actually defined working anarchism."

"Why's it so odd?" I say.

"The world looks to Spain for anarchism, but Barcelona's own young anarchists look to another place — London — for their anarchistic culture."

"But this is another place too," I say. "Some of the same names are still here — the CNT, the Party, the UGT — but they're not the same. And what difference does it make whether inspiration comes from another country or another age?"

"I have that album," says Susan, motioning toward the woman wearing the *London Calling* T-shirt.

"Great album. The Clash," the Cambridge student says.

"I suppose the song in it, 'Spanish Bombs,' is about the Civil War," she says.

I can feel the artist and the anarchist drawing closer, and I say goodbye, leaving them to whatever their Spain will be. I also leave something of my Spain. Reaching into my jacket pocket, I feel a commemorative pin from Valencia city hall, and I pass it to Susan.

FIFTEEN

LEFTWARD HO

Vancouver, 1936–1937

I WAIT OUTSIDE OF SAMMY'S DELI FOR LENA TO END her shift, then we drive at dusk towards the university.

"Jake, I can understand why you wouldn't want to, after the other night, but I would like to continue seeing you."

I am overjoyed, but not wanting to seem overly eager I say, "Well, I don't know anymore."

I park by the beach. "Whenever I'm deciding whether or not to do something," Lena says, "I ask myself, 'Will I be sorry later if I don't do it?' And the answer is I like being with you." She gestures towards the dark water. "Want to go for a swim?"

"That water's freezing," I say, "and I don't have a bathing suit with me."

"Well, I'm going in," she says.

"And," I add, "it's starting to rain."

I watch Lena run along the wet sand, fling down her billowy white dress, and trot into the sea, her knees rising like a high-stepping carriage horse, her long hair flapping.

"Lena," I shout. She stops waist-deep in the water, turns to see that I've exited the car too and am on the sand stripping away dungarees and plaid shirt. She watches as I run to the night sea, stop, tentatively dab my toes.

"Come on!" she says, laughing.

"I'll count," I decide, "and when I hit the number ten I'll run into the water no matter what." I begin a slow, silent count. At ten, I swallow tautly and begin my sprint. I run close to Lena, dive into the ocean, and we swim together, tugging at each other underwater, emerging onto the sand long minutes later. Shivering in the dark, we use our clothing to dry ourselves. Walking back to the car, I reach into my pockets for my key.

"My car key's gone," I shout.

"We'll look for it," Lena says calmly.

We retrace our footsteps, run fingers through the sand, but at night the sand and sea and sky are different hues of the same darkness and there's nothing to see.

At the shoreline, exasperated, I say, "We could walk until we find a phone to call a cab."

Raising her brow, Lena says: "I'm cold and I'm wet and I don't want to do that."

We give the sea a quiet last look, and as we turn away from it, a bronze glimmer in the sand catches Lena's eye and she reaches down to pick up the key.

I wake early at Lena's flat, succumb to an urge to stroke her hair and shoulders. "Oh, Jake," she tosses, half sleeping. "You don't wake up people who sleep in later than you do. Have a little consideration."

"Sorry," I say, moving away.

"It's all right, this time," she says, curling into me. Her eyes dance on me, brows ripple. Lena's face is an open book, each emotion reflected in a twist of her mouth or shrug of her lip or crinkle of her nose. I can see through Lena's face to her thoughts, I am convinced, like looking through a two-way mirror. More often, though, it is she who knows what I am thinking.

I leave Lena's place this morning feeling euphoric, striding alongside the autumn streets, a leafy red-yellow-orange rainbow scattered on the sidewalk, pasted to the curb.

I'm in the same mood a few mornings later when I stroll into Sammy's deli for breakfast. As I'm about to attack a Sammy cheese blintz, a young man's high-pitched voice intrudes on my blissful morning. "Jake," he says. "How are you?" I spin to face my former classmate, Moe Shore, who tells me he's just back from work in a mill on Vancouver Island.

"Now," he says. "I'm going to Spain."

"Spain! When do you go?"

"A week," says Moe. "Lots going from Vancouver. What about you, Jake?"

"I'd like to. I really would."

"Sid Levey, Abigail's kid brother, is in my group going next week. And Art Posner."

"Art?" I say incredulously. "Art?"

"I thought you'd know about that. Aren't you guys like this?" says Moe, crossing his fingers.

"I've been busy lately and he's been out of town. We haven't stayed in touch that much."

I race the two blocks to Art's place, his parents' suite one floor above a drug-and-sundry store. No one's home.

The following day, I return to the Posner apartment, and again no one's there to open the door.

Back at Keefer Street, I'm confronted by Rachel, who has just come from Lena. "Why," she wants to know, "can't you talk about your feelings? You don't have any trouble talking endlessly about revolutions in Spain."

"What else do you and Lena say about me?" I say uneasily.

"Don't suppose you're such a pressing subject that all we have to do is talk about you."

"Did you and Lena talk about how great it's been between us since we got back together?"

"You know, Polly was the one who talked Lena into phoning you. They're not close, but Polly and I bumped into Lena on the street the day after she broke up with you. When she told me about it, Polly said: 'Were you expecting him to be perfection? He's nice for a guy.' I agreed."

That evening, Lena is taken aback when my angsty countenance appears at her door.

"What's wrong?" she says.

"I'm fine," I say. "I'll tell you later."

"O-kay," she says slowly. This morning, before hearing about Rachel's conversation with Lena, I was ebullient. Now, I'm less sure of Lena and wonder if a job and romance has me undergoing a normalization I never thought I was capable of and not sure I want. I'm about to tell her this when she tells me she's thinking about moving back east.

We sit at our coffee cups. "I thought you liked Vancouver," I say. "And what about you and me?"

"If I do move it won't be for quite awhile, and of course I want to continue seeing you," she says. "I never looked at Vancouver as something permanent. I wanted to try some other place for awhile, but in Toronto I can maybe go back to school, look for a more interesting job. I miss my family and friends. And I don't need all this infighting."

At the previous day's Workers Circle meeting, Lena was the subject of an out-of-left-field critique led by Hy Fried. She had, said Fried, an "explosive personality," with an awful lot to say for someone who's a greenhorn when it comes to the city of Vancouver. And he wasn't thrilled that she's the Workers Circle delegate to a socialist congress in Seattle next week.

"Abigail told me later that some of them, especially Hy, feel threatened by a young woman who works hard and sometimes takes the lead in discussions," Lena says.

"I'll bet Abigail's gone through the same kind of stuff," I say.

"That's true. After my first meeting at the Katz place, I met with Abigail and we talked a little about that. She also told me she had a crush on you. I told her I knew you from your visit to Toronto."

"*What?*" I say. "I didn't even notice she noticed me. And I didn't even know you knew my name. But I had a crush on you, since the first time I saw you in Toronto."

"That was obvious," says Lena. "At the Ukrainian Hall, Abigail said you were hanging around me like a schoolboy frightened to speak to somebody they really want to speak to. Sometimes, you act like you're twelve years old."

"No, I don't."

"Okay. I'll give you thirteen. You're thirteen years old."

"Do you get crushes on people, Lena?"

"I certainly didn't have one on you. I never thought about you romantically until you asked me into the Cloverleaf Restaurant."

We laugh, and I'm more relaxed, knowing that any drama between us will probably soon be resolved by the distance between Vancouver and Toronto. That makes our time together now less enduring and, in a way, more endurable.

⁓

When the knock comes, I am in the living room scrutinizing the latest *Life* magazine spread on Spain.

"Wanna shoot a little pool, Feldman?" says Art, and we walk to Macey's Pool Hall. Art racks the red balls and I break.

"I was surprised to hear where you're going. Moe Shore told me."

"I'm surprised you *aren't* going to Spain," Art says.

We haven't seen each other since the night of the *Karlsbad* protest, and our concentration is on the conversation, not the crackling balls. "I'll never be anything like an activist," Art says, "but I can't help seeing stuff and feeling like I have to do something. You know that old Jewish saying 'If I am not for myself, who is? If I am not for others, what am I? If not now, when?'"

"If I didn't know it, I do now," I say. "I like that."

"So I talked with Katz and he helped set it up."

"What about medical school?"

"That'll wait," Art says. "I'm only twenty."

I'm on a hot streak, dropping coloured ball after ball, and as I line up the easy shot that will put the game out of reach, I glance up at Art.

"I'll see you there in a few weeks," I say.

⁓

I pin a map of Spain on my bedroom wall to help me track developments in the Civil War. Then I tell the Katz family my decision.

"The volunteers are a terrific shot in the arm for the Spanish people," Harry says.

"You'll be joining Arthur Posner," Esther says.

"I'd already decided to go, pretty much, before he told me," I say.

"Jake," Alex says. "I'd like to be in on it too. If we don't stop them in Spain, fascism will spread across Europe. And the Civil War will be the start of a world war."

Esther tells me another group will leave Vancouver in two weeks and that New York is the only North American city sending more volunteers to Spain than Vancouver. While many of the volunteers who leave from Vancouver are from the city, others are not — Depression wanderlusters who have been drawn to the West Coast by its moderate weather and militant political climate. Westward Ho is Leftward Ho in this part of the North American frontier.

I know Lena is behind the counter today at Sammy's, so I drop by. At her break, she sits with me at a table, sips soup, lights a cigarette, stirs coffee.

"I'm going," I tell her. Lena does not have to ask where.

"How does your mother feel about what you're doing?" she says, slowly exhaling a mouthful of smoke.

"I haven't told her, or my father. But I know how they think."

Lena does not care what Isaac thinks, but Frieda, she fills Lena with trepidation.

Having given up her dreams, my mother now has her children, and her feelings of joy and sadness and accomplishment are derived vicariously through us. Though we assume our independence, my mother influences us at times so unconsciously that neither we nor she even notices. "*I* wouldn't go to Fort Harold," she tells us, shaping our destinies in more ways than we could imagine.

My mother's parents were children when they left Lithuania. They met in New York and grew up with the city, from an apartment on the Lower East Side to a home in the Bronx, from a scrap-clothing pushcart to "Sidney Pike's Leather and Finery: Manufacturer of Fine Soles." Still in high school, Frieda worked part-time at a tailor shop and earned pocket money designing invitations to recitals and receptions and the opening of a family friend's café. Leaving high school, she graduated to landscape painting and soon had an art school scholarship in hand. Then came Isaac, "a real charmer," Auntie Miriam said, and long before it became conventional, Frieda had married and moved to a suburb, albeit one three thousand miles away. To my mother, Vancouver is a distant suburb, a place between big city (New York) and country town (Fort Harold). After Isaac left her for Fort Harold, my mother's New York family pleaded with her to move back, but she would make her stand independently, in her own place, not her family's city nor her husband's town.

In the Keefer Street house, I cannot but overhear particles of my mother's daily conversations with her friends about, mostly, her children. "Eddie," I hear her say, likes to "schlep around in the middle of nowhere." As for Rachel, I hear my mother say, "She never has any mazel. She tried out for that play, and they're privileged to have her, but they didn't give her the part." I was relieved to be the one exempt from my mother's worries until Rachel said, "She's worried sick about you. She goes on to Mrs. Finkel, Mrs. Tabaka, Mrs. Gizzi, and me about you—*when you're not around to hear her.*"

"Well," I say, "she's worried about you too."

"*What?*"

To my mother, Vancouver is a place to leave. Not for herself. But for her children it is a place to aspire to leave. To refugees from the old countries, Canada's Prairies, or B.C.'s Interior, Vancouver is the Up-To-Date New World, a place to leave for.

To Lena, Vancouver is the last stop in the country, as far as someone can run without drowning — separated from Canada by mountains, from America by border, from most everywhere else by ocean. Is returning — *going backward* — to Toronto, Lena wonders, less courageous than stopping — *not going forward* — in Vancouver? She flips back and forth, unsure whether Vancouver is a place to go to or a place to leave. "Well, I'd be interested to know what your mother says when you tell her," says Lena, sipping the same cup of coffee on her lunch break.

"I will tell you," I say.

"The place is important," Lena says.

"It's not so important," I say. "You can be happy anywhere — it depends on who you're with and what you're doing."

"Oh, I mean the decision about the place," Lena says. "As for your decision, I reckon getting into Spain will be more difficult with the new legislation to stop Canadians from joining the fight. Two years in jail and a two thousand dollar fine, isn't it?"

"I can't think of anything more important to do," I say. "What do you think?"

"What do you feel?"

"Here we go again," I say, my voice rising enough to call attention to the table.

"Don't shout in here," Lena whispers. "Of course, I respect anyone's decision to join the International Brigades, but you obviously have all sorts of reasons — besides the obvious — for going to Spain. You do have feelings, *no*?"

Before I can respond, she's on her feet. "My break's over."

That night, I sit alone in my room sifting through artifacts of a boyhood that will finally end, I sense, when I leave in a couple weeks. In the corner of the room is a cardboard carton of re-read and re-read pulp adventure magazines I haven't looked at since returning from the Interior with Dreiser's *Sister Carrie*, a flattened box containing a worn Snakes and Ladders board game, a stack of swing records. In the drawer, a battered baseball glove bought at Woodward's when I was eleven, the black yarmulke worn home inadvertently from Art Posner's bar mitzvah at Menkus's synagogue, report cards, marbles, the *Baseball Magazine* cover of Hank Greenberg that came off my bedroom wall to make room for the map of Spain. A studio still of the family — I'm slim, curly-haired, arms hanging with hands clenched, wearing knickers, feet on a chair to lift me to the height of Eddie, who's standing stiffly on the other side of the shot. In between the brothers sits Isaac, unsmiling under a fedora with a white feather, wearing a tweed suit, spectacles, shirt buttoned at the neck without a tie; Frieda smiling slightly, skirt draped to her shoes, brown hair flowing over her knees, holding Rachel, who's holding a stuffed kitten.

"Letter from Fort Harold," Rachel shouts the next morning, a moment after the envelope falls through the front-door mail slot.

"Rachel, you're the only one who writes Fort Harold," I say, seated across from Sam at a chessboard in the living room. "You share his letters to you, but we never get to see what you write to him about us."

"What's to say? Contrary to what Sam here thinks, Jake, your life *is* an open book. No dark secrets there," Rachel says, moving towards the kitchen where she'll read the letter to my mother. "And you're wrong. I write Eddie and Joan, not Fort Harold. I'm not in touch with my father anymore."

As I turn back to the board, Sam smiles. "In Fort Harold, your father once told me, 'I was always faithful to my wife as long as the marriage was alive.'" Sam knows, like me, that the marriage was never alive.

"I guess," I say. "My father never caught whoever broke his windows."

"Whoever broke his windows," Sam says through a soft chuckle, as though repeating a punchline, while his eyes continue to analyse the chessboard.

"What are you laughing at?" I say.

Sam looks up from the board quizzically. "You mean," he says, "you don't know."

"Know what?"

"Isaac broke those windows. He wanted us — no, *you* — out of the house that badly at night so he could sleep with Kitty in his bed."

As I enter the kitchen after being checkmated, my mother's seated at the table with Rachel. "Eddie's with him again," she informs me.

Rachel gives me a quick synopsis of Eddie's letter to her — our father was feeling overworked following Sam's departure, the seemingly endless line of wandering employable relatives apparently finally ended. So, Isaac called for Eddie, who declined the invite at first, but relented when Kitty wrote to tell him our father was verging on a breakdown. Kitty, by the way, is now living with Isaac, in the house with Eddie, Joan, and their son, Richard.

Sam is in the kitchen now, too, and he asks Rachel, "How do Eddie and Joan like the living arrangements?"

"Not at all."

"There are all sorts of reasons why Eddie keeps going to that place," I say.

The four of us are silent. Then I say it.

"I'm going away for awhile. Spain."

Silence again. Sam nods as though he has expected this news. Rachel watches our mother. There is a flash of worry on my mother's face, then she stands, speaks impassively.

"When do you leave?"

"Two weeks." They know my resolve, that the place I have to be, for now, is Spain.

"Did you hear if Artie got there all right?" my mother says.

"No one's heard yet," I say. "It's only been a week since he left."

"He's a good boy, a menschen," she says, gazing into the window above the sink.

I've made a decision my mother anticipated. Over the next two weeks, her response is an outward stolidity. She has not followed the events in Spain, but I discovered early that she is steadfastly adaptable when her children's interests are at stake. From premarital sex to class war to Joan the Baptist, whatever we do is, in no time, all right with her, and it is comforting at times for Rachel, Eddie, and me to know that somewhere there is always uncritical love. "You should think highly of yourself," she tells me no matter what. The morning of the night I am to leave, she comes to my room with a new leather suitcase, pants, two shirts, underwear, and heavy socks. "Mom, you shouldn't have done that. You can't afford —"

"If I want to buy something for my boy, I will. It can get very cold in Spain."

No one in the family has mentioned what we all know — Luigi Mundello, one of the first to leave from Vancouver, died in the Battle of the Jarama River Valley. His death was followed by word of other fallen Vancouver volunteers.

I leave the station that night with Billy Sweeney and three volunteers I do not know. We will be joined by others along the way to Toronto, then journey on to New York where we'll board a steamer for France. My mother, Sam, Rachel, Polly, and Lena are at the train to see me off. As I get set to board, they pace, look away from me, then back again. There are handshakes and hugs. It is the first I have seen of Lena since the restaurant. We hug dispassionately and, as we draw apart, I ask when she will leave for Toronto. "I'm not sure I'm going to Toronto," she says, a twist of uncertainty in her face.

On the train's first step, I look back a moment, one hand gripping a bar above my head, swallow.

"Loyf un freyen zikh," my mother says. "Run and be happy."

"Good luck," Rachel says. "We'll miss you."

SIXTEEN

RIGHT AND FREEDOM

Barcelona, fall 1986

'M EARLY FOR DINNER WITH REBECCA, SO INSTEAD of waiting for her in the lobby of her hotel, I stroll down the Ramblas, a long boulevard festooned with flowers and newsstands and artworks. After a few blocks, I head back to Rebecca's hotel, a half-block off the Ramblas and a world away from the modern hotel where I'm staying. Step into this hotel and you're inside a circa 1936 black-and-white photograph, except it's in colour. The aging dark wooden chairs and tables in the dim bar — barely retouched since the Civil War — are remainders from consumptive marathons with Russian-speaking advisors and English-writing authors and *sardana*-dancing Catalans.

Rebecca's hotel is Lincoln Battalion–central, and in its lobby are the people whose names fill the history books and documentary films about the American volunteers. Near the hotel's entrance, Lincoln Sonny Abrams gabs with Kate Quigley, volunteer for Spain-turned-NYC Teachers Union organizer, and Pauline Blum, volunteer nurse turned short story writer. I almost stumble over the outstretched legs of Pauline's husband, Simon Berman, sunk deep into a couch. Simon arrived in Spain as a wire service reporter, enlisted in the Mac-Paps — an American combatant in the Canadian outfit — before joining the Lincolns. After the Civil War, he was an Oscar-nominated screenwriter for *The Mere Idea of You*, a movie that touchingly captured the idealism and decency of so much of the North American generation that fought in World War II. Screenplays like that and his socialist affiliations were enough to get Si blacklisted in 1950s Hollywood, so he survived back in New York writing press releases for a theatre troupe and a trade union, freelance features, a novel. The Toronto reporter is at a coffee table interviewing David Zinn. From Poland, he fought in Spain as a member of the International Brigade's Jewish Botwin Company. Later, David joined the French Resistance organization, the FTP-MOI, participating in an assault on the military compound near the Eiffel Tower. He's lived in Chicago the past forty years and came to the reunion with Illinois Lincolns.

In a corner of the lobby, Mel Fox, the Lincolns' final commander, stoops to huddle soberly with two fellow veterans. One of the men with Mel is author Richard Lillard, a history professor at the University of New Hampshire who lost a hand in Spain during the retreats. The other Lincoln with Mel, Sal Scarsone, is in demand at the reunion, too, but because of the regular long-distance World Series updates his son sends.

"Sarah Koch has been mugged!"

When this cry comes from the hotel entrance, I turn away from the faces in the lobby. Mel Fox leads the charge to the entrance with Jim Heathcott and Sal Scarsone. I follow, too, and see that Sarah Koch is the L.A. woman who I met at the Fuencarral cemetery in Madrid. I also learn that Sarah was about to enter the hotel when a Spanish teen grabbed her bag and knocked her to the sidewalk.

"I came *here* for this?" Sarah wonders as I help ease her onto a couch.

"For this, you could have gone to an American city," says Sonny Abrams, who had a brief career as a nightclub singer after Spain, then a lifetime scrubbing the outer walls and windows of Manhattan skyscrapers.

The Mac-Paps and Lincolns are different but more alike than any other two battalions at the reunion. Both stepped out of Depression-era picket lines and bread lines, ballparks and movie houses, hobo jungles and boxcars. The first Canadian volunteers to reach Spain served in the Lincoln Battalion until their own Mac-Pap Battalion was formed six months later. While I know of some of the Lincoln volunteers here, I scarcely *know* any of them, so I go alone to the bar to wait for dinnertime.. I'm soon followed into the bar by a heavy-breathing Mel Fox, back from an unsuccessful chase after Sarah's mugger.

"Couldn't catch the guy?" I say as Mel collapses into a chair at my table and we introduce ourselves.

"Jim, get over here. Have a drink with us," Mel barks the moment Jim Heathcott sets foot in the bar. But Heathcott stands still, oblivious to Mel, staring at me I believe for an instant, then I realize that he is looking through me.

"No thanks, Mel," Heathcott says. "No, I've things to do."

"What's eating him?" I say to Mel as Heathcott leaves the barroom.

"Who knows what the hell he's been through," Mel says. "Vietnam. It was different. Where are you from?"

"Vancouver."

"Ah, *Canadian*," he says. "The Mac-Paps were the best."

"So were the Lincolns," I say.

"I know one thing about Vancouver — that's where the Industrial Workers of the World got their nickname the 'Wobblies.' I just found that out watching a documentary about them. Were they ever something. When the movie ended I couldn't get up from my seat in the theatre. I'd sweated so much my shirt was stuck to it."

"Have you seen this, Mel?" says Richard Lillard, setting a photocopy of a letter on the table in front of Mel. "Copy of a letter about John Scott. I received it in Spain from his mother after he died and put it up on the wall of our trench so the guys could read it."

"Dick Lillard," says Mel, "this is Jake Feldman, from the Mac-Paps."

"Then you should read this letter too," Richard says as we shake hands.

"I loved your book," I tell him.

"Thank you."

Richard is in demand for interviews at this reunion, having just published his Civil War memoir, *Free, Black, and 21: On the Line from Memphis to Madrid*. The Lincolns were the first American military battalion that was integrated and Richard's book weaves his personal story into this history

"He's doing another one," Mel says. "A collection of letters to and from Spain during the war."

"Been collecting this kind of thing for years," says Richard, pointing towards the photocopy. "John was a friend of Mel and mine."

Mel begins to read the letter aloud: "My dear comrades of the Abraham Lincoln Battalion, I have been a long time in writing to you, but I have not been well. Please forgive me. I am the mother of Inver Marlow—your dear friend John Scott. I just send you a message of great love and my deepest wishes for the great cause that he and you give your lives for. I most sincerely trust that all is well, especially with those who so splendidly helped my son and so kindly have written to my other son, Denis. He is abroad in Poland, but I know he will write himself. There is nothing to say. My son is gone but I am very proud of him and so grateful to him and to all the other splendid men—the living and the dead—in this horrible struggle for Right and Freedom. All your kind and tender messages to me have touched and helped me so much. From your sincere and affectionate friend, Sylvia Marlow."

Mel is visibly moved. "That's some letter," he says.

I'm touched too. I thank Richard for sharing the letter with me, then I'm on my feet explaining that I have a dinner engagement to go to.

Time to see Rebecca. The discovery of leftover bullet holes, from a battle for Barcelona, in the wood-panelled walls of the hotel's stairway would not surprise me. But there are none, and it's quickly up the broad stairway to Rebecca's second-floor room.

"I'll be ready in just a moment," she says, opening the door. "Come on in."

"A woman with the reunion was mugged right outside the entrance to the hotel."

"Oh my God. Do you know who it was?" says Rebecca.

"Sarah's her name. From L.A."

"Is she all right?"

"Seems to be," I say.

"Sarah Weintraub's a nurse."

"I think her last name's Koch."

"That's the name of the Lincoln she married," Rebecca says.

"I met her once and liked her a lot," I say.

I follow after Rebecca along the hallway to Sarah's room. Seeing that her friend is okay, we're on our way to dinner, back through the lobby, crossing the wide Ramblas into a maze of side streets. At the end of a side street so narrow it is always shaded dark, we find a quiet seafood restaurant, where we drink a white wine and an icy almond gazpacho soup, then pick at a paella platter of short-grain rice cooked with vegetables and fish. We speak briefly about Spain, then we talk and talk about our lives afterwards in B.C. and New York. I tell her about returning to Keefer Street. She tells me about Pitkin Avenue in her Brooklyn neighbourhood

"I stayed on at a hospital in Mataro as long as I could after La Pasionaria's Barcelona farewell," Rebecca says. "When I did leave Spain, I rested a week in Dover at the invitation of an English nurse I met here, then back to Brooklyn." Rebecca finds work at Manhattan's Mount Sinai Hospital, resettling in Greenwich Village. On the night of VE day in 1945, she goes with friends for coffee at a Village café. Rebecca slides into a wooden booth as Bill Rivers, just discharged from the army, is about to begin a somewhat drunken poetry reading about his father, who disappeared before his birth. Rebecca goes home with Bill that night. They are a couple of months into seeing each other when Rebecca, after a shift at the hospital, approaches Bill's place just off Second Avenue and 4th Street, and it is so murky outside that she stumbles over him, out cold on the sidewalk.

"Bill," Rebecca says the next morning as he sips from a chipped coffee mug in a quivering hand. "I'm pregnant." For nearly a month, they talk of a future together, a place on the idyllic island Bill would find for them. But she's never certain about him. Besides his drinking, Bill is perplexed by her activism in the New York State Nurses Association.

"Rebecca, tell me, what has a century of earnestness accomplished for the human race?" he says.

"What has self-absorption accomplished for the human race?" she says.

Then he is gone. No word, no note. Like the father he wrote about, he would be a mystery to Rebecca and to his daughter, Janice.

"So I became a single mom," Rebecca says.

"How is your daughter now?" I say.

"Wonderful. We're extremely close. Your children?"

"They're great... but I didn't always come through for the people I love."

"Did you always try?" she says.

I quietly consider Rebecca's question for several seconds. "I think so."

"I've been disappointed in myself too," says Rebecca, "especially when Spain fell."

"You put blame on yourself for that?" I say. "That wasn't on us. I'm old enough to know things don't always work out."

"I know it was irrational, but that's how I felt," she says.

"I felt that way too," I say. "I was devastated when Spain fell. What does your daughter think about you and Spain?"

"My children are like my parents were," she says. "They don't know everything about it, of course, but some things about Spain are easy for them — a *good* fight. You know, if the Spanish Civil War hadn't happened, I probably would have found another Spain. I was determined to devote myself to some revolutionary cause back then. I had a conviction — a moment of clarity, of truth — that touches some of us and is difficult to explain to anyone who hasn't experienced it."

"Maybe they've felt that way about something else," I say. "Jazz or architecture or whatever. I don't know. But the thing someone is passionate about doesn't have to be politics, does it? For you, for me, it was. We share that, Rebecca."

She smiles. "I wonder if Spain was the first time people were so passionate about the freedom of someone else," she says. "It certainly wasn't the last. I was in Nicaragua last month with other American volunteers for Spain to present the people there with an ambulance from us. In Managua, Kate Quigley, Mel Fox, and I met with Americans and Canadians and other internationals helping to harvest coffee and cotton. Kate was a nurse in Spain too.... Jake, we better go."

Rebecca is looking through the restaurant window at the pitch-black night. The crowded streets when we arrived in early evening are gone as we begin the four-block labyrinth back to the Ramblas. Unsure of the way out, Rebecca does a pirouette in front of the restaurant. "I think," she points, "it's this way." And we begin our walk up the middle of the dark street. The way to the Ramblas seems farther than it did before we lost ourselves in conversation for hours. A block along, I notice a small young man, with the rumpled appearance of someone who lives without roofs, walking slowly thirty feet ahead of us. A further half-block, he lets out a whistle, and I turn and see another man emerge onto the street behind us as if he'd crystallized from cobblestone pavement. Rebecca and I walk on in the night chill, not sure we're headed in the right direction, passing dark doorways. The man ahead of us leans to scoop up an empty wine bottle.

He is twenty feet away running his fingers across the bottle as though admiring a newly acquired firearm. The man behind us steps up his pace.

"What's going on here?" Rebecca says.

"We're being set up for a mugging," I say, moving close to the buildings, reaching for Rebecca's hand, still walking. Two blocks from the light of the Ramblas, no one in sight, the man ahead stops ten feet away, his eyes on Rebecca and me, bottle poised. Suddenly, a British woman's voice declares with delight, "Absolutely splendid meal."

"Quite," a man agrees. The woman and man step from a barely discernible doorway into the unlit street in front of us. Their post-meal banter is a beautiful symphony to Rebecca and me as we merge with the British party exiting the ground-floor entrance to an upstairs restaurant. The two men who had been sizing us up vanish, but Rebecca and I don't feel entirely safe until our strides reach her hotel and we stop for breath at the barroom table of Mel and Hildy Fox, the Toronto reporter, Jim Heathcott, and the tour guide from Portland.

"We were just about mugged," Rebecca tells them.

"Where the hell did that happen?" Mel says.

While the others listen closely to Rebecca, Heathcott is pre-occupied with staring intently at the tour guide.

"Off the Ramblas," Rebecca says.

"Okay, then, I'm going back to my hotel now," says the guide.

"These creeps could knock you off," Heathcott says, "and escape through those streets like rats through a sewer."

"There but for fortune, Jim," says Hildy.

"What!?" Heathcott says. "You like the creeps?" He goes back to staring at the guide.

"You enjoying the view, Jim?" the Toronto reporter asks.

"What kind of a question is that?" says Heathcott. "What kind of reporter are you? Are you an objective reporter?"

"Yes," the reporter says. "My objective is to destroy capitalism."

"Very funny," Heathcott says.

"I think it is," Hildy says.

Heathcott glares at the guide as she rises from the table.

"What happened off the Ramblas isn't unique to Barcelona," Rebecca says. "You know how many times I have felt as vulnerable as Jack just felt?"

"Are you sure you want to walk around out there by yourself?" I ask the tour guide. "I'm leaving now. I can walk you to a cab."

Heathcott shifts his stare from the guide to me, then back to the guide.

"It's fine," she says to me while spitting a look at Heathcott. "I can walk by myself."

"I don't understand this place anymore," Heathcott says.

Rebecca and I say our goodbyes and I quickly walk the half-block to the boulevard, where others madly ramble the night, and with my own mad urgency wave down a taxi.

"I was waiting," Peter Krawchuk says, slumped in a chair in the Hotel Condor lobby. "But they never came."

The Toronto reporter is recording The Truth Behind the On-to-Ottawa Trek According to Peter Krawchuk. "How many others were waiting across the country?" the reporter asks.

"I'd say thousands of us," Peter says. "I had gone back east for work, but the Trek never got to me because somehow the government found out what the real plan was and they stopped it in Regina."

"What real plan?" the reporter says. "I thought the objective was to march on Ottawa to put pressure on the government to improve wages and conditions for relief workers."

"No, no, no," Peter protests, as though everyone knew something bigger was on the agenda. "The plan was to start at the Pacific Ocean and hit Ottawa with enough protesters to overthrow the government and declare Canada a socialist republic."

"That's the first I heard of it, and I was there," says Henry. After a long pause, he adds: "*Nah*, I don't believe it."

"Not everyone knew about it," Peter says, "but there were thousands waiting to join the Trek in Regina, more waiting in Winnipeg, and even more in places all over Ontario. We would have hit Ottawa maybe fifty thousand strong, and those comrades heading up the Trek, they weren't, you know, liberals."

"Agreed. Slim Evans was as radical as they come," says Henry, who paces a couple steps with a grin, wondering whether he has just been told actual history, albeit unknown, or Peter's wishful thinking. The reporter fumbles with his recorder. "Let me make sure I got this on tape," he says excitedly, having struck what could turn out to be oral history pay dirt.

"Maybe we should ask Irene about it?" Henry says to me quietly.

"What for?" I say. "What Peter said isn't going to change anything now, and I don't doubt that he honestly believes it all." I have my doubts about some of Peter's assertions, but not enough to intrude on his memories as he records them for posterity and the Toronto reporter.

"Irene knows everything about the Trek, so I'm going to ask her about it anyways," Henry tells me. But not now, because the reporter, having finished with Peter, is turning his attention back to Henry. The reporter's been wanting to speak with

Henry since hearing that he gave a talk about the Ebro offensive on a tour bus. Some of the reunionists, the reporter says, are comfortable talking about Depression-era Canada and its protests but have never spoken to anyone about the Spanish battlefields. "I'm game for anything," Henry says.

Between events, back at the hotels the reunionists still want to be with each other, so we congregate in a bar, a restaurant, a lobby. Sometimes the Toronto reporter unwittingly provides our entertainment. Watching him interview Henry, for instance, is a bit like being in the studio audience of a smart talk show — *Dick Cavett*, say — and several of us sit at an adjoining table, listening.

"The retreats?" the reporter says.

Henry removes his grey overcoat, moves to a chair across the table from the reporter. "Our lines break across the Aragon, and we're just moving, moving, moving," he begins, the big man struggling for the words that will make his testimony matter as much as Peter's On-to-Ottawa Trek revelations.

"March '38. It wasn't just soldiers retreating. We come to this highway, and as far as the eye can see there are people coming from the villages. Mostly on foot, taking what they can carry. Some furniture's piled on donkey carts. We're carrying our company commander, Phillip Shaw, shot through the chest. He was one commander who never rested on ceremony — salutes and that kind of B.S. At dusk, we see soldiers on a hill. A guy from the Thaelmann Battalion, retreating with us, shouts up at the hill and someone shouts back in German. 'Nazis,' the Thaelmann guy says. And the bullets start coming. Shaw says, 'Keep moving. Leave me here and just keep moving.' Understand that this wasn't just a Spanish fascist offensive. There were many, many German tank companies and bomber squadrons. The Italian army."

Several of us form a ring around the reporter and Henry, listening closely to his memories, which are intact, like an elderly ballplayer who cannot tell you what he ate for breakfast this morning but can recall each pitch in a bygone at-bat.

"Every time we stop, the goddamn fascists attack. Nothing much to eat so we eat anything we can find — unripe almonds, raw turnips. In this village, there's a warehouse, and we find cases of marmalade."

I have no memory of Henry in Spain, but I do remember the marmalade. My retreating Mac-Pap unit found the same warehouse. Probably the same day. *In minutes, the marmalade tins are ripped open and the Mac-Paps's fingers and faces and clothing are drenched in ecstatic stickiness. Crouched over two tins I have wolfed down, I'm eating a third, deep yellow stuck in beard bristles, smeared on my khaki coat sleeve. The unit slowly falls back from the marmalade, and in the broiling breezeless afternoon, the fatigued troops, stomachs full, crumple lifeless under trees and against the warehouse wall.*

"Never tasted anything so good," shouts Henry, adding quietly, "Never even liked marmalade before that." Then, to no one in particular, "You know, there's no one here," Henry says. "The village is a ghost town."

On to the seaside village of Caspe. "On the outskirts of town, we meet up with others from the International Brigades and make a stand," Henry says. "At one point, it looks like we're going to be routed. Fascists coming at our line, hardly any arms. And this Spaniard who's with the Mac-Paps jumps to his feet screaming, 'Estes Battalian Canadiense,' and spraying machine-gun fire. 'This is the Canadian battalion,' he's saying. 'Damn it, you can't defeat us.' His gunfire stops the rout for a bit, and we hold Caspe for a few days, but we're under such heavy fire—bombers and artillery and tanks—that we have to retreat again." On to the village of Marçà. "On May 1, 1938, we have a May Day parade on the river at Marçà. Rafts and banners and everything. I still got the photographs."

Henry falls back in his chair, stops talking, spent. But he has one more thing to say.

"We had our victories too, especially early on," Henry says quietly. "Like Belchite. It's door-by-door, hand-to-hand, with bayonets, grenades. The only way to take Belchite is to storm it, moving our barricades up a couple feet at a time, from all directions. It seems impregnable. Machine-gun fire everywhere. Snipers. To advance we're busting holes through walls, fascists are retreating through tunnels. This goes on six days—exhaustion, collapsing, but we fight like hell. And we take that town."

Henry falls silent again and the recorder is pressed off.

"The first time I returned," says Tom Barkley, "they stopped our bus at the Valle de los Caídos, that gigantic monument to Franco just outside Madrid. I was in a busload of tourists. Everyone else looked at the monument, took photographs, heard about how it took almost twenty years to build into a hillside. I stayed on the bus and I felt sick. I knew that after Franco won, he rounded up Republicans. Mass executions. Women were raped, had their heads shaved. A half-million Republicans were put in jails and concentration camps. Thousands sent to German concentration camps. Forced slave labour. Franco forced Republican prisoners to build that monument at gunpoint. After a few minutes on the bus, I had to get off and throw up."

The reporter reaches for the recorder so Tom can repeat for the record this visit to the Valle de los Caídos. "Somebody should blow the damn thing up," Henry says.

"Wonder why the so-called people's government that's been elected here hasn't done something about it," says Tom.

"Probably figures that getting rid of it would cause too much of a stir. Too many old fans of Franco still around," Bob surmises.

The group turns quiet, reflective. Finally, I say softly, "The retreats. Absolute terror on faces of the people evacuating those villages."

"I've never seen anything like it since," Henry says.

I stare down. Others sag, silently.

"Anyways," Henry says, "they're serving breakfast. What are we waiting for?"

SEVENTEEN

JACK FIELDS

Vancouver, 1939–1942

O N ANY DAY IN THE 1930S OR '40S, VANCOUVER'S Canadian Pacific Railway station is a bustling monument to the Train Age. On the February day in 1939 that I returned from Spain, ten thousand fill the station and spill outside into the snow. There are another thirty returning Mac-Paps with me. We climb methodically from the station's waterfront tracks as if rising from the ocean, and up the stairway to the waiting throng. The moment I step into it I'm enveloped. "Jakie, Jakie, Jakie," my mother cries, embracing me, as Rachel leaps at me, knocking my navy blue beret into the cheering crowd.

The crush of bodies sways in the warmth in the cold. They're stilled by a voice, belonging to Nat Nemirovsky, the Spanish Republic's consul in Vancouver. To Mac-Paps from Strathcona, he is one of our own—from the neighbourhood, welcoming us home. "On behalf of the government of Spain, I want to thank you all," he says into a megaphone. "It's good to have you back home."

"It's good to be back," shouts Mac-Pap John Kolchynsky, speaking after Nemirovsky on the makeshift plywood platform that's been erected at one end of the station. After a pause, Kolchynsky concludes: "Now, we come home to carry on the struggle with as much determination as we did in Spain."

Amid the cheers that erupt in the crowd, a voice booms: "Viva la República Española."

"Viva Kolchynsky," calls another.

The new mayor, Lyle Telford, follows Kolchynsky. "It has not been in vain," he says. "This great crowd feels that you have fought for them and for humanity. Some day I hope this country will be worthy of heroes like you."

I hear "Jake!" and turn to see Claire Gordon reaching out to squeeze my hand. "Have you," she asks, "seen Art?"

"No, I never did."

Claire drops her hand and I'm swept away from her by the pressing crowd, to outside the station, through slushy snow to waiting cars that take us to dine on beef stew and make toasts to the falling Republic. At the dinner, I am approached by Hy Fried to address a Workers Circle meeting at the Katz place the following evening. "We would have won this war and stopped the spread of fascism if the so-called democracies hadn't blockaded arms to Spain," I tell the meeting, "but they saw the Civil War as a fight between left and right, and they chose the right, they chose fascism. So now we have lost the first battle in what will be a war of the world."

A week after my return, Rachel is off to New York. Sam left earlier, out east to try again to make music for money but instead he bartends.

Returning home from someplace never seems to take as long as getting there, and travelling back to Vancouver I was calm with anticipation. The exhaustion comes after the first days back as Spain's afterglow begins its fade. I've been on the go non-stop since leaving for Spain in 1937 and now, back on Keefer Street, I am deflated — worn-out, saddened, bittersweet. These last days between wars a pall has fallen. Not only has Vancouver lost Art Posner, Luigi Mundello, and more than one hundred others, but the Mac-Paps who survived and returned feel helpless watching the unfolding of our world war prophesy. In September, Canada goes to war.

"Essen," says my mother, handing me a bowl of her matzo ball soup. "What are you going to do now?"

"I want to join up," I say, and the next day I tell this to a recruiting officer.

"Any experience?" he smiles.

"I fought in Spain."

"Well, come back tomorrow."

"I want to join," I say on my second visit to the recruitment office.

"Come tomorrow."

"You said that yesterday."

"We don't have any openings."

"How can an army not have openings?"

"There's nothing for you here," the recruiter says flatly, adding with a snap, "because you fought in Spain."

Spain disappears when World War II begins. It is a part of the Dirty Thirties, rear-viewed by some as an extreme decade filled with misguided idealism and outright sedition. The 1940s and its War Years would belong to new veterans, not the volunteers for Spain. Those who supported Spain's Republic are now called "premature anti-fascists." Even Jimmy Cagney, Warner Brothers' choice to star in a movie about University of Notre Dame football coach Knute Rockne, loses the role because the school will not countenance an actor who had supported Spain's "godless" Republic.

"Nothing." At the docks. At Red Top taxis. For days I walk along the shoreline by the university, through neighbourhoods I don't know, averting eyes or crossing streets when encountered by a familiar face. Before Spain, I was young and inexperienced and felt I had no past. Now, I'm beginning to feel I have no future. Passing Sammy's deli, I glance up from the snowy sidewalk barely in time to avoid a collision with Georgie Leonard, the first I've seen of him since returning from Spain. "I was just in the neighbourhood so I thought I'd get something to eat at Sammy's," he says. Georgie lives on the West Side, he tells me, attends the University of B.C. law school, has his future set with a firm specializing in commercial properties.

"That was rough about Art," he says, but I will not discuss Art with Georgie. I miss Art, left behind in the Spain left behind in me.

"Got to go," Georgie says. "Got to be a go-getter, Jake. A word of advice from an old friend — don't stand around with your finger up your ass while the parade goes by. Let's get together sometime and shoot the breeze." Both know we will not. Georgie has places to be, and goes on his way, thankfully, and so do I, with nowhere to go.

On the day the rains wash away winter's last snow, I walk aimlessly, pause in front of the stucco box where Lena had lived. When I turn onto Keefer Street, Alex Katz is standing in front of me.

"Jake, how you been?"

"Not so good," I say.

"Found work?"

"I fought in Spain, don't you know?"

"I know, it's been tough for a lot of the guys," Alex says. "I got something on a trawler. So it's not like absolutely no one will hire us, and some Mac-Paps were able to enlist. But these sorts of things are harder for us now and some of the guys have changed their names to make things easier. John Kolchynsky became John Cole and found work right away up north, in a mill."

"You think I should do that?"

"It's something to think about," Alex says. "By the way, don't tell anyone about John."

"How can I? Haven't heard a word about him in ages."

"My name," I tell my mother that evening, "is now Jack Fields. I'm leaving town as soon as I've got some money."

"Where are you going, Jakie?"

"Jack. Call me Jack. I don't know, but there isn't anything in Vancouver."

Jack Fields finds work in a Yellow Cab. The plan is to drive seven days a week for a month, then buy a ticket eastward bound to start over. At first, my mother is entertained by the name change, but is disturbed after a week of it. "Jakie," she says. "I've got an appointment for you with Rabbi Menkus this afternoon."

"Why would he want to speak with Jack Fields?"

"Fields, schmields, *abi gezint*," she mutters. "He's someone to talk to."

"Jack Fields does not know a Rabbi Menkus. Jack Fields is a non-believer."

"And Jake Feldman wasn't?"

I do not see Menkus. "Jack Fields is the only way," I tell my mother, "the only way I know of."

I am moving on adrenaline down Keefer Street.

"Jake."

I keep moving.

"Jake!"

The voice follows, then a hand tugs the tail of my jacket. I stop.

"Where are you going like that?" Polly Siegel says.

"Just walking," I say.

"How have you been?" she says curiously.

"Pretty good, I guess."

"Have you heard from Rachel?"

"Yeah, she's taking dance classes and living with our relatives in Brooklyn. You must know all this."

"We stay in touch. Want to go to Sammy's for a coffee?"

Polly and I follow the neighbourhood side streets to Sammy's. When I first returned from Spain, I thought I'd come home to the same neighbourhood, and the neighbourhood thought I had come home the same person, but the neighbourhood and I had both changed more than either of us knew. Some of the sounds have changed, with much of the old Jewish quarter, in short years, moving to parts of the city south and west of Strathcona. Sammy is one of the holdouts. He works and he waits, and his former neighbours come back to Strathcona for his challah and pickles and knishes. Polly and I sit at a table splotched with mustard.

"I haven't seen you for so long, Jake. Where have you been?" she starts, reaching for a dill pickle.

"Right here. Just haven't felt very sociable," I say.

"I thought you were going to walk through a wall on Keefer Street, Jake."

"I'm not Jake anymore," I say impatiently, gazing past my sister's friend. "I'm Jack. Jack Fields. I'm going away soon so I'm driving cab to get a few bucks for a ticket out."

"Where to?"

"Don't know."

"Rachel saw Lena in Toronto. She's doing well as a graphic artist. Her stuff's been in *MacLean's* and other magazines. She's seeing a lawyer, left-wing lawyer."

"He would be."

"This name thing," Polly says, "you want to pass for gentile?"

"No. That's not it at all. People who fought in Spain aren't so employable these days. So some have changed their names."

"You should be proud you fought in Spain."

"I'm fine with it."

"Are you okay?" she says.

"I told you, I'm okay. Pretty good."

"That's good."

We sit quietly for a moment.

"Well, I'm getting out of here," I say, tossing down a coin.

"Holy cats." My mother is on the telephone puffing a cigarette when I come through the back door.

"What's the matter?" I say as she hangs up the receiver. "You shouldn't smoke."

"I don't even inhale. I don't know how," she says. "That was Joan. Your father is sick — heart attack."

"How bad is he?" I say anxiously.

"He's sick but he'll survive. A mild one. Joan is running the store. She talked to Eddie from Camp Borden and he said maybe she should ask you to come up and help."

"I'd love to spend the next forty years of my life in Fort Harold."

"She said just until Eddie gets out of the army or your father is back on his feet."

"No thank you. I've got other plans and I've just about got the money I need."

"You're in a dream world, Jakie. He's a bum, your father, and he ran away, but even he didn't run like you. You used to say you love the world so much that you have to make it better, then you decided to hate the world."

"I wouldn't talk, Ma. You have your children, but they're leaving, and even the neighbourhood's leaving you. But you stay put here. You're in the dream world. What have you got?"

"*Gornisht mit gornisht*," she says softly. "I've got nothing but nothing. And you think I'm silly."

"No, no I don't," I say quietly, reopening the back door.

"Where are you running to?"

"Out."

"Run, run," my mother shouts as I close the door behind me. "Run your meshuggena head off."

I take long strides down Keefer Street.

"Jake!"

I stop. Polly again, walking home with a small bag from Sammy's.

"Are you sure you're okay?"

My body sags and I hang my head. "Gornisht mit gornisht. That's what I'm sure of."

"Let's walk," she says. We begin a long stroll through the neighbourhood and beyond. For the first time, I talk about the war, not everything that happened, but about my despair over friends lost, a cause defeated, a people vanquished, nothing for me here. And I tell her about my plans to move east by myself. "I've been thinking that maybe someone back from a war has to be left alone for a while."

"When something's healing, you let it be," she says. "And I'm sure it takes time to regain your self-esteem once that's been battered."

"Don't you think certain things won't — shouldn't — ever heal?" I say.

"Probably. There's nothing wrong with being justly angry or sad about something."

Since finishing high school, Polly has been living with her parents and sister, working at a Woolworth's soda fountain, taking a dance class, spending long hours at home choreographing routines. She'd like to join Rachel in New York. In the meantime, every Tuesday evening at the canteen in the Jewish Community Centre, she's a volunteer, singing as well as playing cards and checkers, talking, and dancing with World War II soldiers passing through Vancouver.

Polly and I walk and talk across the city for the next few days. One afternoon downtown, as we walk to a matinee, a camera snaps, and a man reaches towards us with his card as someone else's hand offers us a leaflet. "Read this," the leafleter says, shoving the paper at my clenched hand.

"Did you take our picture?" I say.

"No, I did," says the other man as Polly takes his card. "You can pick it up at that address in a few hours."

"I'm passing out federal election information for the Liberal Party," says the man with leaflets.

"I'm way to the left of the Liberals," I say, stepping up to the theatre wicket.

"I would be a leftist," the man calls out as we disappear into the theatre, "but I can't stand Trotsky." I contemplate the leafletting Liberal as I eat popcorn during the previews. The schmuck wouldn't know Trotsky from Stanislavsky, I'm thinking, but after all we've been through, from the Ballantyne Pier to the Ebro River, the only thing that guy absorbed about the left is its sectarian banter. Is that sad commentary on us or him? The feature begins and I leave the leafleter behind and move on to Rosalind Russell and Henry Fonda. Afterwards, Polly and I go to the address on the photographer's card, laughing at the shot of us nearly colliding to avoid the leafletting Liberal, his hand covering Polly's face, all under the movie marquee for *His Girl Friday*.

"Are you really going to leave," Polly asks when our laughter subsides, "and do this Jack Fields schtick?"

My mother is alone at the kitchen table, coffee cup trembling. "Your father," she says, as Polly and I come through the back door. "He's dead." I embrace my mother, Polly embraces me, the three of us clinging in the kitchen in the house on Keefer Street. Joan makes funeral arrangements, phoning to ask if the body should be sent south for burial at the Jewish cemetery, but my mother says no. Isaac chose Fort Harold to live and in Fort Harold he should remain. He was almost happy there, sometimes.

"I really didn't know him well," I tell Polly at Sammy's the day of the funeral in Fort Harold. "Maybe every family — everyone — has someone or something they don't talk about."

My mother is melancholy for a morning. But all is not forgiven and she will not let Isaac's passing rewrite her sentiments. "Your father," she says a few days later, "he was a stinker."

During Joan's phone calls to my mother, she again passes on Eddie's plea for me to go north to help with the store. "No

Mom," I insist. "I've got other plans." Eddie writes me directly from Camp Borden, the southern Ontario army base where he is stationed. My mother is overjoyed that Polly and I are with each other, already suggesting we marry, knowing we talk about leaving town together. New York? Toronto? California? Never Fort Harold.

"Just until I get home from the war, Jake," says Eddie, in a phone call from Toronto, where he's on leave before being shipped out to Europe. "You're the one to do this. *Family*."

"I'm sorry, Eddie, we've got plans. I'm sure Joan's doing a good job."

"She's good, but no one can do it on their own, and she's got the boy. I think she hates it there too."

"At least it would be a job," my mother says after the call. "And you can forget about this Fields business. It is *Feldman's* Mens' Wear. And think of all the postage and phone bills you'll save your brother Eddie."

I will not go. Won't follow my father's footsteps. For me, any curiosity Fort Harold held with Isaac's life left town with his death.

Whenever I pass by the railway station, my thoughts return to the Mac-Pap homecoming. But on this rainy day in 1942, I see that a farewell is underway. This time the friends and family of the people on the train are mostly on the train too. There had been rioting against Asians in Vancouver in the early 1900s; they still do not have a vote, and now, with World War II, Japanese Canadians have had their belongings confiscated and are being forcibly removed to internment camps in the Interior and eastward. I stand at a wall, easy to slip from unseen, away from the handful here to say goodbye. The train begins to move. Mrs. Tabaka, from a window, waves a hand in a white glove, holding a handkerchief. I follow her eyes to Mrs. Finkel and to my mother, in brimmed hat and heavy coat, waving, face crushed. My mother is crying. In another window, I see a man looking out at the station in the city where he was born. I have seen him before, beckoning me into his backyard during the Ballantyne Pier riot. There is nothing for him here. Nothing for me. Was there ever anything, I wonder, turning to make my getaway.

Three hours later, I'm with Polly at the White Spot dining room at Granville Street and 67th, where I've taken her for a birthday dinner.

"It's time to leave this city," I say, over an order of Chicken in the Basket.

"What you witnessed today at the station isn't just about Vancouver," she says, over an order of Chicken in the Straw. "The world has gone mad and that's happening to Japanese people up and down the coast."

"I know this," I say, "but, still, it's time we moved on. I thought we'd be long gone by now, but we keep *putzing* around."

"That's because there's no one place we both want to be," she says. "We talk and talk but we still haven't settled on a place to go to. "

"It doesn't have to be forever," I say.

"Happy birthday *to you!*" Three singing White Spot workers have interrupted our travel plans with a chocolate cake singalong.

"Happy birthday, dear Polly," I sing too.

Frieda is back on Keefer Street when Polly and I stop by after dinner.

While eating her slice of the birthday cake, my mother tells us that she spoke with Eddie today and he's still eager for me to go to Fort Harold. "I don't want to interfere," she says, "but I would go up *there* for a little while."

"All right!" Polly and I finally shout out in unison. After all, I want to run and hide, and Fort Harold is the traditional family place to do it. Jack Fields has passed. Polly and I do a quick ceremony with Rabbi Menkus, leave to Victoria for a weekend honeymoon of tea and crumpets at a mock British hotel, then it is onto Fort Harold. "For a couple of years," I say.

"Loyf un freyen zikh," my mother says.

EIGHTEEN

TOM'S BERET

Barcelona, fall 1986

THERE IS A MAD CIRCLE OF MOTORISTS RACING around the Plaça de Catalunya as if manoeuvring a demolition derby, but the vehicles do not collide. They don't, at least while Tom Barkley and I wait for a pause in traffic so we can snake across the wide street to the relative safety of a sidewalk lined with businesses. Tom said we would find a beret on a street just off this plaza. He didn't know which street, though, and emerging from the underground into the plaza is like ascending onto the hub of a beat-up bicycle wheel with side streets shooting out like bent spokes.

Tom chooses a side street for us to walk down in search of the hat shop where he bought a beret on his first return to Spain. So we walk beneath the wrought-iron flower holders, scanning tiny store windows for hats. Before the reunion, I did not know these Eastern Canadian Mac-Paps who have returned to Spain with me, but from a distance at the airport terminal in Toronto I recognized them by Tom's beret. Now, Tom and I search for the old Barcelona of berets and bandoliers. We enter into a square. Four women in black, with ruby lipstick and sunglasses, are browsing a bookstall, waiting for a fifth friend who has stopped to greet a man in a group of men in black leather jackets and Levi's jeans. Slipping through the leather and lipstick to reach the young man selling old books, I stumble for words about the whereabouts of Tom's beret store. The bookseller stares unintelligibly, but one of the women in black decodes enough of my groping Spanish to respond with physical contortions that point to a hat shop one block away.

"It's my store," Tom says, finally, looking in the window at the grey glass display berets share with black broad-brimmed hats and festive feathery headgear. I buy two adult-sized berets, one baby beret. "My daughter in L.A. recently had a girl," I say. Tom grins and says, "That beret's cute as hell. She'll get a kick out of it." He buys another black one to replace the worn ten-year-old beret on his head, and we trace our steps back to the subway, stopping at a shop to buy a blue-and-yellow glass butterfly for Tom's wife, Susan. The clerk notices the International Brigade pin on Tom's jacket and refuses to let him pay.

As we continue to the plaza, Tom adjusts the new beret as he tells me that the people in the apartment where he lives don't know he fought in Spain. "Oh, one or two know, and they've asked about it once or twice, and I'll talk about it if they do, but I don't say much." Tom was never married, and Susan was a widow when they met eight years ago at a retirees' bowling league in suburban Scarborough, where he'd recently moved from Montreal. "I like to bowl. She enjoys it too. But Susan likes square dancing more, so we do that. We do things together. Try different restaurants. We don't talk politics. Don't get me wrong. I still get browned off with the system. It just so happens that I no longer believe you have to be a devout left-winger to be a decent person." We quietly walk the last block to the station. "We love each other a lot," says Tom as he's about to go underground to the Barcelona Metro.

Alone now, I enter an El Cortes Inglés department store in search of a camera to replace the one borrowed from my daughter before I left Vancouver. There was no retrieving her camera, and its roll of film, once I left it on the subway after the visit to Park Güell.

"Canada," says the smiling young clerk in the store's electronics department. "A tourist?"

"Not a tourist...I guess I am," I say. "I'm in Spain for the reunion of the International Brigades that were here during the Civil War."

Her black eyes study me with the intense curiosity of someone with a personal interest, so I continue. "The young people, today, are they interested in the Civil War?"

"Oh, no. Most of my friends know hardly nothing about that. They're more interested in getting a job or going to school or the disco. Only some are interested in that."

"Are you?"

"One of my grandfathers in the war was fascist, the other anarchist. Both my grandmothers vote for socialists."

Beneath the oft-times generic European surface this country presents in 1986, there lingers the polarization of fifty years ago when Spain was divided by political ideology as passionately as some countries divide by ethnic or religious differences.

"Your grandfather, the anarchist one, is he still alive?"

"No, he died defending Madrid in the war. He was a baker, in the anarchist union. My grandfathers never met. The fascist one died in the war also."

The war means Spain's war only to Spain and the international volunteers. To almost everyone else of my generation, it means World War II.

"It really was the beginning of the same one," I say distantly. "I mean, the same war." The clerk does not hear this because the line of shoppers is showing impatience for an end to this conversation that is bottlenecking transactions, and she turns her attention to the next customer.

When I return to the hotel it is late afternoon and Tom Barkley is in the bar recalling, for the Toronto reporter, the moment he learned of Spain. "'Revolt Breaks Out in Spain.' That's what the headline said." That news came to Tom in a newspaper he found in a boxcar he hopped on, in the outskirts of Calgary. Tom was riding rails to the West Coast to look for work. He had never been a joiner, but that day he read about Spain he crossed the tracks to jump on an eastbound freight car. "Back home in Montreal I had the wherewithal to get to Spain," says Tom, seated across from the reporter in our hotel's bar.

I sit down at an adjoining table with others from the travelling reunion. "It's kind of funny," Tom continues. "We went halfway round the world to fight in the Spanish Civil War, but most of us didn't know even one Spaniard before we left. But I did. Had boarded with a Spanish family in Montreal and they were good to me when I lost my job driving a truck for a meat packer. The Peiro family. They were pretty happy about the Popular Front getting elected."

"You," the reporter said, "went to Spain for them?"

"No, I'm just saying I knew some Spaniards. I wasn't real active, politically speaking, but I wasn't wet behind the ears either. I might have gone even if I didn't know the Peiro family. But I did, that's all."

"I'm tired," says Susan, warily watching her husband, who's still wearing the beret he bought today. She has never fully understood his preoccupation with Spain, and now she slowly withdraws from the table's conversation as if pleading with Tom to leave with her, to forget his passion with this place that seems to her to moderate any he could have for anywhere, or anyone, else. But she stays, as Tom ships from Montreal to France to the International Brigade training base at Tarazona.

"After training," says Tom, "I was assigned to transport, moving around the front, delivering supplies, evacuating wounded. I left transport. I was in the trenches at the last International Brigades battle, at Serra de Pàndols, a range of rocky hills south of here. The Spanish troops we relieved on Hill 609 left bodies all over the place because the ground was too hard to bury anyone. At sunrise, the fascist bombers started circling. We were just sitting ducks. All we could do was try to bury our faces in the rock. Shell after shell, rock fragments shooting all over. Then the fascist troops came, a few at first, then more and more. We had to get out of there. Same with the battalions on our flanks—the Lincolns were to our right on Hill 666."

"British Battalion on 705," Bob Mitchell says.

Jim Heathcott, with memories of another army, has joined the table. "You give a little hill a number like it's a goddamn New York public school," says Heathcott, "and you think it's worth dying and killing for?"

"What the hell is he talking about?" says Bob.

The rest of the table directs puzzled looks at Heathcott, but the reporter quickly changes the subject. "Hold on a second," the reporter says to Tom. "Let's back it up. Why did you leave transport?"

Tom, for the first time at this reunion, turns mum.

After a long uncomfortable pause, the reporter turns to me to break the silence. "Were you at Tarazona?"

"I do recall," I say, "as we headed to Tarazona, reaching through the window for an orange from this boy who was running alongside the train when it slowed down. He caught up with me. Reached out with the orange. Tasted *so* good."

"I do recall," Heathcott says. "Thuy Bo."

"What's that?" says the reporter.

"My nightmare," says Heathcott.

"It reminds me," says Henry Simmons. "Jack's story about the train. It reminds me…"

"Of what?" I say.

"Of hopping freights, that's all."

"How," the reporter says, "do you hop a freight?"

"First thing," Henry says, "you got to keep away from the yard dicks. They patrol the bull run, the gravel road along the tracks. Pick your car. Boxcars are the best, especially in bad weather. Don't get one with sawdust or fertilizer or grain."

"Straw's nice to sleep on." Bob Mitchell says.

"When you hop," says Henry, "make sure you're running faster than the train. My brother Matt…"

"Okay," Tom interjects, fidgeting with his cold seafood tortilla. "I'll tell you."

Now, he begins to speak about something he's never spoken about. "After the Aragon Front falls to the fascists in early '38, we retreat. The water-supply truck I'm driving with another Mac-Pap breaks down in the town of Batea. The people there know fascist tanks are coming. They're terrified. We continue our retreat on foot. About an hour later, a Spanish Army truck pulls up alongside us and these soldiers wave for us to get on. Then the truck stops in a village and…"

"And what?" I say after a long pause.

"This Spanish Army officer comes over to us…"

"Uh-huh?" says the reporter.

"The officer says, 'You're not with your company.' I say, 'We're transport troops, got lost after the lines broke. We aren't AWOL.' This officer doesn't understand, or doesn't care, and we wind up at a prison."

"You were in prison!" Bob says.

"Why am I not surprised," says Henry, giving Tom a malevolent glower.

"Hey, I didn't know what the hell's going on. We were all retreating and it didn't seem to matter anymore who you're doing it with. We were on the run, like everyone, that's all. Had no choice. I was locked up three, maybe four days. Lost track of time."

"The good guys put him in jail," Heathcott says with a laugh and a scowl. "*Sonofabitch.*"

Henry frowns. Bob looks away uneasily. Susan is distracted, and I wonder if she's hearing any of this.

"Anyway, I'm staring out our second-floor cell window," Tom continues, "see Jimmy James, a Mac-Pap I knew from Tarazona, walking on the sidewalk right across the street. Jimmy's dad is a Party wheel back in Canada. I shout to Jimmy but he doesn't seem to hear, so I scribble a note. *I'm in jail. Innocent. HELP. Tom Barkley.* Drop it through the window onto the sidewalk and call out to him, but he's already walked by and I figure that's that. But the next day I was let out, so he might have heard me and walked back, found the note. I think Jimmy could have had a little pull. I wanted to talk to him, thank him if he did something for me. He died in Spain before I could."

Tom's voice turns barely audible, directed at the Toronto reporter as though he is confiding something personal to just one person, but the rest of us are hushed, hearing every word. "At this point I'm released, sent to Brigade headquarters in Barcelona, then back to the front. In Barcelona, I run into Phil Boudreau, a Mac-Pap from Montreal I was pretty friendly with. He says, 'Tommy, where you been?' I just say Barcelona because no way I'm going to tell anybody I've been in jail. Might get the wrong idea about me. Don't know if I imagined it, but everyone seemed different after that, like they were looking at me funny."

"I'm looking at you funny right now," says Heathcott.

Susan gets up from the table, walks purposefully over to Heathcott and puts her face squarely into his. "What," she says, "is your problem?"

He glowers at her but says nothing.

"You want to know what I'm thinking, Jim?" I say. "You had impossible expectations of us before you met us and now you're disappointed that we have human frailties. Familiarity can indeed breed contempt."

"You want to know what I'm thinking, Jack? You think too much," Heathcott says. He laughs. And we move on from Heathcott.

"Don't know what the others thought," Tom says. "But I didn't go AWOL. I'm proud I went to Spain. I would do it all over again. It's the one thing in my life I've never regretted."

Tom's voice is quivering and the reporter tries to offer him a conversational way out. "Did you see the Peiro family when you returned to Canada?"

"The Peiros sent me tobacco when I was in Spain. Tobacco was rare. Anyhow, I visited the Peiros' nephew, Sandro, when I was on leave once in Barcelona, and we smoked that tobacco. Wonderful fellow. He took me for a drink. Don't know its name, the most beautiful drink you ever…" Tom says, pursing his lips.

Henry is still glaring at Tom.

"I don't see that Tom did anything wrong," Bob says.

"I agree," I say. "And he's got the best beret collection in Scarborough."

"Mistakes are made, granted," Henry blurts, "but when the International Brigades went into a village, the people were happy, not scared. They had big community gardens in the villages and I don't know of any one of us taking a thing. They gave things to us sometimes, but we never just took. We weren't like other soldiers."

"I never saw the Peiros again," says Tom. "They were gone when I got back to Montreal."

"No, we weren't like other soldiers, Henry," Bob says, "but some of us were, sometimes."

"We had to be the same in some ways," I say. "All soldiers are. But we *were* different too. I'm proud that we were among the first to understand the meaning of fascism."

"We believed great changes were coming," says Tom, slumped deep in his chair. "We fought in Spain."

NINETEEN

A BOX OF FEATHERS

Fort Harold, 1950–1960

ROM THE SKY, FORT HAROLD IN THE 1950S IS NOT unlike suburban Los Angeles, its backyards filled with oblongs, rectangles, ovals. In Fort Harold, though, these shapes are skating rinks, not swimming pools.

Polly and I had stuck around the Fort after Eddie returned from action in the war's European theatre including D-Day. By the time our youngest, Molly, is born in 1958, our routine is as rote as my father's minestrone. Backyard skating, backyard funfairs, backyard barbecues. Sunday drives "Around the Hoop," a roadway that forms a circle around Fort Harold, swinging through the old part of town called North Fort Harold. Sometimes we stop at a wilderness trail by the river and pick tiny, sugary wild blueberries and strawberries.

Summertime means a month-long holiday from the store and Polly covering her eyes as we drive through the canyons that slit the Interior Plateau in B.C., taking reprieve in small-town pit stops, then relief in the Okanagan's orchards. There is a time when a city is *the* place, and to much of North America the 1950s and early '60s belong to L.A., with its

Muscle Beach Party and Beach Boys and *77 Sunset Strip*. In parts of Canada's West Coast province, it's *California, here it comes*, working its way northward, turning the Okanagan community of Penticton into a distant L.A.-bedroom beach town, where tourists dress in Hawaiian shirts and Bermuda shorts, eat at drive-ins and fruit stands, and sleep at beach-front motels. Polly and the children and I do much of this, too, on our summer vacations to Penticton. On the beach, our blistered torsos rise lotion-caked from a day in the sand and, after cleaning up at our motel, we spend the early evening playing miniature golf, on amusement park rides, and in a magic, albeit plywood, castle.

Joan's work in the store during the war years was assumed by Eddie upon his return, and she becomes a part-time librarian. "I like libraries," I tell her semi-jokingly. "They're one of the few existing institutions that we'll keep around after the revolution."

"Still into that political crap?" snaps Eddie.

"I'm a card-carrying member," I say, "of the Fort Harold Public Library."

Along with the library, there is the pool hall, which is down the street from the men's wear. My interest in playing snooker is revived in Fort Harold, and often I drop by the hall. One day I'm shooting with a couple of regulars, Bill Winslow and Paul Whitecloud. When Paul reaches into his pocket for a cigarette package, he inadvertently pulls out a five-dollar bill that falls on the floor. A mean big barrel of a man quickly steps on the bill, reaches under his shoe and, clenching it in his fist, sits in a chair against the wall. Seeing that no one other than me has noticed him do this, he gives me a worried look. I silently consider the best way to handle the situation. He mistakes my momentary silence for acquiescence and gives me a menacing grin as if to say, "You're in on this with me now. And I've got you."

I walk over to him. "Give Paul his money back."

"I ain't got nobody's money," he says, surprised that I'm taking a stand against a much bigger man.

"Give Paul his money or I'll tell him right now what you've done."

"You taking a thieving Indian's side over me, asshole?"

Revulsed by this racial hatred so endemic to Fort Harold at the time, I say, "Fuck off," then turn away abruptly and stride towards Paul.

The man chases after me, stops as I near Paul, and leaves the pool hall.

These first post-war years, Fort Harold seemed a part of Isaac to me still, and I looked in the town for hints of the father I barely knew. There was the restaurant at the Fort Harold Hotel, a block from the store up Harold Street, where Isaac's lunch every workday was a heavy minestrone soup. I tried it once, dipping the white buttered bread into the vegetable paste at 12:30 p.m. sharp, just like Isaac always did. "You'd think even he would get sick of having this every day," I tell myself. The restaurant's long-time server Emily told me: "I tried more than once to get your dad to have a grilled cheese sandwich, but he wouldn't go for it. So I just brought the minestrone without even asking." The unswerving single-mindedness that kept my father in the north also gave him tunnel vision when ordering a meal. Finding minestrone agreeable his first time at the restaurant, he ordered the same lunch for the rest of his life without the slightest curiosity about anything else on the menu.

The store itself holds hints. Now that Feldman's Mens' Wear has passed to Eddie and me, with the exception of a framed black-and-white mug shot on the office wall, there is little visible evidence of Isaac's tenure there. But I know. There is Isaac's safe in the office, the counter where he arm-wrestled customers, the ornate cash register he had shipped from Vancouver, and especially, the clothing he wore. Merchants take on the character of the stores where one-third of their lives are spent, and some of the hats and jackets and shirts in Feldman's Mens' Wear still look like Isaac's hats and jackets and shirts. In a dark basement storage space I come upon a pair of snowshoes and a shoebox. "Are these yours?" I ask Eddie, after carting the dusty relics upstairs. "No. The old man's. He liked to go to hills by the river in the winter and he would hike in the snow for hours. So those shoes. Don't know about the shoebox." The cardboard box is tied up tightly by a shoelace. When I open it I know instantly that this was where my father kept the white feathers he wore with his fedoras.

I work in the store six days a week. I live in a flat-roofed wooden bungalow in a new part of town, a neighbourhood of gravel roads and forest trails where Barbara, the firstborn, and Daniel, the second, find endless ways to amuse themselves.

Joan gives birth, and again, and again. Christmas. Eddie and Joan host a dinner, where the two Feldman families sit about a tree-dominated living room and wash down Christmas cake made by Joan with Manischewitz wine brought by Polly. At first, Eddie makes pleasant enough small talk over dinner about hockey and his new car, but he's soon on to his usual schtick. "Is Jack a good lover, Polly?" Eddie barks across the dinner table

204 · DAVID SPANER

with a malevolent smirk. "Is he a Feldman or what?" When Eddie first came back from the war, Polly would groan amiably as he regaled everyone with accounts of his sexual prowess overseas but now she turns to stone when it begins. "I can't listen to this," Polly mutters quietly to me. "He's such a jerk."

"He's my brother." I answer softly enough that only Polly hears.

Now Eddie is on about the physique of the new bartender at the Fort Henry Hotel. "Let's just say, she put lead in my pencil."

"Ick feh," Polly blurts, loudly enough to quiet the table and draw curious looks.

"Kitty was a good woman," Joan says to Polly after dinner. They are alone in the kitchen, leaning against a counter filled with drying dishes. Kitty and Isaac drank their last years together and, with his death, she stopped by the funeral, then disappeared. "She put up with a lot from Isaac and a lot before she ever met him. But she never lost her dignity. She dressed well, kept her head up, and even when she drank, it was never outside the home."

"What did she see in Isaac, for God's sake?" says Polly.

"Maybe a companion," says Joan.

"Did he have any appealing qualities?"

"Not to me," says Joan. "Maybe she didn't want to be alone anymore. I don't understand, to be honest with you."

"Why was Eddie close to him?" Polly says. "He was the only one in the family who seemed to get along with him."

"Maybe it's because they were alike."

"What about them was alike?"

After a long pause, Joan says, "Maybe the way they thought about women."

"I don't know what Joan sees in Eddie," Polly says in the dark on the drive home.

"I feel the same way you do about how he talks a lot of the time," I say. "But he wasn't always like this. Remember the brother I had on Keefer Street? The big brother who sent his relief camp wages to our mother to help pay the rent. He's got a nice side too."

"Why did he change?" Polly says.

"Eddie hasn't completely changed," I say. "As he's gotten older, he's just become more like his father than he thought he was." Eddie, like Isaac, knows how to distance himself from intimacy with people. My father would turn silent and withdraw into himself. Eddie talks. He wants everyone to believe he's one of the few souls bold enough to speak openly about the most intimate of subjects, but I know empty bravado isn't bravery, and my brother's prattle has nothing to do with intimacy.

"Have you noticed that Joan cringes at your brother's jokes," says Polly, "and she and Eddie hardly speak to each other?" Perhaps, Polly muses, they know one another so well that there is no need for words, or maybe it is a bad marriage that never should have been, "Like musicians who cannot be in the same band."

Perhaps, Polly thinks, *it is the same with me and Jack.*

Joan gives birth again.

I'm still a reader but rarely choose books about politics, and I no longer talk about Spain. In a way, it would be easier if I were disillusioned with the left, if I had made a conscious choice, at a particular time, not to care about the same things anymore. But I haven't. Underneath it all, I still profess to myself the same beliefs I had when I signed on for Spain. They have just worn flat in Fort Harold, like the three-pointed star on the Mackenzie-Papineau pin I still keep in my wallet.

Winter, 1960. Sunday morning, 6:30 a.m., the phone rings. And rings. Polly lifts the receiver.

"Jack," she says. "Come to the phone."

"It's Davie Armstrong," says the voice on the line. "They got me in the tank. Drank too much. They give me one call. Can you help?"

"What do you need?" I say, but Davie's interrupted by a cop's voice. "Do you know this Indian guy? He says you're his friend."

"I know him. What can I do?"

"A hundred bucks and the guy's out this morning."

"Okay, okay," I say. "I'll be down."

The ringing has awoken Daniel, who stands in pajamas by the telephone watching me talk. "Want to keep me company?" I say when I hang up the phone, touching Daniel's shoulder, and the two of us ride the icy roads to the lock-up, where I sign papers and a cheque and Davie Armstrong is released.

"How you doing, Jack?" says Davie Armstrong, giving me a gap-toothed smile as he reaches to shake my hand.

On the drive home, Daniel asks, "Is he one of your best friends?"

"I kind of remember him buying something in the store a few months ago."

TWENTY

RED SOX AND SOCREDS

Barcelona, fall 1986

OM AND SUSAN CAN'T WAIT TO TELL ME. I'M ALONE
with my breakfast and a *Herald Tribune* when they approach
the table excited about a message he found when they
retired to their room last night.

"You know I've been looking to reach Sandro Peiro, the
nephew who bought me that drink, ever since you told me
about finding your old comrade Victor," Tom says.

"Yeah, I knew you spoke to the organizing committee about it."

"Found out last night he was executed in Franco's roundup
of anti-fascists after the war."

"It's sad," Susan says. "Tom was very sad."

"I've got a phone number for his family," says Tom. "I'd like
to see them while I'm here, tell them what kind of a guy I
thought he was."

"Goddamn sonofabitch." Henry Simmons walks jerkily past
our table in the busy hotel restaurant. "AWOL," he mutters,
looking straight ahead as he passes.

"What the hell…?" says Tom, instantly diminished, face
sagging, as Susan shrinks.

A man approaches me and reaches out his hand. "I'm Frank Murphy," he says, eyeing the empty chairs at our table. "Mind if we join you? We're with the reunion."

Frank and his parents, Deirdre and James, settle in across the table from me as Tom explains, "Hank and I, we never got along. He has always been, always will be, a party-line man. Me, I'm too independent for that bull."

"I knew there was some tension there," I say, "but I never thought…"

"The line is that Tom Barkley did *something* in Spain," says Tom, "so Simmons has never liked me, and last night, well—"

"I thought he acknowledged yesterday that what happened with you in Spain was a mistake."

"He said that yesterday, granted. But today's another day."

"Maybe you two should try to patch things up," I say. "I mean, we have a few more days together and—"

"It's like Howard Carpenter," says Tom. "He didn't have a lot of politics but he hated fascists, so he came over, got tossed in jail like me by some little Stalin, and he wanted out of Spain. So he escaped that jail and he got out. Some of the guys never had any use for him after that. I bumped into him on the subway in Montreal years later when he was a big-shot writer. He remembered me."

Although Frank Murphy and his parents don't know what Tom is going on about they are visibly uncomfortable with the gist of what they are hearing. "There was more comradeship than conflict among the volunteers, at least the ones I know of," says Frank's father.

"Lots of guys, besides yours truly, weren't affiliated with any organization," Tom continues, "but most were in the Party, I think, and by and large it made the travel arrangements."

"There were other socialists, anarchist internationals too," contributes Frank, a history professor in Indiana, and still carrying a thick Celtic lilt after ten years in America. His parents still live in Ireland.

"I know that, and there were volunteers who made their own way to Spain," I say. "For the most part, whatever their particular politics, the volunteers were very decent guys."

"Most of the Communists I knew were good guys who joined the Canadian Party because it was organizing unions and fighting fascism," says Tom. "But I'm no fan of the Soviet Party. It really got to me when I heard that some of the volunteers in Spain, after the Republic fell, couldn't go back to their European countries — they were occupied by then — so they went to the USSR looking for refuge and the Soviets tossed them in jail."

"It wasn't just the Soviet Union," says Frank. "After the war, the internationals were treated badly by a lot of countries. Did you know that the FDR administration indicted Americans who helped recruit volunteers for Spain?"

"Look, I'm still a socialist," says Tom, "and no way am I going to defend the Western governments, but I just expected more from the Soviets at the time, that's all. Now, I know better and don't trust political parties — not a Communist Party in the Soviet Union, a Democratic Party in America, the Conservative Party in Canada."

"Spain was about a lot bigger things than party politics," I say.

"Idealism, that's what," says Frank. "My dad, he was with the James Connolly Section. There weren't enough of them to form an Irish battalion so they got stuck in with the British. After a while, some of the Irish and British were going at each other like cats and dogs."

"No," Frank's father, James, says faintly. "We got along fine."

"One of them told my husband," adds his mother, Deirdre, "you may be anti-fascist and we may be anti-fascist, but you're still Irish and we're still British."

"It got so that the Irish section left the British Battalion and joined the Abraham Lincoln Battalion," Frank says.

"Still, most of us got along fine," his father says impatiently. "After all, the whole point of it was international solidarity. Differences are natural but it was bigger than that."

"My dad," says Frank, "is admirably non-sectarian. His knee-cap was shattered during the Ebro offensive."

Henry Simmons is across the room at a table with Peter Krawchuk and Aaro Ononen.

"Well, there they are, the central committee," Tom sniggers, watching Henry's fingers dart as the others listen. Peter stands up, makes his way to our table.

"Hi, Jack," says Peter, facing me, looking at Tom from the corners of his eyes. "Hi, Tom, Susan."

"So," says Tom, "what's the chairman of the central committee blathering on about?"

"Don't know who you're talking about," Peter says.

"Henry."

"Henry talks," says Peter, pointing his thin crocked finger towards Tom, "and Henry is proud he fought the war with valour, becoming a lieutenant, never being sent to jail — by either side — but he's a sad old man, and he just believes —"

"In toeing the party line, he does," Tom says.

"As a matter of fact, Henry hasn't been in the Party for thirty years," Peter says. "I still carry a card, mind you. Henry just believes in not letting go of grudges. Not letting go of anything."

"Well, will you get a look at those two," Susan says, eyeing Henry and Aaro huddled inches apart. "Getting along just famously, and a few nights back they were just about ready to take each other's heads off."

"I guess," I say, rising from the table, "there must be some things that are even more important to Henry than grudges."

I cross the room to the animated pair, ask, "Are you two planning world conquest or debating lunch?"

"Jesus," Henry says, "everybody's a goddamn comedian."

"Maybe you and Tom should try to patch things up," I say.

"Always bellyaching," Henry grumbles, glaring at Tom.

"Does anyone know who won yesterday's ball game?" shouts a Lincoln standing on a chair.

"New York, but Boston's leading the Series three games to two," a woman shouts back.

"No, it's New York, three games to two," I shout too. "I read it in the *Herald Tribune*."

When Aaro rises to leave the restaurant, the Toronto reporter slips into his chair and places a recorder in front of Henry.

"You," Henry says, "are getting to be a pain in the ass with this taping gizmo."

Henry thought his interview was through, but the reporter says he has a few more questions. "I never asked you about your life after the war," he says. "That's really why I want to talk again. A little personal stuff. How did you wind up in Victoria?"

"After the war, I found my first steady work. Construction in Victoria. Me and Millie been happy there a long time."

While we wait for the tour bus, some stand or sit near Henry's table, half-listening to his testimony about life in postwar Victoria.

"What else?" the reporter says. "Children?"

"Terry ... I don't talk about him and he doesn't mention me."

"Why's that?"

"I embarrass him," says Henry. "My politics. Actually, we kind of embarrass each other." Henry's son, Terry, is Canadian spokesperson for the born-again I Found Out cult and a candidate for B.C.'s governing Socred Party in the upcoming provincial election.

"What's with this Red Sock Party?" Joan from Boston interjects.

"Sock red," Bob corrects.

"Soak red," I correct. "Now that Franco's gone, it's the last of the 1930s right-wing movements still in power, and it's in B.C."

Jim Heathcott interrupts. "You," he says, looking at me icily. "We got to go! Bus is here. The guides are fed up with the backtalk. Everyone be at the frigging bus in five minutes."

As we join the line for the bus, the reporter continues: "The other day, Henry, you started talking about riding the rails."

"If you want to wake up when the train pulls out," says Henry, "put a spike on a rail and when the wheels move, it will ring just like an alarm clock."

Henry, taking a window seat, and the reporter, sitting beside him, are the last to board the bus.

"Well, let's move out," Heathcott says.

"Any other travel tips?" says the reporter. Henry says nothing for more than two minutes, contemplating, before resuming with the reporter. "Me and my brother Matt, we tried to hop a train at Saskatoon, and Matt missed the ladder, fell between the boxcars. I reached out for him, touched his hand, couldn't grip it. He lost a foot, brains got scrambled."

Other voices on the bus turn quiet. Henry is still again. Finally, he says, "All I had to do was grab his hand instead of his fingers. Couldn't hold him. Matt was something else. Jesus, could he ever skate. Like the bloody wind. Like a Bentley boy. Everybody thought he could of played in the NHL. Good politics too. He is the one other one in the family who *would have* fought in Spain. I know this." Henry's large hands cover his face, then he fumbles for the reporter's recorder, flabby fingers fighting to turn it off. Inconsolable. The reporter stops the taping.

"You *did* fight in Spain," I say.

"You did good, Henry," says Tom. "You did your best."

TWENTY-ONE

THE DECLINE OF
WEST COAST CIVILIZATION

Vancouver, 1960–1962

THIS SUMMER, AFTER OUR ANNUAL HOLIDAY TO
the Okanagan, Polly and I take the children to Vancouver.
We drive into the city along Kingsway. If the Okanagan is
a facsimile of Malibu or Ventura or whatever beach town
a California-dreaming tourist wants it to be, Kingsway is L.A.
without palm trees, a broad, interminable street — lined with
fast food and fast-talking car dealers — that slashes across the
city's East Side. Vancouver's outskirts are streaked with look-
alike Kingsways, the model main street for a post-war suburbia paved with shopping centres, cul de sacs, and tract housing.
For me, my mother is all that is left in Vancouver, but Barbara,
Daniel, and Molly revel in the place. There are the wonders
of Stanley Park and network television, amusement park rides
at the Pacific National Exhibition, lunch downtown at Scott's
Cafe or, better, the White Spot drive-in restaurant with pasto-
ral murals I can contemplate while awaiting, to come through

the car window, a long green tray of hamburgers with "secret" sauce and walnut-coated butterhorns.

Whenever we come to Vancouver now, I miss Rachel. In New York, she studied dance and waited tables, then found chorus spots in *The Girl from Nantucket* and *Are You With It?* before three years of *Annie Get Your Gun*. She was a lead understudy in *Pal Joey* before moving to Toronto, where she directs and performs in musical theatre. There are phone calls on birthdays, but it has been years since Polly or I exchanged letters with Rachel. I did see her once, when she returned to Vancouver last year to appear in *The King and I* at Stanley Park's Theatre Under The Stars. Polly stayed with the baby, Molly, in Fort Harold while Barbara and Daniel accompanied me on a brief working holiday to select the store's winter inventory at the garment factories in the Gastown district.

The children, my mother and I sat in folding chairs, on a sloping park meadow surrounded by cedars, watching Rachel traipse the Malkin Bowl stage in the warm early evening. As the sky went as black as the mountain backdrop, we shrouded ourselves in blankets, sipped hot chocolate, and watched the bright stars and incandescent stage lights shine on Rachel. There was a drizzle and Rachel kept dancing. Then the rains came. Daniel was wearing a Davy Crockett–simulated coonskin cap, but Barbara and I were handed strips of brown wrapping paper to fold into pointed hats. The conductor, in yellow plastic raincoat and floppy fishing hat, waved his baton at the orchestra pit. Rachel sang "Shall We Dance?" The rains lifted just before the finale, bringing an elation to the Bowl that would not have come without the downpour, and everyone rose to their feet in ovation as Rachel and the rest of the cast stood on stage applauding the audience.

Now, at my mother's apartment, Polly asks nobody in particular: "Why does it always seem to rain whenever we come to town?" We're holed up at the apartment on our first afternoon back in town. "This is a dull, grey place, and if you have a sense of humour they think you're *meshugga*," says my mother, looking out at the splashed pavement beneath her second-floor window in the West Side's South Granville area, having recently, finally, moved out of the old Strathcona neighbourhood. "I'm *oysgemut-shet* — worn-out and harassed and bothered and just all —"

"You're pretty good at talking Jewish," Barbara says.

"I used to was," my mother says.

She plies Daniel, Barbara, and Molly with kasha smothered in chicken gravy, then she is on the phone to a friend as the family eats, and I turn the television to a Seattle station broadcasting the U.S. presidential election debate.

"Thank you very kindly," says my mother, rattling the receiver down, glancing at Kennedy and Nixon. "Yap, yap, yap. It's a yappy world."

After the debate, Barbara changes channels, stopping briefly at Guy Lombardo's orchestra.

"Canadian," I say.

"Don't they ever get tired of it," says my mother, "the same people in those bands?"

Frieda walks the family to our car, linking arms with Polly and Barbara.

"*Geshmak*," she says, cupping Molly's cheeks.

"Isn't that a *punim*?" Polly says.

"She's got Rachel's face," my mother says. She kisses each child, then turns to me.

"The children can do anything anyone else can do if they have the opportunity. But not in that town. "

"Polly agrees with you," I say. "But Fort Harold's not so bad."

"*Much*," says my mother. "Jakie, you are your father's son."

The Vancouver we visit is mostly a place where we never lived. Polly's parents and her sister have left, moving to California while California was coming to B.C. Polly and I come as tourists and leave with a cardboard box we fill at Rubin's downtown delicatessen. When we get home, the children open the box and offer their neighbourhood friends bagels and kosher salami and other delicacies unknown to Fort Harold.

Three blocks from the Feldman bungalow in Fort Harold there is the Thrifty Food store, where Daniel and his friends buy Popsicles, baseball and hockey cards, comic books, and Pez candies. Across from the store, there is a slightly unkempt black-and-white shingle house where everyone knows, "the Russian" lives. Daniel has never seen him, but eyewitness reports have him pot-bellied and slim, tall and short, Einstein wild-haired and Khrushchev bald.

If in early 1960s Fort Harold, California is the dream brought to our living rooms in a "living colour" we're unable to see on our black-and-white televisions, Russia is the nightmare, as colourless as our TV sets. The Russian evokes terror among neighbourhood children, and some adults too. Lorne Lawrence, who lives across the street, is Daniel's lone playmate unafraid of the Russian. Lorne is an American whose father was a scientist at the Los Alamos Laboratory but angrily resigned after Hiroshima and Nagasaki, and left the States a few years ago. "Yankeeland," Lorne calls it. I wonder if Lorne's father, Bill, who teaches high school science here, might have been blacklisted before leaving the U.S., but I don't ever mention this to anyone. Bill seems like the kind of guy I might have been close to a couple decades back, but not in Fort Harold in 1960, where I go about the business of being a father and husband and shopkeeper. I tell myself that I will never hide what

I am or stop believing what I believe but, still, I know I have assimilated into post-war North Americana much more than my neighbour Bill. Polly knows this too. Watching *Leave It to Beaver* and *Father Knows Best* and other family sitcoms of the time is a bit like watching home movies, I tell Polly. Except, she notes, "You're Jewish and a socialist."

The Halloween after the Russian's arrival in Fort Harold, only Lorne dare approaches his door.

"But I heard the Russians don't believe in Halloween," Daniel says, the day after Lorne's bravery.

"Sure they do," says Lorne, showing Daniel the Russian's candy kisses. "That's just Yankeeland propaganda."

Later that day, Daniel holds a new mirror for me as I screw it into the bathroom wall. "How come I never see the Russian, Dad?" Daniel says. I smile at our mirror reflections. "Daniel, my father was from Russia," I say.

"I feel so isolated," Polly says, back in Fort Harold after the summer holiday. Feeling increasingly stifled, antsy, she auditions for the lead in *South Pacific*, this year's community production at the high school auditorium. "Once you have found her, always let her go," she sings, practicing for the audition while she dusts.

"Why not get out of here?" she tells me. "This was supposed to be for a couple of years. That was twenty years ago. I'm not going to be a martyr like Joan or Kitty. I'm not going to do it. The kids have to experience more so they know the possibilities out there. It's all in what you're exposed to. And they need some kind of Jewish identity before they get much older."

"You mean like we had living on Keefer Street," I say.

"I learned growing up in Strathcona," says Polly, "that every-one should know where they came from, and it's important for everyone to be happy to be whatever they are."

"Yes," I say. "People are people, as my mother says."

Polly ponders her reference to identity while she makes Molly's bed the next morning, "Was it just my reaction to feel-ing like a nonentity here — *an identity, please* — or did I mean it?"

I know she meant it. And that she's certain moving on would be best — in innumerable ways — for the children and her and even me.

"You told your mother that I agree with her about Fort Harold," she tells me that evening. "I do in some ways, but I don't. There are things I like about it."

"That's because you like me more than my mother liked my father."

Polly laughs. "Everything isn't about you, Jack. Or your parents."

"I'm just saying my father gave my mother a bad time in this town and that's part of the reason she hates it."

"There isn't anything particularly wrong with this town," says Polly, "except it is too cold in the winter and there's nothing much to do here any time of the year. I think I've figured out why you're so comfortable with it. Back in Vancouver, I thought of you as a city boy from Strathcona. I realize now that you're also a small-town boy with childhood memories of this place."

"Yes," I say. "I'm both."

"You're also a creature of habit, and even though you were resistant to coming here in the first place, now that we've been here for twenty years you feel snug and safe in your routine and your surroundings."

Polly does not get the role in *South Pacific*. She finds other outlets. Dancing every morning for an hour after I've gone to work and Daniel and Barbara are at school. Polly enters a rhyming jingle contest sponsored by a London, Ontario, olive oil company. "Don't let your dinner spoil in oil. For a tasty broil use London Oil." Polly scribbles this during a coffee break from household work, and it wins a talking Bugs Bunny for Molly.

Another morning, Polly writes a song with Ken Lubitsch, an aspiring singer hired on as a disc jockey at local radio station CKFH. The twenty-ish Lubitsch had ventured into Feldman's Mens' Wear his second day in town, told me he is second cousin to Mrs. Finkel, and I invited him to our place for dinner.

"Jack says you sing and dance, Polly. I'm a singer," he says over roast beef and mashed potatoes.

"I've pretty much given up on that," Polly says. "The kids are the talented ones. You should see the drawings Daniel does."

"Mom won London Oil's poetry contest," beams Barbara.

"There's a studio in St. Louis that records your song if it's good enough," Lubitsch says.

The next day, Polly and Ken's "Blondes and Brunettes" is composed and posted to St. Louis. Polly waits for the letter that says for $75, "recording artist" Merv Douglas will put their composition on vinyl. Polly sends the money and the song comes back forty-five revolutions per minute. "I can sing way better than that," groans Ken. He leaves Fort Harold determined to be Kenny Silver, saloon singer.

Barbara, Daniel, and Molly are in the yard applying a carrot nose and stone eyes to a snowman when I get home after work and park my blue-finned Chrysler in front of our yellow bungalow.

"Where's Mom?" I say.

"In the kitchen," says Barbara.

After dinner, wood crackles in the fireplace, its shimmer lighting the room. I press back the recliner chair and open the drape a crack to the dark outside. Summertime, the children are out with neighbourhood playmates, shouting in a game of hide-and-go-seek or go-go-go-go-stop. But it is winter and outside looks like midnight by 4 p.m. I'm leafing through *Look* magazine's illustrated projections of a near future of airborne automobiles and moving sidewalks. Daniel is curled on the couch after a bath, engrossed in the biography of the 17th U.S. president that's inside the pictorial encyclopedia Polly purchased "for the kids" volume by volume at the local SuperValu supermarket. Molly is on the hardwood floor, gouging pick-up sticks into Tinkertoy wheels, stopping at irregular intervals to tug at the cord on her stuffed Bugs Bunny.

"I want a carrot," says Bugs.

"Wonder if Bugs Bunny was named after Bugsy Siegel, the gangster," I say. "Subconsciously, I mean."

"What a cheery thought," says Polly.

Barbara is in her bedroom, door closed, faint sounds of "Hand in Hand with You" seeping through the walls. Pop singer Bobby Curtola enraptured much of Fort Harold's adolescent population when he visited last week, signing Barbara's arm, which remained unwashed for days afterwards. Polly sits beside Daniel on the couch, gazing glassily at flickering television images. June Cleaver has roasted beef for Ward and the boys, bought a corsage for Wally's date, got Beaver out of a fix for erecting a lemonade stand without a permit, impressed Eddie with her newly purchased cashmere sweater, and visited the beauty parlour and supermarket — all in thirty minutes minus commercials. Polly does not laugh with the laugh track.

"What's up, Doc?" says Bugs.

Polly stops watching the TV, turns her eyes to me, and says she's narrowed to three the places we might move to. "I've done this because I've come to the conclusion that you never will. There is Los Angeles, where my family lives and the sun shines; Vancouver, where your mother lives and is in the B.C. that you love; and Australia, which for some unfathomable reason you've become interested in lately."

Outside, there is the sheltering storm. I step from the house. From the rooftop, icicles form an upside-down picket fence around our home. The snowman with broken-branch limbs and sagging carrot nose stands in the snowfall. Flakes blow at my face. I hike along the gravel street, lit by street lamps and Christmas lights, paved by snow crunching under my Feldman's Mens' Wear working-class boots. I turn down the hill towards downtown, stop under a lamppost, television glimmering in the living room window of a brown shingle bungalow. At the bottom of the hill, the lovers cuddle beneath the projectionist's dusty shaft at the Royal Theatre, the chickens shiver in the town zoo, the men's wear on the downtown corner, with its work shirts and coveralls, is locked closed, panes intact. And the ones on the run still come to these parts. Tonight, some huddle by fires in remote cabins, others by televisions, watching California, but there is something about this northern British Columbia cold pinching my face that heals as well as the Southern California sun. I stay a while, beneath the warmth of the lamppost, before turning back. But this time there is no music.

TWENTY-TWO

A LARGE THING TO FIGHT OVER

Barcelona, fall 1986

THREE BREAKFASTS FROM LEAVING SPAIN, I BRING a sweet snail-shaped roll and café con leche to the table of Irene Blair and Bob Mitchell, my only fellow travellers in the hotel restaurant this morning in Barcelona.

"Well, Jack, it's just about over," Bob says.

"I'm tired," I say.

"I'm a little sick," says Irene, sniffling over her coffee.

"I've been asking myself how come," I say.

"How come?" Bob says.

"Don't you ever ask?" I say.

"I do," says Irene.

"How come what?" Bob asks. "I've never asked how come we came here, if that's what you're getting at. We came to oppose fascism."

"And that is definitely reason enough," I say. "But I'm asking, 'Why else?' Every one of us has many reasons of our own."

Aaro Ononen has entered the restaurant and is alone at a table deep in reading.

"One does what one can," Bob says with a shrug.

"I do ask questions," Irene says. "But at the same time I know and, despite everything, being here only reaffirms my feelings. We have to try. We do not always win but we never will if we don't try, and would the world be a better place if we don't?"

Irene is at the reunion from her cottage on an island off an island off an island off the West Coast, but in 1935 she lived in Regina and was on the welcoming committee when the On-to-Ottawa Trek came to town. "I thought they were going to pass through town quickly, en route to Ottawa, that my job was to help prepare a couple meals, and that would be that," she says. The day after the Trek protesters were stopped in Regina by bullets and billies, Irene was among a group of volunteers bringing sandwiches into a jail housing 148 of them. A sudden tug at Irene's blouse sleeve nearly caused her to drop the sandwiches. There was a soft smile behind the hand reaching through the bars. "I'm going to marry you," Doug Blair told her. "I don't expect you'll be attending many weddings today," Irene said with a laugh. Doug was one of seven Trekkers charged with conspiring to incite the Regina riot. He was acquitted after a heavily publicized trial, and Irene and Doug moved to the West Coast, where she taught school, he caught fish. After Irene settled on the coast, there was Spain, then ban-the-bomb petitions, picket lines, civic elections, anti-war parades, no-nuke protests, and now, finally again, Spain. When Doug died, Irene sold their bungalow in a Vancouver suburb and left a lifetime of school teaching for Hornby Island, off the east side of Vancouver Island. Following this reunion, she plans to travel on to Ireland to visit friends. But for now her attention is on war in Spain.

As Irene and Bob and I depart the restaurant we pass by Aaro, too absorbed by his book to notice us. In the lobby, Irene says: "*The Dialectic of Sex*. I saw that's the book he's reading."

"I don't know that book," says Bob.

"I've heard of it," I say, "but haven't read it."

"I've read it," Irene says.

"Don't look so surprised," Bob says with another shrug. "Just because he's rough around the edges doesn't mean he's stupid. Aaro is a very intelligent guy."

It's a crisp morning in Barcelona so I ask Bob and Irene if they'd like to go for a walk.

"I think you're in an existential mood this morning," Irene tells me with a laugh, then suggests we subway to the Ramblas and visit the Picasso Museum.

The sun glistens off a Ramblas newsstand as Bob plucks the latest *Herald Tribune* and opens it to a headline that has Boston leading the World Series three games to two. "I'm not interested in sports," Bob tells me as he turns the page. He returns the newspaper to the newsstand when Irene steps from a shop with a jacket for her grandson.

"I've got a granddaughter in San Francisco," Bob says as we begin the walk to the museum.

"My daughter Molly used to live in the Bay Area, designed sets for a theatre company there," I say. "She's in Vancouver now. I have grandchildren in Los Angeles and Vancouver."

"She's a teacher," Bob says as Irene rejoins us, "my daughter in San Francisco."

"On the plane into Madrid I asked Jack about his children," Irene says. "Now let me ask you, Bob, what does your daughter think about your politics?"

"She's supportive, but she's not active. Took her to demonstrations when she was younger."

Shards of natural light shoot through the windows of the stone building dedicated to Picasso. We peruse unhurriedly, stopping a while at *Mother and Child*, the painting of a ragged mother's drawn face sagged protectively against a small vulnerable head with blazing brown eyes. Then we stand before our Spain — on the wall of the museum's shop is a print of Picasso's painting *Guernica*, its pained arms reaching, out of horribly contorted beings they are reaching, despite everything they reach, at war but reaching. As we are leaving the museum, I purchase post-card versions of *Guernica*.

After Picasso, we return to the Ramblas and rest on a bench. "Think we can smooth things out between Henry and Tom?" I say. "Spain is such a large thing to fight over now."

"I wasn't put in prison wrongly, never saw a deserter shot, but I'm sure some things like that went on," Bob says. "They do in a war."

"That's no excuse for anything," Irene says.

"Not saying it is. Just saying the Republican side wasn't a monolithic movement, and I'm aware of its wrongdoing as well as its righteousness. And a lot of it was pretty righteous, especially within its International Brigades. The rest I wasn't really involved with and doesn't bother me that much now. It's the little indignities from years ago that eat away at me."

"Like what?" I say.

"A racist slur I let pass, a phone call I should have returned, some mean-spirited comment made by me. Those things can keep me up nights. But never Spain."

"Tom and Henry fighting over the war is so senseless at this point," Irene says firmly. "I don't know what happened fifty years ago, but Tom is proud he came to Spain, so why rehash it all?"

"It's the most important thing for Tom and Henry to rehash," I say. "Maybe the most important thing for all of us."

"I was overwhelmed by Spain too," says Irene, "even though I never set foot in it. Since the Spanish Civil War, there have been many political things I have felt strongly about, but never have I felt quite that deeply again. I'm not sure why. There was so much hope then. Maybe it was the age."

"Maybe it was our age," I say.

"Friends of mine went over to fight," Irene continues. "I heard Norman Bethune speak about Spain at the Orpheum Theatre in Vancouver. I was active in Friends of the Mackenzie-Papineau Battalion. We collected food and reading material to send over. I held the Mac-Pap banner at the May Day parade in 1938. I've got a picture. My friend Rose Barrett is standing beside me with her little boy, David, dressed as a Spanish war orphan. So, no Jack, I never questioned why. It all seemed so clear."

"Compared to everything else it was clear," I say. "Now, there's a man who isn't clear at all." I nod towards Jim Heathcott, who's on the other side of the Ramblas gesturing furiously at an elderly woman selling books from a kiosk.

"There's something off about him," Irene says.

"He's all right," Bob counters. "Vietnam."

"Fuck you," Heathcott screams. Then he stalks away, past Irene, Bob, and I without seeing us, the reason for the outburst lost, another excuse to detonate. We rise from the bench as Heathcott passes, following behind him down the Ramblas. There is something in his explosiveness, his unpredictability, that draws us down this street too, our old footsteps struggling to keep pace behind this madly damaged Pied Piper. Unlike the volunteers for Spain, Heathcott did not return home to crowded train stations. He returned from Vietnam to America for a moment in 1972, then left for Thailand, then Spain, where he has lived, in Valencia, for a dozen years. Now he is on the march again, down the Ramblas like a kinetic ten-pin bowling ball, pedestrians — civilians — be damned. Where the boulevard meets the Mediterranean Sea, Heathcott stops, muttering profanities. He turns and sees the three of us standing dwarfed beside a statue of Columbus that towers above the harbour. Heathcott shrieks, "You phoney bastards."

"Calm down, Jim," Bob says. "Get a hold of yourself."

Heathcott does not figure he has a self worth holding and, instead, stands inches from Bob, pounding finger darts into his chest and spitting words into his face. "You're no better than we are. Thuy Bo! You're no different from the fascists. Than *Franco*. We are all warriors."

A crowd is gathering. I motion at Heathcott to calm down, at Bob to walk away. Irene tugs at Bob's sleeve. But Heathcott's rant is too much for Bob. His face spotted with the Vietnam vet's spittle, he replies, "How dare you fucking say we were no different from the fascists. We came here to fight fascism. We came to build a new world. How dare —"

Heathcott reaches inside his leather jacket and pulls out a pistol. "Time to kill," he says, waving his weapon in front of Bob. "You knew you'd die in Spain didn't you, Charlie?"

"Don't," I shout.

Heathcott turns from Bob, grabs the nape of my neck with one hand, and presses my mouth to the tip of the gun's barrel.

"No," Bob beseeches. "Jim, no!"

Other voices plead, in Spanish and English. I am numb to the danger as though I've gotten inside some slow-motion cinematic moment I'm watching on a giant screen. Then all goes silent in my mind. And we are motionless. Monuments to Spain. In the autumn sun. On the waterfront.

"Atten-hut!"

Heads turn past me to a tall solitary man standing upright behind Heathcott.

"Attention, Corporal Heathcott," shouts Mel Fox, last commander of the Lincoln Battalion. Heathcott cocks his head towards Mel, maintaining his grip on the pistol and me. Then his fist opens and I stumble forward, then tumble into the surrounding crowd. Heathcott stands at attention.

"Corporal, surrender your weapon," orders Mel, reaching his long arm towards Heathcott's gun. Mel has a commanding presence and Heathcott starts to comply, but then he draws his arm back, hangs it limply at his side in defiance of the order. He lifts the gun to his own head.

"Atten-hut!" the Lincoln commander orders.

"Don't," Irene says.

And Heathcott fires.

Bob and a bystander rush to Heathcott's body, its blood spurting onto the pavement. Mel slumps to the ground. I stay standing, unable to speak, still not entirely convinced the episode has actually happened.

Finally, I say quietly, "He fought in Vietnam and he died in Spain."

"And," says a surprised Bob, shuffling through Heathcott's I.D. for kindred names and numbers, "he was born in Canada."

"What does Thuy Bo mean?" says Irene.

"I know," Mel says. "Villagers massacred there by marines. Vietnam."

There are wars the whole world watches and private wars. Civil wars and uncivil wars. Bob puts his hand on my shoulder and we take a few steps towards the Mediterranean. We stand silently, numbly, staring at the sea. A short distance away, an ambulance and police cars have arrived. Finally, Bob says quietly: "Jim was right about one thing, Jack. I always thought I would die in Spain."

"A lot of us did, but not that way."

"It doesn't matter how I go. I'm dying anyway," Bob says.

We sit at a bench facing the sea, and I draw the *Guernica* postcards from my jacket pocket and begin to write love letters to my children.

TWENTY-THREE

LIKE SUPERMAN, BATMAN, AND FELDMAN

Toronto, summer 1962

ANIEL STARTS TO SPRINT WHEN HE SEES US IN the car in front of the house. Barbara and Molly are waiting for him in the back seat, Polly and I up front, the trunk packed. When Daniel reaches us, breathless after a half-block dash home the last day of school, the blue-finned Chrysler begins our summer vacation along the gravelly streets, up the highway overlooking Fort Harold, then away.

I have not been in Toronto since the Mac-Pap homecoming stopped at Union Station in 1939. But it is time — the relatives are middle aging, and Polly said it would be a good experience for the children, and she wanted a city. In the back seat, voices call out the states and provinces on passing licence plates. In front, Polly passes tuna sandwiches back to the children, then finally relaxes, reading *Star Weekly* magazine. I adjust the radio dial as frequencies rise and fall, and read aloud the emerging road signs. "Radium Hot Springs — 88."

Daniel supposes someone from Europe might think that sign means the population of Radium Hot Springs, not how far away it is. "Fat chance," Barbara scoffs.

"Calgary — 249,641," I say.

"We'll need a rocket ship to make it there," says Daniel.

"That's the population, not the distance," says Barbara. "Don't you know anything?"

"He was making a joke," I say. "I think."

"From here to Toronto it looks real boring," says Barbara, as we push through Alberta. "I'd rather be going down to Californ-I-A."

"I don't want to go to Yankeeland," Daniel shouts.

"Oh, you're so immature," Barbara sighs.

"You're ten times worse than that," Daniel says.

"Well, you're even worse than that," Barbara says.

"You're ten times worse than that."

"Well, you're a thousand million zillion times worse than anything."

"You're ten times worse than that," he says.

"Mom!"

"Just get along back there," Polly says, without expectations, twisting her face into the back seat and handing out chocolate bars as pacifiers.

"You know, Daniel, we could visit Disneyland in California," Barbara says.

"I guess there are some things that are all right down there, but I still wouldn't go," Daniel says. "And, besides, Disneyland's in Los Angeles, not California — don't *you* know anything?"

"*Oh, brother,*" Barbara says.

Molly has been quiet, content to scrawl in colouring books or nap. Now she awakes, yawns.

"How's Molly?" I say.

"I'm carsick," she says, rubbing her eyes, unsure where she is. "And where's my baby?"

Polly passes Molly's "baby," an abundant golden soother, to her in the back seat.

"I'm looking for an angel, but angels are so few, so until the day that one comes along, I'll string along with you," I croon off-key.

"You know what the biggest book in the world is?" Daniel says.

"Webster's... I dunno, what?" Polly says.

"The Empire State Building," Daniel says. "It's got a hundred and three storeys."

"Where did you get that from?" Barbara says.

"I made it up myself."

"Always thinking," I say, slicing through a wheat field towards a rising grain elevator.

And so it goes. Polly is quiet. I will occasionally point out a deer or a cow or a crop, but the sights grow familiar and the front seat is still, while in the back they push and jab for space, and voices erupt, then go still with Daniel (Batman) and Barbara (Archie) immersed in comic books and Molly looking at Yogi Bear on her View-Master.

"I can't wait to see Rachel," Polly says, gazing through her open window to the passing wheat fields. "Don't think I'll look up anyone else. You lose touch over the years."

"C'mon. We'll see the whole family," I say.

As we fly through Northern Ontario, Polly sings. "In olden days a glimpse of stocking..."

When she stops, I turn on the radio.

"On Wolverton Mountain..."

As we weave the narrow two-lane Trans-Canada Highway through Northern Ontario, windows are rolled up to block the

234 · DAVID SPANER

stench of mill-town pulp. Daniel shoves his superhero comic books aside and does Elvis Presley doing "Blue Suede Shoes," which has Polly, Barbara, and Molly dancing in their seats.

"Toronto the Good," I say as we begin the final stretch to the city. Before checking into the Conroy Hotel, we stop at Lawrence Plaza, home to Max's Toy House. My cousin Max is not at the store, so I phone his actual house, and cousins are on their way. To fill the time it takes Max to pick up Florence and drive here, we browse, the children as wide-eyed at this sizable shopping centre as Rachel and I used to be at Woodward's department store. When we visit the plaza's department store, Morgan's, in search of a bathing suit for Barbara, we step from the escalator onto the second floor and into a flurry of voices and embraces. "Jake," shouts Max as I am bear-hugged by Florence.

"I've got Toy Houses in three shopping centres now," Max says as we walk back to his store. "Three. It's the future. This shopping centre's nothing. They're building one that's all indoors."

Six hours later the family fills a long table in Chinatown.

"Save a seat for Rachel, beside Jake," Florence says.

"Where the hell is Rachel?" Max says. "She moves to Toronto and I don't see her, but you'd expect her to show up for her brother."

"I see her," says Florence.

"We got tickets for you to see Tony Bennett at the O'Keefe Centre," the youngest cousin, Jerry, tells me.

"Thank you," I say.

"I love those songs," Polly says.

"They don't have food like this in Fort Harold," says Milton, the oldest cousin.

"As a matter of fact, the Fort Harold Hotel has the best Chinese food I've ever tasted," I say.

"Lots for you to do in Toronto," Max says. "You got to take the kids to the Ex, Jake. The new Hockey Hall of Fame is something."

"Blueberry buns," suggests Florence's daughter Nita. "The Health Bread ones."

"And Yorkville," says Florence, "is getting really interest-ing — little galleries, boutique shops, offbeat places. Beatniks. Folk singers too."

"Bring the kids by the store, Jake. I'll let each of them pick out something for themself," says Max.

Assimilation came so easily in post-war Fort Harold that I didn't even have to try. Jake Feldman did not become Jack Fields. But Jake became Jack. On visits to Vancouver, the chil-dren took little notice when Frieda called me Jakie, assuming it was some affectionate name a mother gives a son. In Toronto this summer, though, I am Jake, a puzzlement to my own chil-dren, supposing it must be the Toronto word for Jack or the family nickname for their father.

I'm immersed in the menu when Rachel arrives and embraces Polly. I look up as they unclinch, and it is my turn to give Rachel a hug. She is working on CBC TV's *The Wayne & Shuster Hour*, responsible for the musical numbers that some-times fill the holes between the comedy team's parodies of U.S. popular culture.

"What's that like for you, Rachel?" Max says.

"Johnny and Frank are a lot of fun to work with," she says.

"Johnny Wayne — his real name's Louis Weingarten — was a real cut-up in class," says Florence. "One time we had a falling out at school. I don't remember over what. We were in grade 4.

So I wrote him a note that said 'I'm sore at you.' He sent back a note. 'Use Zam-Buk for sores.'"

"What's Zam-Buk?" Barbara quietly asks, with a pull at Polly's bare arm.

"Something you put on sores."

"I knew Frank Shuster a little," Max says. "He lived in the neighbourhood too."

Molly and Barbara are seated beside similar-sized cousins, but none of these relatives are Daniel's age, so he and his comic books are squeezed between Max and me. "That comic you got there," Max says, pointing to the issue of *Superman* that Daniel's reading at the table. "Frank Shuster, of Wayne and Shuster, has a cousin named Joe, and Joe invented Superman. Joe moved down to the States but he grew up here in Toronto on the same street as us. See, Superman is from the neighbourhood. Like Feldman and Silverman."

"Some days I feel like a strange visitor from another planet," Rachel says with a smile.

"I *was* from another world," says Bessie. "The shtetl I came from was like another world."

"We watch Wayne and Shuster's show in Fort Harold," Polly says.

"I'm glad someone watches those putzes," Milton says.

"No. The show is very popular," Florence says.

"Milton's just kidding," says his wife, Esther. "He watches it all the time."

"And we see Wayne and Shuster on *Ed Sullivan*," I say.

"Did you see 'Gunschmuck,' their send-up of *Gunsmoke*? A hilarium," says Esther.

"I think my friend Al Bochner has a relative on *Wayne and Shuster*," notes Florence's husband, George.

"Al was at Christie Pits," says Max as he passes along a large plate of shrimp fried rice. "I was there. Jake too." Max turns to Daniel. "Your father and I were real pals at the time."

"All my girlfriends had crushes on you, Jake, that summer you came out here," Florence says.

Barbara and Daniel look at me with bemusement. This, too, is something about their father they haven't imagined.

"No," I say. "You're just saying that, right Flo?"

"Uh-uh," says Florence, shaking her head.

"I guess I was the lucky one," Polly says with a smile.

Polly and I laugh.

"Is she eating her food or just playing with it?" says Milton, eyeing the chow mein on Molly's plate.

"I'm eating it," Molly says defiantly.

"Don't listen to him, Molly," says Esther. "He's only pretending to be a schmo."

"Such a cutie," says Auntie Bessie, giving Molly a big grin. "A *zeesa meydelah*."

"My grandmother talks Jewish like that," says Daniel.

"Your grandmother and I speak the same language in more ways than one," Bessie says. Frieda and Bessie know each other well from a lifetime of letters back and forth, but they have never actually met. Neither of them does much straying from the cities they've found themselves living in.

The Toronto relatives insist on divvying up the bill among themselves.

"Tell everyone your Empire State Building joke," I urge Daniel as we depart the restaurant, and he delivers it with gusto in the adjoining parking lot.

"A hilarium," Florence says amicably. "Another comedian in the family."

"What street were we living on that summer you came out here, Jake?" says Jerry. "We were always on the move. We moved whenever the rents went up. Now we stay put, more or less, touch wood."

"We were on Keefer Street. You were on Clinton Street."

Now, mostly these relatives live spread apart in detached split-levels in nearby northern suburbs, having left the semi-detached houses off College and Spadina, doughnut shops about to rise in Toronto where bagels were. Our days with the Toronto family are busy—Casa Loma castle, the Noshery deli, the CNE, movies, music.

One evening, Rachel takes Polly to a Yorkville coffee house to hear a young woman from small-town Ontario and a young man from Vancouver Island who've teamed to make beautiful folk music together.

"How do you like being alone," Polly asks over cappuccino.

"Doesn't bother me," says Rachel.

"I don't know," Polly says, "but I would be lonely."

"I don't want to get married, and I'm not sorry I made the decision to not have children."

"But is there something missing there?"

"There's something missing almost everywhere, with you and Jack too, I notice."

"Sometimes," Polly says, "when I'm alone after the kids have gone to school and I've done the housework, I put on a record, a Broadway soundtrack, and just dance alone. I imagine I had gone to New York with you and I'm up on stage with Yul Brynner, and I sing 'Shall We Dance?' and leap from couch to chair. Whirl from room to room. One time a delivery boy from the Hudson's Bay came with a new table, and I couldn't hear him because of the music, and as I did my pirouette, I saw him shading his eyes, looking at me bewildered through the living room window. And I was embarrassed. Now when I do it I close the drapes."

"I don't know," Polly tells me after the coffee house, "that Rachel is that happy."

The day before leaving Toronto, we visit Bessie alone in an apartment on North York's Bathurst Street, and her arms engulf me again. Afterwards, Polly and I and the children, along with Florence and Nita, take the subway downtown. We emerge near Simpson's department store, Barbara still looking for a bathing suit, Daniel determined to buy a Toronto Maple Leafs sweater, having toured the Hockey Hall of Fame at the CNE. Everyone else disappears into the store.

I walk awhile on this warm morning, then hop a streetcar, Toronto's among the last on the continent. As the tram jerks easily on the track, I contemplate the drive back to B.C., first dipping into the States at Niagara Falls, then across through Cleveland and Chicago, up to Winnipeg and home. Polly and the children will take the train from Winnipeg because she doesn't want them to miss an opportunity to experience Canada from a mobile bunk bed. Recalling my train trips across Canada in the 1930s, I agreed it would be a good experience for the children. Polly is always looking for experiences for the children, I muse, enjoying my solitude in the back of the tram as it trails past the Royal York Hotel and other sites that countrywide radio has transmitted into national monuments. The week in Toronto kindles Polly's desire to leave Fort Harold. "The children need to broaden their horizons," she says.

The streetcar is in traffic, slowly approaching an intersection. I turn to the window, see the back of a head, long dark brown hair dangling against a summery lavender dress, bobbing along the sidewalk. I stand, walk quickly down the aisle, following her movements. When I reach the front window, I see her face for the first time as she turns at the intersection's crosswalk and passes in front of the streetcar. I argue with myself whether to get off, my eyes fixed on her passing profile. After crossing the street, Lena pauses a moment at a curb, facing the same stop signal as the streetcar, then she walks through the red light.

"You've got too many nightmares," says Polly, waking beside me our first morning together in Fort Harold after Toronto. "Far too many nightmares."

"I wasn't aware..."

"You twisted and turned and shouted all night."

"What did I say?"

"The same as usual. A lot of swearing."

This December 1962, Polly will insist we do Hanukkah instead of Christmas with Eddie's family. We will call the tree a Hanukkah bush and on Christmas Day drive downtown for Chinese food. Christmas is why so many Jews like Chinese food so much, having acquired a taste for it because it is readily available this one day of the year when they're looking to eat out and every other kind of restaurant is closed. Skipping Eddie and Joan's annual dinner is another way of Polly saying how badly she wants out of Fort Harold and its routines. I ponder this for a day or two but don't say anything about moving.

A month into the new year, the family fills the car for the Sunday drive Around the Hoop.

"Some enchanted evening," Polly sings.

I turn on the radio.

"You don't like my voice," Polly huffs.

I say nothing.

"Nature Boy…" comes through the radio.

"That's odd," Polly says.

"It's the CBC," I say.

Polly points to a sedan parked at the side of the road. Welded from two cars, it has six doors, is hand-painted a thick mustard yellow, with antlers fastened to its roof.

"It is an odd car," I agree.

"I meant that song on the radio," she says.

Polly snaps off the radio and sings. "I'm going to wash that man right out of my hair."

I turn the radio back on.

"Being that we only have one life to live," Polly says that evening in bed after the lights are out, "do you ever think about trying to do everything you've dreamed of making of yourself?"

"I don't know if anyone does that."

"Some people do," Polly says. "Einstein. Albert Schweitzer. Leonardo da Vinci."

"Sammy Davis, Jr.," I say.

Silence.

"We're leaving. You're welcome to come. But we're leaving."

"What can I do in L.A.?" I say the following day. "And we've made a pretty nice life for ourselves here."

"*Nice*. I hate that word, nice," Polly says. "I want the kids to have every opportunity to be themselves and everything they can be. And I wonder if maybe I can do something."

"I've become comfortable here."

"You and your father are birds of a feather. He had it wrong when he said you're another Sam. You're actually another Isaac," says Polly, adding apologetically, "Listen, in most ways you're not like him. You're kind. You're really not like him but..."

"What?"

"You are alike in one way. You're both drawn to this town or what it represents. Did you ever figure out why your mother never mentioned his name once he left? She was nothing, mit nothing, to him, and it was her way of returning the compliment. And the funny thing is, he was the one who was nothing much, not really. You've always looked at him as a big mystery to solve, this human whodunnit. Now, I realize you could never solve it because there was no solution — Isaac was empty. There was no one home."

"Give him a little credit," I say. "It took courage to immigrate. The boat almost sank, for Christ's sake, then he travelled across a continent, broke, everything foreign to him. I went to Spain. But the old man outdid me. He went to North America."

"He was a *schtunk*," she says, "and you think more of him than you do of your mother even though he never had the time of day for you. You don't see that she has always been more courageous than him and she's smart as a whip. She would not let Isaac turn her into him. Frieda thinks she doesn't have much to offer, but she has given more than she realizes."

"Much more than she has taken."

"That's for sure. I love your mother but I will not be her — anyone else."

Barbara is excited about the move. "She's going into her last year of high school, which is another reason to move now," Polly says. Daniel has reservations about living in the U.S., although he does like the new California home's proximity to ballparks and theme parks. Molly wants to go with her mother and stay with her father. "Why don't you come?" she says.

Polly has wanted to move on pretty much since we arrived in Fort Harold. Last year, I relented to her prodding, sending for brochures on Australia and Los Angeles, but after talking fleetingly about moving I never broached the subject again. Finally, after our trip to Toronto, Polly made the decision alone, and when I said I wouldn't be going she withdrew, not speaking with me the final week as a moving company's truck was loaded. I watch Polly and the children leave on a Sunday morning train, and later that day I am alone when I drive Around the Hoop. It is on this drive that I say aloud, for the first time, that I don't like myself. Still, I continue driving.

TWENTY-FOUR

LIKE ANY WAR

Barcelona, fall 1986

"I CAN UNDERSTAND HIS DESPAIR," REBECCA SAYS, AS we exit a subway near Park Güell the morning after Jim Heathcott's eruption. "But I thought it was illegal for Canadians to fight in another country's war, so how was it that he fought in Vietnam?"

"I guess that law was only for Canadians who wanted to join with the Republican army to fight fascists in Spain," I say, beginning the sidewalk climb to the park. "The Canadian government didn't mind at all if you wanted to join the U.S. Army to fight in Vietnam."

Near the entrance to the park, Rebecca points at a wrought-iron balcony filled with flowers and creeping plants. We pause to examine the whitewashed building, its red-tiled roof and intricately carved coat of arms above a window. "Gorgeous, huh," she says.

Stopping to look at Spain is something I've not done on this trip. "I guess I don't appreciate Spain like a tourist would," I say. "Hardly see anything here but the war."

We stroll on into the park and come upon a long serpentine bench shooting around an open terrace, where we stop, and Rebecca tells me about the photographs on the wall in her Greenwich Village apartment. Next to the bed where she sleeps, the oldest photo, taken in the 1920s, is of a girl, five years old, crossed legs dangling from a park bench, eyes bright, smiling. There is another girl, in a much later snapshot, running, black hair in a ponytail, devilish glint in her eyes which are turned slightly from the camera. Behind her stand two other children, smaller, eyes directly into the camera lens, expressionless.

Rebecca and I sit on the Gaudi park bench as she tells me about these three children. First daughter, Janice, is born on Rebecca's birthday, in 1946. At a party almost a year later, Rebecca is introduced to Edwin Rogov, stocky and stolid, a young engineer with progressive views. After two dinner and movie dates, he proposes. David is born. They live the postwar's new-style domesticity in a series of houses on Long Island. At first, they leave suburbia to attend benefit concerts and martyrs' funerals, but this becomes less and less frequent. In the 1950s, there is scrutiny on those who hold on to 1930s values, and it is a comfort to be married with a prefabricated house and fabricated lives. Susan is born. It seems that the television sitcom family of the '50s has always been, that the founding "fathers" stepped from the Mayflower with children wearing pedal pushers and twirling Hula Hoops. But no matter what is said, Rebecca knows this model family is new, unlike any in the Brooklyn neighbourhoods she knew before. It came with the post-war and has no politics, no culture, no history — things to be ashamed of now, discarded in the wholesale assimilation. Names are changed, pasts concealed, neighbourhoods abandoned, languages lost.

Not everyone is absorbed. Rebecca occasionally travels into Manhattan for lunch with Max Scheinblum, a childhood friend who continues to write poetry in the Village. Max is excited about another 1950s, one with Jackson Pollock art and Beat books, Charlie Parker riffs, and Brando movies. After one such lunch with Max, Edwin tells Rebecca, "I don't want you meeting with any other men." She nods and has another lunch with Max. When Rebecca starts working again, part-time at Manhattan's Mount Sinai Hospital, Edwin snaps, "Why don't you stay at home like a wife?" She nods and does another shift at the hospital. Edwin shows little interest in David and Susan, and in Janice, another's child, even less. David and Susan withdraw quietly, but Janice's bright, mischievous eyes wince at Edwin's sullen silence.

When Bill Rivers comes knocking again, it is the 1960s and Rebecca is living with Susan in a small house on Long Island. "I think of the past, what I could have done differently," Bill says, holding Rebecca the first night back. "I've admired your political convictions. It would be nice to have a rock in my life when I'm buffeted about. But I don't know that I could ever believe in anything. For me, nothing is black and white, or red, white and blue, or red all over. What's true to everyone else is a lie to me."

"That's true," Rebecca says. And they laugh. Bill lives between her place on Long Island and the East Village. Still in love, no longer drinking, he claims. But she's not sure what to make of him. "I don't know if I can trust you."

They talk of a life together, maybe, he says, on the Mexican island he knew would be there if he kept looking. Isla Mujeres. The Island of Women. The beaches are powder smooth, the water crystal blue, the streets sand. "At night, I'd sit eating seafood in a hillside restaurant overlooking the sea."

The first time Bill shows up drunk she's surprised, the second time confounded. When it's repeated, she's ready for him to move on again. He's gone for a couple of weeks, then shows up one night drunk and convulsively sick. Rebecca wants to take him to the hospital, but he refuses. Finally, he relents and is taken to Mount Sinai. Two weeks after Bill dies, his daughter, Janice, who's been living on the West Coast, comes back to Long Island to find Rebecca's eyes small with sadness, her deadened body curled in the corner of the unwashed kitchen.

"This? Over my father?" Janice asks.

"No," Rebecca says. "Everything."

Janice kisses her mother's high, delicate cheekbone. "I can't do a thing," Rebecca murmurs as Janice helps her to bed.

"That picture," Janice says, glancing at her mother, five years old, with dangling legs and bright eyes in the old photograph beside the bed, "isn't you."

"And where," says Rebecca, pointing to the photo of her daughter with mischievous eyes, "is your ponytail?"

The two laugh.

Rebecca slowly rises to her feet. She soon moves to a flat in Greenwich Village, continues working at the hospital, attends demonstrations again, this time to end the war in Vietnam and the wars on women.

The past few years, Rebecca has spent much of the time with her daughter in L.A. and was in California and Seattle before coming to the reunion. Now, she stands in a thicket in Gaudi's park, in the temperate fall day, overlooking her Spain.

"What about Heathcott's despair, Rebecca?" I say.

"He was trying to make some sense of it," she says, "like any war."

"Like soldiers do," I say.

"And he couldn't," she says.

"Going for a ride today with Aaro and Tom. Want to come?"

Back at the hotel after my second visit to Park Güell in three days, there is this message waiting for me from Henry Simmons. I knock at Henry's door. Look for him in the restaurant. He isn't there. Bob Mitchell is.

"Two days to go," Bob says with a sigh. "Have you seen Aaro?"

"He went somewhere with Henry this morning," I say, settling into a chair.

"This kerfuffle could incite a conflagration over everything," says Peter Krawchuk.

"What conflagration is that?" I say, and he hands me a front page splashed with photographs of commandos training machine guns on workers with arms raised above their heads in surrender as they leave an automobile assembly plant. The troopers had stormed the Aragon factory held for a week by strikers, leaving two dead, seven wounded, the rest arrested. In response, there is talk of a general strike.

"I'd like that," Peter says. "I'd also like to sleep in my own bed for a solid week."

After a few minutes in the bar, I go to the hotel's auditorium where Rebecca sits waiting for me with Pauline Blum. Whenever Rebecca visits her daughter in L.A. she sees Pauline, her friend since Spain.

Pauline's husband, Si Berman, is on the auditorium stage. Mel Fox finishes introducing Si ("a mensch and a scholar") and he begins a presentation about a documentary film project he's developing called *The Return*. "Along with everything else the Civil War stood for, it meant a Jewish return to Spain after centuries in exile," Si says. "During the Spanish Inquisition of the fifteenth century, the country's considerable Jewish population, though it had lived there for eons, was given the choice of conversion or expulsion. Many were expelled. In the 1930s, Jews returned to Spain, volunteering in disproportionately large numbers — over half of the American nurses, for instance, from a country three-point-something percent Jewish. One personal note. In 1937, I crossed the same ocean going to Europe that my parents had fled across, coming from Europe just a generation earlier. My parents fled the barbarism of pogroms, inquisitions. I came back to fight it."

Si reads a 1937 statement by Luigi "Gallo" Longo, Inspector General of the International Brigades. "We must gather together the magnificent examples of self-sacrifice and heroism of the Jewish fighters and reveal them for the admiration of the world."

Si turns the microphone over to David Zinn, veteran of the Spanish Revolution and the French Resistance. "Why did so many Jews fight in Spain?" Zinn says. "We were twice motivated — as leftists and as Jews. Let future generations know how we fought back, rallied to join the first armed resistance to fascism."

Afterwards, at the hotel restaurant, Rebecca and I are seated next to Irene Blair and Bob Mitchell's table. Bob, I'd noticed, left the auditorium partway through Si Berman's presentation.

"Saw that you left before it was over," I say.

"Well…yeah," Bob says. He shrugs.

"I thought Simon Berman's presentation was terrific," says Irene.

"See, Bob, you don't have to be Jewish to enjoy what Si has to say," I say.

"I am Jewish," Bob says. "Real name's Mitchell Silverstein. Before I went to Spain I changed it because Eaton's department store in Toronto wouldn't hire a Silverstein."

"How did you feel about that? Changing your name," says Rebecca.

"If that's what you had to do, that's what you had to do," says Bob with another shrug. "I like one thing Si Berman said — *equality and justice for all*. But I'm not religious."

"Being Jewish has nothing to do with religion," I say.

"A religious Jew would disagree," Bob says.

"How many of the Jewish veterans at this reunion are religious?" I say. "Very few. But none of them would deny they're Jewish."

"Religion means nothing to *some* Jews," says Rebecca. "Everything to others. Growing up in a Jewish neighbourhood in Brooklyn, it was obvious that we are a cultural-ethnic group — like the Irish and the Italians — as much as a religion."

"Not everyone in your neighbourhood was a left-wing Jewish atheist," Bob says.

"Of course not," Rebecca says. "But quite a few of us were. There's that Jewish left tradition, you know — from Emma Goldman to so many Lincolns to Abbie Hoffman. But the neighbourhood had all kinds. Religious or not, every Jew shares one thing: the lies about us."

"Of course the stereotypes are lies," says Irene, "about any group of people."

"Yes, this is not just about Jews," Rebecca says. "There's a whole set of different lies about women that I share with every other woman. And I have no doubt that it's the same way for Blacks, gays, anyone who's picked on."

"A lie can be a powerful thing to share," I say.

"I understand this," Bob says softly, sipping black coffee. "I know why I fought in Spain. A lot of the other things I've done in my life are just part of the compromise of living. Learning to choose your battles. I mean, changing a name. So what? A name's just an accident of birth. It's not important to me."

"*Redn di narishkayt*," Rebecca says.

"No, Rebecca. It's not nonsense," says Bob. "Like Jack said, I would never deny what I am, because that would be giving in to the bigots. But if I truly identify with anything, it's with the international proletariat."

"I've been a socialist forever and a Jew even longer," I say.

"What do you mean by that?" Bob says.

"That everyone is everything they are."

"I agree with Jack," Irene says. "You can't separate your life into categories. It's all intertwined."

"Your politics have everything to do with your personal story," Rebecca says.

"That's right," says Irene. "Of course, Spain was a class war as well as a civil war, and a storied event, but I'm interested in its individual stories too. What moved a person or a particular group of people to volunteer? So I was fascinated with Si Berman's presentation, I was fascinated with Dick Lillard's book, I'm fascinated with my own Irish heritage. I was Irene Ryan, you know, before I was Irene Blair. I've visited Ireland, I don't know how many times since I retired."

"I've been to Ireland," Bob says. "My wife was Irish."

There is a moment of silence, then Rebecca says: "I knew you were Jewish, Bob."

"How?" he says.

"You look just like a boy from the old neighbourhood. Talk like him too," she says with a laugh. "You sure you're not from Brooklyn?"

"I met someone the other day who said I look like I'm from New York," I say.

"Doesn't the bible say 'Jews are the Children of New York'?" Rebecca says.

Irene laughs. "Is that in the Old Testament or the New Testament?" she says.

"The *Mad Magazine* Testament," I say.

"We are all New York in the eyes of America," Bob sings quietly.

"Is that a line from a Dylan song?" I say.

"Jefferson Airplane," says Bob.

"*You*...listen to *that*?" says Rebecca.

"You're full of surprises, Bob," I say.

"I still like the Weavers. And Harry Belafonte," Rebecca says.

After lunch, Rebecca and I are sitting in the lobby when Irene steps from the elevator with the Toronto reporter and Susan Barkley. "Are you folks coming to the demonstration?" Irene says, and Rebecca and I are on our feet.

As the taxicab nears our destination, block after block is crowded with protesters headed towards an enormous rally against the government and its commandos.

Bob, in the front seat between Susan and the driver, pronounces contentedly, "Finally, we're in Spain."

"This," says the reporter, "looks like the social-*ist* event of the year."

"Maybe they're rehearsing another farewell to us," I say.

"This is really something," says Bob. "Think it will amount to anything?"

"I don't think there's going to be another civil war if that's what you mean," the Toronto reporter says from the back, with Irene and I. "It is just a demonstration."

"It is *something*," Irene reprimands him.

"What do you think about it?" I ask Susan.

"I guess it's what you came here for."

With the streets and sidewalks jammed with protest, our cab driver pulls over and says we'll have to walk the last couple of blocks. We make our way out of the cab and through the crowd to an Abraham Lincoln Brigade banner where veterans of every international battalion are congregating, including other Mac-Paps. While there are hundreds in this International Brigade contingent, it's a speck in the crowd filling the street like a gigantic block party. Two drum-pounding clowns in bright red-and-yellow costumes march into the middle of our contingent of veterans, who clap along to their thumping. "Meet the new Spain, same as the old Spain," one of the drummers shouts into my face. I smile back, recognizing under the face paint the anarchist from West Bengal. He's with the artist from D.C. In an instant, they vanish into the hubbub.

There is a kind of protest that brings a city street to life in a visceral way that you have to experience to fully understand. It is a heightened sensation that I first felt running through the streets at the Ballantyne Pier riot of 1935. And now, again in Barcelona, I'm overcome. This is no longer a lifeless concrete thoroughfare taking Barcelonians to their transactions. Today, its colours are more vibrant, its pavement for people. Although other individuals here and I would be strangers if we crossed paths in any other setting, now we are in total alignment. Invincible. I look at Rebecca standing next to me and know she is feeling the exact same thing.

"You seen Henry and Aaro?" says Bob, who slips away before I can answer. I did see them on the periphery of the crowd, called out their names, but my voice was lost in the din and they were gone. Henry and Aaro have oddly become almost inseparable since their barroom confrontation in Valencia. Last night, I was surprised to see them at the hotel bar with Tom and a young Spanish woman.

Now, from a makeshift stage on the street, a man in a white suit addresses the protesters, hammering his fist into his hand, attracting a smattering of applause. Most protesters are focused on the street party-protest, not the stage. "A las barricadas," sings an impromptu chorus behind me, "To the barricades."

Tom, meanwhile, has joined the contingent behind the Lincoln banner. "Hell," he stammers, his breath touching my ear, "it is her."

La Pasionaria is stepping slowly, erectly to the front of the stage. The old woman dressed all in black reaches the microphone, stands quietly observing the multitude. As one by one the protesters note her presence, the street party goes quieter until it is silent. Surrounded by the reunion's volunteers for Spain, I see that they're all looking at this stage, on the same street as the farewell, fifty years removed. She begins in Spanish, speaking deliberately, body still. First, she decries the assault on the strikers, then in French, then English, she reads aloud: "A special word to the international comrades who stand with us today. We welcome you back. Some of us who were here the day you left are here again today. We are still with you. You are still with us."

She leaves a riveted crowd for the next speaker, a young woman who speaks faster and calls for a general strike. Half-cocked arms with full-clenched, pumping fists pummel the sky, then bodies sway to "The Internationale." Tom introduces me to the young Spanish woman who was at the bar last night with him and Henry and Aaro.

"Jack," he says. "This is Sofia Peiro, the niece of Sandro Peiro."

"Pleased to meet you," I say, shaking her hand. "I've heard much from Tom about your family."

"I've heard much from my family," says Sofia, "about your International Brigades."

TWENTY-FIVE

ONE PART PARADISE

*Los Angeles, spring 1964,
and Fort Harold, 1965–1972*

AT NIGHT, THE PHONE RINGS. POLLY, FROM L.A.

"The guy who sang 'Good Morning' with Debbie Reynolds and Gene Kelly in *Singing in the Rain*, that was Donald O'Connor, right?"

"Yes."

"You were supposed," I hear a man's voice in the background, "to ask who it was, not give the answer."

"Oh," she says. "What was the name of the guy who sang 'Good Morning' with Gene Kelly and Debbie Reynolds?"

"I said it was Donald O'Connor."

"I'm having a bet with a friend over this," Polly says. "He is sure it was someone who became a famous director."

"Maybe it was Ingmar Bergman," I say. "You were going to be a dancer. I mean, how could you not know..."

"I just wasn't sure. I said Donald O'Connor, okay, and I am a dancer. I'm dancing again."

"Next, you'll be calling long distance to ask who played Rick in *Casablanca*."

"You're sarcastic," says Polly. "Oh, fuck you."

When I finally visit Los Angeles, six months after Polly and the children leave Fort Harold, they are staying with her sister, Ida, and brother-in-law, Stanley, in the San Fernando Valley's Encino neighbourhood. I drive a rented car from LAX, anxious that I might be travelling in the wrong direction because on the freeway I can't find a skyline, any demarcation between suburbia and city. I continue, however, on this expressway to nowhere I'm certain I want to be and arrive in Encino. As I pull into the driveway, I tell myself again how badly I messed up by not moving to L.A. with Polly and the kids, and maybe, just maybe, there is still time to do it. There is no response to my door-knocking and bell-ringing at the sprawling ranch house, so I walk around back to find Polly and Ida lounging by a swimming pool.

"So, you've managed to pry yourself out of that town," says Ida, stretched out on a lawn chair.

"The town of Fort Jack," Polly says, rising to peck my cheek. "It's good to see you again, but I want to tell you right off, so there are no misconceptions, I have no interest in resuming our marriage."

"The chemistry wasn't right," Ida contributes. "Fred and Ginger had it. You don't."

"The marriage had its moments," I say tersely.

"Possession is nine-tenths of the law," Polly says, "and since marriage is legal, possession is nine-tenths of marriage."

"Did you bring a bathing suit at least?" Ida says. "It's ninety-five degrees in the shade today."

The Valley is one part paradise, with its February sunshine and lush groves, and one part Kingsway with palm trees. I get a room in a nearby Travelodge and the next day we all go to the Farmers Market and Grauman's Chinese Theatre. Mostly, though, they've already seen what I want to see in L.A. and have moved on from touristy sites. Polly is taking a dance class, Barbara has fallen in with a UCLA dental student, and Daniel and Molly are busy with new friends.

I spend an afternoon at the Olvera Street Mexican market-place. L.A. is wonderfully multicultural, but it has a different diversity than the other American mega-city. I do not see anything here of New York's Italian or Puerto Rican or Irish neighbourhoods. The Westside of L.A. has two ethnic groups: Jews and blondes, and half the Jews have dyed their hair blonde, and half the blondes have converted to Judaism, so they are fast becoming one.

One morning I drive by myself to Disneyland, where the other adults all seem to have come with children. While they line up for rides, I'm content to find a cozy corner on Tom Sawyer's Island to sit on my own and read *Catch-22* in the sun for an hour before sauntering onto Main Street for lunch. After a chicken sandwich, I step into a shop with ready-to-wear Donald Duck beaks, Cinderella crowns, and Mickey Mouse ears.

Wearing my new mouse ears, I mosey in and out of the theme park's Wild West replications, including a saloon, a stagecoach, and a train ride through cowboy country. Leaving the 1880s behind, I take the Jungle Cruise featuring brand-new, mid-twentieth-century technology, and it all seems so real. When a robotic alligator rising from the muddy water splashes children on board our small riverboat, the young girl seated beside me rears back in astonishment. "Oh my," her mother says.

When I return to Encino in the early evening, the family is eating pizza and watching a W.C. Fields movie on TV.

"What did you do with yourself all day, Jack?" Ida says

"He went to Disneyland," Daniel says.

"How would you know that?" I say.

"You," says Polly, "look more like Mickey Mouse than Mickey Mouse himself."

"Oh," I say, taking the mouse ears from my head. "I forgot that I was still wearing this."

"By yourself, you went to Disneyland?" Ida says.

"Isn't that for kids?" Daniel says.

"Why didn't you take me?" Molly says.

I hand Molly the ears.

"For you."

And she puts them on.

I had come to L.A. thinking about reconciling with Polly and moving south, but having awkwardly moved through my family's lives for a week, my last morning in Encino is spent in front of a colour television in Ida and Stanley's den, asking myself whether I am still a part of my family. I take Daniel to a matinee at the Encino Theatre to see *Robin and the 7 Hoods*, stopping afterwards at a pinball arcade where he hovers intensely over thumper bumpers and ricocheting balls, roundly defeating me and the machine. "That looks like Eddie Fisher," I say, watching a man angrily tilt a nearby machine. "Big deal," says Daniel. "Saw Vince Edwards yesterday just standing at a corner on Ventura Boulevard." As we leave the arcade, I take a quick glance at the Eddie Fisher look-alike — or is it Eddie? — now pounding the face of the pinball machine.

In the front yard, I watch Molly play catch with Stanley. "But they left me, I didn't leave them. I'm visiting them, they aren't visiting me," I tell myself unconvincingly. "You should have been a boy the way you catch," says Stanley, softly tossing an arching ball towards Molly. Chasing the ball, her foot catches a sprinkler and she falls crying into wet grass. I jump up from the lawn chair and rush to Molly, but she looks past me to her uncle. Stanley starts towards her, then pauses with uncertainty, aware he may be encroaching on father-daughter territory. Her face is round from crying, smudged with tears and sprinkler water. I reach for Molly's hand. She looks to me and I lift her into my arms. I will always be there for you, I tell her. When I came to L.A. last week I thought I might move here. But Polly and the kids have moved on. When Polly and I were together, I tried to do whatever my father hadn't done. Now that we are apart, I damn sure will not distance myself the way my father did. So I distance myself in ways he didn't. Before leaving for the airport, I tell the children and Polly that I'm thinking of relocating to L.A., but I don't. I will write, I say, and I do for a while.

Most every day the store closes at six o'clock and I promptly disappear into the front door of the yellow bungalow and have my hastily prepared dinner in front of the television. This day, there is an envelope waiting for me inside the door, and I stand in the hallway's dim light, snow melting from my coat onto the hardwood floor as I read Polly's letter.

Polly is dancing. She taught at an L.A. dance studio called I Won't Dance, Don't Ask Me, then joined a troupe called the Dancing Women's Battalion. Its tour of the States just ended with packed performances at the Lower East Side's Anderson Theatre. "I'm not sorry I spent those years in Fort Harold," her letter tells me. "I feel like I have been released and I think that shows in my dance. In that town I felt old, but here I am, dancing with women of all ages and people are loving what we do.... Molly is here, and she says hi.... Barbara's Sam looks like me, everyone says.... Daniel is travelling across country, thinking about university in Toronto."

I no longer motor Around the Hoop just on Sundays but get up at any odd hour to drive and listen to the radio or cassettes. I still read. Often buy newspapers and magazines at the newsstand in the Fort Harold Hotel. Recently liked Pierre Berton's *The National Dream* and Simone de Beauvoir's *The Mandarins*. Joined the Book of the Month Club. Every day except Sunday I go in to work and my occasional outings usually have some connection to the store. The manager of the new hotel, the Fir Tree Inn, is a customer and he invites me to use its indoor heated swimming pool, the only one in town. Some sleepless nights I go to the hotel so early there is no one else in its pool. The editor of the *Fort Harold Citizen* is another customer, and when he shops at the store we talk about writers and movies. So he asks me to review Woody Allen's latest, already several months old when it arrives in Fort Harold. "Why am I the only one laughing in this theatre?" I scribble into my notebook during the movie, then labour over the review, driving twice Around the Hoop to mull its contents, which I finish and the *Citizen* publishes. But I don't submit another review.

Eddie is determined to remarry me.

"I've got a babe for you," he says one morning as I fold shirts in the store.

"Not interested."

"Don't be a schmuck, Jack. Get a grip on yourself. At least get a grip on your schmuck. She's a waitress at that new restaurant, hotter than a firecracker for me, but I've got more than I can handle. I told her she could have my brother, even though I'm the good-looking one."

"Eddie, I'm not interested in meeting anyone right now."

"You still pining over Polly? Okay, go home and jerk off or whatever you do. Are you a Feldman or what?"

They reunite backstage, embracing while Polly catches her breath after a Dancing Women's Battalion performance at L.A.'s Pantages Theatre. Polly has just returned from Europe with the troupe. Rachel is in town to direct a theatrical production of *Pal Joey*. They talk for hours over coffee at a café near Polly's apartment off the Sunset Strip.

"After we went to that coffee house in Toronto all those years ago," says Polly, "I told Jack that Rachel says she doesn't want kids or a man and I can tell she's unhappy. Later, I was so embarrassed for saying that."

"Don't be," Rachel says. "I made my choices and I'm glad of it. You know I've had my share of relationships, but I've never been one to settle down, or settle."

"You think all husbands are interchangeable?" Polly says with a laugh.

"I don't think I'd say that, but on the other hand would life be much different if it was spent with Bill from Buffalo instead of Cal from Calgary."

"Or Jack from Vancouver?" says Polly.

"No, my brother's... one of a kind," says Rachel.

"Anyway, I'm excited that we're together," Polly says.

"And I'm excited about the work you're doing, Polly. As much as I appreciate them all, I am tired of re-staging Rodgers and Hart and Hammerstein and choreographing Wayne and Shuster."

Polly and Rachel begin that evening and into the morning — *Ginger and Ginger*, a musical collaboration — fusing the dancing battalion's unshackled movement with the Tin Pan Alley melodies they performed in the house on Keefer Street. I learn this in a letter from Molly. She's with her mother in New York. Barbara has a son and a daughter and a home in the San Fernando Valley. Daniel is active in the war against the war in Toronto. "Mom says he is his father's son," Molly writes. "Does that mean he'll wind up in Fort Harold too?"

"Dad, I'm at the Fort Harold Hotel. Just passing through."

Surprised by the phone call, I leave the store immediately and meet Daniel at the hotel's coffee shop. He's in B.C. for a few weeks, he says, staying with friends in Wells.

"Still wearing Davy Crockett's clothing," I say to Daniel, who's dressed in a buckskin jacket with fringes, patched jeans, braided belt, his dark-brown hair curling down his chest.

"What do you do all day?" he wants to know.

"Not much," I say.

"Mom said you're comfortable here."

"Yes. I'm okay with it."

Can someone who withdraws from the real world, and just watches, have a better sense of it than its participants, I wonder? Daniel has no doubts that it is those on the front lines who understand the world. He's dropped out of the University of Toronto and lives off Spadina with fellow members of the Vandals, a New Left group named from a Dylan song. "We're building a liberation movement, like in Vietnam," he says.

"Only our movement is made up of freaks, the hippie counter-culture. We're building a beautiful, cooperative new nation in the belly of the dying old one."

"You're going to have to speak English if you want to get anywhere, Daniel. What does this freaks stuff mean to a working stiff?"

"The *workers*? They've been bought off by the system. Give them a colour TV and a two-car garage and they're happy. We're organizing *youth*. Just before I left Toronto we did a fighting action. The Bay Street Bash. Trashed the financial district. We're bringing the war home."

"But you live in Canada."

"America's client state. It's a pig nation too."

"I'm opposed to the war too," I say, "and any Canadian complicity in it."

Daniel writes for *Morning Breaking*, an underground newspaper named from a Dylan song.

"My life's pretty boring compared to your Dylan songs," I say, "but I'm okay with it."

I accept a copy of his newspaper and open it to a photograph of Daniel and other Vandals strapped in bandoliers, armed with toy machine guns.

"Is that what you're going to overthrow the system with," I say, "an arsenal made by Mattel?"

"By Marx," says Daniel. "The Marx toy company is our supplier." And we laugh.

"How many members in this Vandals organization?" I say.

"I'm not a headcounter," Daniel shrugs. "I'm a headhunter."

"The difference between our movement in the Depression and this culture of yours is that we didn't have a choice," I say. "You and your friends can cut your hair and go back to school.

We were a movement of unemployed working people who needed to make social change just to survive."

"If someone *chooses* to live outside the system," says Daniel, "maybe their commitment is greater than someone who felt they *needed* to join a movement. The way we live is something people want to do, aren't forced to do for survival."

"People can quit your movement like that," I say with a snap of my fingers.

"And you couldn't leave Spain? What about the people who lived in Barcelona when the fascists marched in. Their lives depended on a Republican victory. Yours didn't."

I wake up the next morning hoping that it is later than I know it is—too early to go to work, too late to go back to sleep. I try to kill time reading Daniel's newspaper. Still restless, I take the aged snowshoes from a shelf in the basement, bundle in winter clothing topped by a fedora, then step into the Fort Harold snowfall. The heavy wooden shoes leave a pattern of teardrops in the snow as I trudge down the middle of the road in the dark.

TWENTY-SIX

INTERVIEW WITH A TORONTO REPORTER

Barcelona, fall 1986

"THERE ARE TWO THINGS I KNOW ABOUT THE Vancouver of 1986," the Toronto reporter says when we meet in the hotel lobby. "You've got a real left-winger running for mayor and you've got a world's fair going on." That real left-winger, Harry Rankin, has topped the aldermanic polls forever but will lose this year's mayoralty race. That world's fair ended just before this reunion started. There are people who like to say Vancouver wasn't a city until this fair arrived in 1986. There are others who say Vancouver wasn't a city when they moved to it, *whenever* that was, as if their personal arrival had everything to do with its citification. Truth is, the Vancouver I've known has always been a city. Third biggest in the country since the 1920s. To the Fort Harolds in B.C. it was *the* city. Our neighbourhood, Strathcona, and our street, Keefer, gave me hope. Other cities had ethnic neighbourhoods but Vancouver had a neighbourhood of ethnic neighbourhoods. And we all got along, more or less.

It turns out that the Toronto reporter is far more interested in the Spain of 1936 than he is in the Vancouver of 1986 or, for that matter, the Vancouver of 1936. He is sending articles on this reunion to a daily newspaper and magazines in Canada. Says he started out as a writer working on underground newspapers. Says he has uncles who fought at Christie Pits. We've already talked some about my Vancouver background, but he says he'd like something from me about being in Spain's war. Not sure why I trust that whatever the reporter will write will honour Art and the others I left in Spain, but I do. So two days before the reunion ends I meet with him for a mid-day interview at our hotel's barroom.

"It's good to be here with you in Spain, Jack, fifty years after you fought in Spain," he says into his recorder. "Tell me about getting into the country in 1937."

"At French customs, we say we're going to the world's fair in Paris. They wouldn't have let us in if we had mentioned Spain. So, we're twenty young men wearing cheap suits, carrying cardboard suitcases, going to the Paris Exposition of 1937. I don't have time to actually go to the fair, or explore the city much at all, because we convene that day in the basement of a Paris restaurant with another two hundred volunteers from all over the place. That night, Republican guides take us through the Pyrenees Mountains and into Spain. Just being together in Spain is extremely moving. I mean, it's exciting to finally be in Spain."

"When did you first see action?"

"After training at Tarazona, I'm with the Mac-Paps sent in to replace a Spanish company on a hill near Teruel. Republican forces are trying to retake the city from the fascists. There's lots of frozen bodies on the ground between us and the fascist line. The wind is so icy that it pierces you. My feet turn blue and I can barely close my hands. My friend Billy Sweeney, from Vancouver, gets gangrene and his left foot is amputated. I help carry Billy on a stretcher to a medical truck. It's tough to see him leave Spain that way. The food trucked into us is frozen. We're digging trenches in the hill and it's like excavating an iceberg. And the bombs rain down."

"What was morale like there?" the reporter says.

"Despite these horrific circumstances, we are extremely motivated to be in Spain and morale is good. I'm no longer the quiet teenager I was at the relief camp a few years ago and participate as ardently as anyone in the singalongs and conversations. Around the fire at night a couple of Wobblies sing Joe Hill songs. We have fiery but friendly group conversations that go into the night, mostly political such as 'Spain, is it a revolution or civil war?' I say it's both considering the collectivization occurring in some areas of the Republic. Or 'the international consequences of a Republican victory?' Everyone says it would embolden progressive movements and deflate fascism.

"There are lighter topics too, like 'Best Canadian welterweight boxer: Frankie Genovese or Sammy Luftspring?'

"'I like Sammy because he fought in the Christie Pits riot,' I say.

"'So did Frankie,' says Lou Bonetti, a Mac-Pap from Toronto.

"'Then I'm not picking one over the other,' I say.

"'I declare this debate a draw,' Lou says. And we all laugh.

"There is a visceral camaraderie and sense of purpose in Spain that will always be hard for me to explain to anyone who wasn't there with us. That is why it is so gratifying, fifty years later, to be at a reunion where no one needs an explanation.

"Lou Bonetti doesn't survive the Battle of Teruel. Of the eight hundred or so Mac-Paps that go into Teruel, less than two hundred come out."

"You were terribly outgunned," the reporter says.

"We're fighting brand-new Nazi artillery and warplanes with old broken-down rifles," I say. "Some work all right, but others jam. Some were made before the First World War. We are always short of supplies, always promised guns and air support. It is always too little, too late. We don't blame the Republic for this. We know that aid to Spain is being blockaded by the Western governments."

When the Toronto reporter pauses the interview to change his recorder's batteries, I notice for the first time that Tom Barkley and Henry Simmons are seated on the other side of the barroom with Sandro Peiro's niece, Sofia, and a young Spanish man. The four are huddled closely in what looks to be intense conversation. I am intrigued by what those two seventy-something Canadians in berets and two twenty-something Spaniards in black from head to toe could be talking about so animatedly. The Spaniards rise from the table, exchange clenched-fist salutes with Tom and Henry and depart. Concentrated on his recorder, the reporter is unaware of the Spanish-Canadian goings-on across the room.

"Ready," he tells me and the interview resumes. "After Teruel?"

"Not long after we leave Teruel, I am in the Battle of Caspe. I'm in the thick of the fierce fight to desperately hold that town when I...I'm shot. Catch a bullet in my lower back. I can't...it is...Victor is there, kneeling beside me in the rain. See his face and shout his name, then I black out. When I come to, I'm in a hospital train, fading in, fading out, but it is always black because the train travels at night, spends daylight under cover in tunnels. We reach a town on the coast where a school has been turned into a military hospital. Shivering, skin oily sticky, feeling in my left leg gone. How helpless and hopeless I feel.

"I'm in bed in an upstairs room, unable to move, the day Paul Robeson comes to the hospital and sings.

"'*There's an ol' man called de Mississippi.*'

"Robeson's deep, pain-powered basso wafts through the floor to my second-story bed, where I'm in sweat-soaked sheets, lips caked with medicinal congealment, skin oiled by fever.

"'*That's the ol' man I don't like to be.*'

"I've been half-delirious, half-visionary for days when Robeson's voice rises through the fever.

"'*What does he care if the world's got troubles?*'

"Not sure that I am actually hearing Robeson sing, or if it is a recording, or in my dreams.

"'*What does he care if the land ain't free.*'

"I'm the only one in this eight-mattress makeshift hospital room who isn't able to be at the performance on the ground floor.

"'*Ol' man river. That ol' man river...*'

"Robeson — Shakespearean actor, all-American football player, folk singer, lawyer, movie star, writer, opera artist, political theorist, blacklisted activist — has come to the Spanish Civil War, like some Bob Hope flip side, to entertain the troops. The International Brigade's troops.

"'*You an' me, we sweat an' strain. Body all achin' and wracked wit pain...*'

"Alone, I hear Robeson sing to us.

"'*Tote that barge and lift that bale. You show a little grit and you lands in jail...*'

"The day Paul Robeson comes to the hospital, I'm not too disoriented to notice he has changed the climatic lyrics of his signature song 'Ol' Man River.' Instead of *'Ah gets weary an' sick of tryin', I'm tired of livin' and scared of dyin',*" the words he now sings: '*I keeps laffin' instead of cryin', I must keep fightin' until I'm dyin'.*'

"That day, a hand with a cool towel comes, too, soothes my face and body.

"That hand comes again and again. I close my eyes and imagine Lena Horowitz's hand holding the towel. But when the fever breaks, I see that the hand has a face, its own face, belonging to a petite woman with long braided brown hair and huge hazel eyes. She is an American nurse who volunteered when the war started and is now a veteran of mobile blood units, ambulances, medical trains, instant hospitals. I watch her hand soothe each patient, anxious for my turn as she comes down the line. She and I barely talk with each other the first few days, then one morning as she reaches my bed I tell her how I had at first visualized her hand belonging to Lena. 'Do you compare all women to the image you have of this Lena?' she says. 'Do you even compare Lena to this image?'

"Doctors at the hospital say I'll likely never regain the feeling in my leg. Don't want to scare my family with this, so I write home saying I've had a minor flesh wound, which I know is still enough to give my mother conniptions. I also write Lena, saying I love her and miss her and when I'm able will go to wherever she is. Letters come from Lena and my sister Rachel on the same day. Rachel asks about my wound and provides a family lowdown — she's still working at the delicatessen, my mother as a seamstress, and they follow reports from Spain in all three local dailies. Word from Fort Harold is even my father keeps up with developments in Spain. Lena's letter is less convivial — 'You write of meeting "anywhere on this earth," but your inability to feel or share feelings makes a future together unlikely. Nothing is not possible but it shall not be the same as it was.' Lena and I left on pretty good terms, I figure, so why this? I resolve to write a bitter letter in response.

"Surprised to open a *New York Herald Tribune* to find Rosey Goodman hitting .328 with the New York Giants. The other wounded in this room are mostly Lincolns. Feeling so down some days I don't speak, just sit in bed re-reading box scores, particularly Rosey's, which seem to have replaced Lena as my great escape. Then a Lincoln who's heard of Rosey is put in the next bed. From Newark, New Jersey. Morrie Stern tells me he goes into Brooklyn to see the Dodgers but mostly watches the Newark Bears, minor league club of the Yankees, and the Newark Eagles of the Negro National League. He has joined protests against the game's segregation. Some great baseball in the Black leagues, Morrie says, predicting that the big league colour line will be broken 'before you can say Jack Robinson.' As the days pass, my wounded leg doesn't improve. There are times I accept this. At least I'm alive, I say, but other times I'm frightened.

"'You might have a better chance of improving if you tried to do something physical,' the American nurse tells me.

"'I doubt it,' I say.

"'What good does that do?' she says. 'Everybody has problems. You're lucky that most of yours came after you were born.'

"I'm in bed reading a *New York Herald Tribune* when the next letter from Rachel arrives. Overcome by the letter, I show it to the American nurse and she begins to read it aloud: 'We are all full of sorrow about Art.' She stops. After a brief silence, I say, 'So I learned my best friend died in Spain in a letter from

Canada that I read in a hospital bed in Spain.' She takes my
hand. Her face is filled with grief. My early days in Spain I
tried to reach Art, learned he was shuffled from the Abraham
Lincoln Battalion to the Mac-Paps, to the 35th Artillery bat-
tery at Teruel just two days before I arrived. Art's death on top
of my lifeless leg, the letter from Lena, the impending defeat of
the Spanish Republic. All of it overwhelms me. I stop reading
newspapers. Distractions die too. Now, I see my preoccupation
with Rosey's batting statistics as just another diversion from
things I didn't want to think about. Never followed the game
after that. Never sent the bitter letter to Lena. After thinking
it over and over again, I concluded she wasn't wrong that we
weren't right for each other.

"Worn down by the nurse's urgings, I finally relent. She helps
me out of bed and I soon take my first steps with crutches. Each
day I walk a little farther until I am outside. Like to sit under
the olive tree in the hospital's schoolyard, alone, sometimes
with her. Victor comes to visit one afternoon, and he and she
and I sit under the tree. Feeling slowly returns to my leg. In late
summer, I am dispatched to Barcelona. I stay around the barracks for awhile and they consider sending me back to Canada
because of the wound, but I don't want that. I am sent to the
front for the last battle. Serra de Pàndols. Hill 609. After that,
I'm sent to Ripoll and wait to be repatriated. I'm at the farewell
in Barcelona. Don't feel all that heroic, mind you — spent a lot
of my time in Spain in a hospital bed feeling sorry for myself."

"Come on," the reporter says. "You weren't in that bed by
choice." He presses the stop button that ends the interview.
"Thank you, Jack."

Funny how a short time can define a lifetime. For a lot of the volunteers, the Spanish Civil War years are the big memory, but when you think about it, the war lasted less than three years. I was there about a year and a half and so much of it's a blur. Before today, I didn't know I remembered some of the things I told the reporter. Never talked about most of it before. Haven't even thought about it. As the reporter and I begin to make our way out of the bar, he says, "By the way, did you get a chance to say goodbye to the American nurse?"

"She was away from the hospital when I received word to leave immediately for Barcelona. Saw her again just once before I was repatriated. She reached for my hand through the thick crowd at the Barcelona farewell and gave me a black rose. Before I could say goodbye, I lost her in the crowd and was swept away by the parade."

"Is she at the reunion?"

"Yes," I say. "Rebecca is at the reunion."

TWENTY-SEVEN

THE OTHER RETURN

Vancouver, 1983–86

W E HAVE COME TO VISIT FRIEDA AND EACH other. Molly, from her apartment in L.A., made the calls for a family get-together after she was hired as set decorator for a U.S. television movie being shot in Vancouver. I have missed other family gatherings, but as soon as Molly called I knew I would come to Vancouver this time. What is calling me back to Vancouver? I had to leave Spain and I had to leave Vancouver. Abruptly. Afterwards, I tried not to think about either. Lately, though, I've been thinking about both. So I will do things on this visit that I haven't done since I lived here.

Staying at the Sands Hotel downtown, I rise early and drive out to the university the morning of the day we are to reconvene. Technology will soon send the city into the twenty-first century, but a monorail that's being built to practically nowhere is all the city has to show for the flying cars, mobile sidewalks, and other futuristic forecasts of post-war magazine spreads. For now, the future is not what it used to be. Still, in some ways the Vancouver I drive through today is startlingly different from the city I knew. The intricately designed

granite and brick, wood and limestone buildings have begun
to be demolished to make way for characterless glass high-rises.
Neighbourhoods are now often named for the nearest mall.
The open-air shopping centres that postdated my Vancouver
are already being reconfigured as indoor malls — generic cities
that erase practically anything distinctive about the community they're located in. Stroll through these malls and Seattle
is Toronto is Philadelphia is Vancouver. They are places where
ethnic edibles such as pizza, sushi, and bagels are now bland
staples paper-dished out in food fairs. Their bookstores are
indistinguishable, each with a wall of Top 30 paperbacks and
tables heaped with large picture books named *Great Tanks of
World War Two*, destined to decorate some den's tabletop like
a porcelain lapdog. And outside, by the light of the all-night
convenience store, the young huddle, devouring microwaved
burritos and dyed-blue ice cones. The B.C. premier, like the
U.S. president and U.K. prime minister, thinks social progress
is the work of the devil. Shelters for the most vulnerable have
been closed by government decree, so the streets are asylums,
and sidewalks fill with the sick and the homeless and the abandoned, fashions by Smithrite. The writing is on the wall, and
on the bus stops, benches, and billboards: "We play in the fields
of freedom" and "Fuck the world, I want to get off."

None of this is to say that the up-to-date city I am visiting
on this spring day in 1983 is any less or more Vancouver than
the version of the place I knew a half-century ago. There are
things, too, about the city that have stayed the same or are better. I park my white Honda at the beach near the University
of British Columbia. Today's temperate weather is so comfortable that it's barely noticeable, not a hot or cold intrusion,
prompting some strollers to bundle in coats, others to wear

short-sleeved shirts. I begin the walk I used to take to be lost in contemplation. It's along a dirt path to an ocean trail of stone and washed-up wood blistered with barnacles. I step log by log and look across the sea to the most unusual of city skylines, a mixed marriage of mountains and skyscrapers. I turn away from Vancouver's downtown and continue to the sandy walls I could never scale, sit on dampened wood partially hidden by bush near the remains of a searchlight tower erected during World War II. When I first saw these towering walls, with Art and Georgie, they looked unyielding. After awhile, they looked surmountable and now, again, they look unyielding. I stand motionless, sizing up the challenge, turn to walk away, then spin around to attack the wall, hands clawing into the wet pasty sand, feet churning, bending twigs, climbing. Barely making headway, I slip back, muster one last heave upward, and slide down the wall's crumbling face.

On previous visits to Vancouver, I avoided Strathcona. The neighbourhood's Jewish streets were gone and the Japanese were gone too, but this time, this place, not by choice. This visit, though, I park and walk the old neighbourhood, past unknown faces on familiar sidewalks. As I walk on, the songs and the scents of the shtetl still rise from Menkus's synagogue, now the shell of a condominium, and from Sammy's Delicatessen, now a Vietnamese bakery. "Loyf un freyen zikh," my mother still tells me. "Run and be happy." My parents would have conversations in Yiddish. I don't speak as much Yiddish. My children less than me. In one of the linguistic oddities of modern times, there was the transformation of a people's everyday language, Yiddish, into a religious language used primarily by the Orthodox, while their religious language, Hebrew, was becoming an everyday language. But my generation, my children's generation, their children's generation, all carry a trace of Yiddish in our voices, even those without a word of it in their vocabulary. Heirs to inflections passed through the generations. How can a language be lost if it is in us all?

How much I know about this place. It is inside me, its past, like an unused language that will not die. Up Keefer Street, past the brick apartments and sloping wood frames, is the house, porch drooping. On Hastings Street, the destitute still do the dance, rubbing hands grown cold from being outside too long even though the day is not especially cold. So many passersby glance but don't see these people surviving on the street in fraying coats and worn-out shoes. When I pass by them, I think of veterans of World War I. That's who my father told me they were. But on this visit to Vancouver, I look beside the shadows on the sidewalks and see faces my age and much younger, veterans of later wars. Sometimes I'm surprised at how quickly I've become this old, but despite the aches, aging is nothing to be bothered by, and I tell myself I'll never be as young again as in this moment and probably never healthier. I wait at a corner's red light, by the domed library-turned-community centre.

Then, it happens.

A stout, grey-haired man comes up beside me, waiting for the same light to change. I look at him for a moment, turn away, but drawn back by a pin with a star on his navy blazer, I look again.

"I've... I have one of those," I say.

The man shoots me a curious look. He is a veteran of my war, on his way to a meeting of Mac-Paps, and on his chest is the pin we received from Friends of the Mackenzie-Papineau Battalion.

"Do you want to come along?" the man asks.

"I can't today. I'm meeting family for dinner." We exchange numbers, though, and he tells me his name: Henry Simmons. He also mentions that plans are already underway for a fiftieth-anniversary reunion of the volunteers in Spain.

I arrive at my mother's apartment building to take her to meet Molly and Daniel for dinner. When I walk in on her, she's on the couch watching *60 Minutes* on television and eating an orange. Her hands and pink flannel housecoat are dripping juice from the orange, hair is flattened, squinting eyes filled with sleep. But none of this embarrasses her — the very old and very young are perfectly unselfconscious. When my mother goes into her bedroom to change for dinner, she shouts to me through the wall: "I've got such a headache I can't even think straight. There's matzo ball soup in the fridge for you."

"Mom, we're going to dinner," I say. "Supposed to be there in fifteen minutes."

Before we leave, she hands me a cellophane-wrapped variety pack of vitamins. "I would take these with your meal," she says. "They'll give you strength."

The family convenes at the Gas Station, a trendy restaurant built into a service station abandoned a few years earlier during what headlines called "the oil crisis." Its enormous plastic-coated menus list designer potato skins and deluxe nachos, and gourmet burgers named after celebrated bergs, such as the Steven Spielburger and the Ingrid Burgerman. Its walls are papered with movie posters, record sleeves, and glossy autographed photographs, including one of Kenny Silver. By the time he left Fort Harold, Kenny's saloon-song style had been almost entirely shoved off the Top 30 by rock 'n' roll, but he's managed to make a living playing small clubs and hotel bars. While perusing a local entertainment weekly at the hotel,

I noticed that Kenny is at Chardonnay's, a downtown restaurant, "before his European tour."

Molly's dressed in black, a sling holding one arm, having broken it yesterday when she slipped in front of the hotel where she's staying. Daniel's hair is shorter than it was when I saw him in Fort Harold, but he has that casual West Coast way that tells you he is, or was, countercultural.

"How you feeling, Molly?" I say.

"I'm okay. Went to a preproduction meeting today."

"Rachel, Barbara — I mean, *Molly* — I would be careful working with that arm," my mother says.

"What do you think they're going to do," Daniel says, "slam dance at the preproduction meeting?"

"You're looking handsome as ever," my mother tells Daniel, and her fidgety grandson looks away. "It's a shame Barbara couldn't be here," she adds. "And Joanne. Where's that daughter of yours, Daniel?"

"Joanne and Grace get back late tonight from a week in Cuba," he says. "I'm going over to their place in the morning to see her."

"She's such a *shayna kleyna meydelah*," my mother says. "Beautiful girl."

A man at an adjoining table speaks loudly over a business meal. "When will you start the work?" he says.

"I'm an idea man," his youthful dinner companion shouts back, wagging a finger at a quiet third man. "He'll start the work."

"Where do all these people get all their money?" says my mother, inspecting the business diners digesting their baby-boom pablum.

"Stockbrokers, lawyers, I don't know," Molly says.

"Consultants, accountants, I don't know," adds Daniel.

"I don't like this place," my mother says. "You know, the Leonard boy owns it."

"Georgie?" I say in a pique. "If I knew that I wouldn't have come here."

"It's all right," she says. "Don't make a magilla."

"How was your day, Dad?" Molly says.

"Good… to be back on Keefer Street," I say. "I'm thinking of leaving Fort Harold."

"That'll be the day," Daniel says.

"Danny!" Molly says, admonishing her brother with a glare.

My mother gives Molly, then Daniel, disapproving looks. "*People*," she says, "fight over every little word." Then she lights a cigarette.

"You should quit smoking," Daniel tells her.

"I don't even know how to smoke," she says, butting her cigarette.

"You know, Daniel, there was a time when I was all set to move to L.A. to be with your mother and your sisters and you," I say.

Daniel looks surprised, then quizzical.

"And you didn't," he says.

"I have an announcement," Molly proclaims. "I am moving to Vancouver, for now. I've already got a job on another project after the TV movie wraps. And get this, it's a Film Board documentary about Mom and Auntie Rachel. *Ginger and Ginger* took Polly and Rachel more than a decade of starts and stops. There was collaboration between themselves and with other artists—writing and choreographing and workshopping—but their persistence eventually paid off with a successful New York run. Polly has moved to Toronto, too, where they operate a dance company, and their next show is about to open.

"We start work on the documentary in Vancouver, go back to where they grew up," says Molly. "Then we move everything out east, shoot at their studio, other places around Toronto. We'll be at the opening of their next production, *The Other: Woman*."

"They're the perfect subject for the National Film Board now that they're both living in Canada," Daniel says. "In America, performers know they've made it when they're booked on *The Tonight Show* with Johnny Carson. In Canada, they know they've made it when the NFB makes a documentary about them."

"That's wonderful news, Molly. This girl has got such a kop," says my mother, beaming at her granddaughter. "Such a mind. And she looks like a movie star."

"Which one?" Daniel says. "Ernest Borgnine? Edward G. Robinson?"

"Molly looks like her aunt Rachel," my mother says. "She's a doll but she needs to meet the right man."

Other eyes roll, but the old woman's twinkle, and we all laugh.

"I don't mean no fancy-schmancy," my mother clarifies. "A jeans guy."

As she hands Molly another packet of vitamins, I retell the story of Eddie and Joan's secret marriage, and we laugh again. Daniel, though, has quietly drifted away from the rest of us and slumps back in the booth. He lived in Vancouver for half a decade before moving back to Toronto two years ago. Now, he lives with friends in Kensington Market, gets by writing freelance.

"Danny," my mother says, "if I were you I'd think about moving here too."

"Thanks but no thanks. I've spent enough time on the West Coast. Not sure where I'd go if I left Toronto."

"How long are you here for, Danny?" Molly says.

"For the week," he says. "Staying with friends just off Commercial Drive."

"I like that neighbourhood," my mother says. "Italian."

"It's not as Italian anymore," Daniel says. "I suppose the young tragically hip have to live somewhere, and the Kitsilano neighbourhood that had epitomized hipness was now too gentrified for them, so it was on to *Life in the Espresso Lane*. And that's how so much of Little Italy got young and hip and dressed in black."

"I don't think anything of it," Molly says. "Change comes and change goes. That's still a great neighbourhood. And it's still pretty Italian."

"I know that," says Daniel.

"So Daniel," I say, "tell me, what's this I hear you're writing?"

"I'm working on a screenplay. It's a B-movie about a drug turf war between bikers and the mob. It'll be big at drive-ins."

"If they still had drive-ins," Molly says.

"This drive-in movie for a post–drive-in world will end in revolution," Daniel says, "and the people banish the bikers and mobsters to an island, without food except once a day, at dinnertime, a right-wing political prisoner is parachuted from an airplane. The perfect mealtime treat. And the perfect punishment. One day it might be an almost-impeached president, the next a prime minister or business executive, dropped into fifteen thousand starving bikers. The movie will be called *Devil's Angels Island*, or how about *Devil's Food Island*? Molly, you're in showbiz, think Hollywood would buy it?"

"Might do. Depends on the writing."

"I'm just kidding," Daniel says. "My values wouldn't allow me to write such a movie. You see, I'm socially responsible, downwardly mobile."

Before Molly's work brought her to Vancouver, she was holidaying in Jamaica. She's the family nomad, travelling through Europe with her mother's troupe, Asia more than once, and Jamaica the past two winters. "I feel I really belong there," says Molly, swallowing a Vitamin C capsule provided by my mother.

"Is Jamaica your Spain?" Daniel says. "I think that having uncritical affection for some other place gives people an anchor. It might be Jamaica for Molly or, for someone else, Nicaragua or India, or the Soviet Union, even Vancouver."

"I don't think it has to be a place on a map," I say. "There are reasonably intelligent people who lose all critical faculties when it comes to a certain thing in their lives, could be a place, but also a religion or an ideology, a people or a person. Or themselves. You can be insightful about everything but yourself, Daniel. But I think you're right — it can be a place. The place you choose is important."

"Yeah, it shows whether you've sold out or not," says Daniel, turning to me. "So what brings you out of exile?"

"Don't bother me with this crap. I still believe..." I start, stop. "Hok mir nisht kayn chainik."

"What does that mean?" Molly says.

"Hit me in the head with a frying pan," translates Frieda, turning to Daniel: "You worry too much about nothing, everything."

That stops the talk for what seems like forever but is maybe fifteen seconds. Daniel breaks the silence. "I'm sorry," he says. My mother gives him a broad smile.

"I like Jamaica — the culture, the music," Molly says. "I'm more comfortable there than any place."

"You don't have to explain," my mother says. "Molly's an ofen bukh. Sam always said 'Don't be an open book.'"

"That's okay to be," I say. "I like how open Molly is about herself. There are too many people with lots to say about everyone but themselves."

"Jake!" shouts a familiar voice.

"Jack," I say, looking up to see a chortling Georgie Leonard breathing over our table.

"Georgie," I say.

"George," Georgie says. "How are you?"

"Alive and kicking."

"We're alive," Georgie says. "Never mind the kicking. Alive's enough. Death is nature's way of telling you to fuck off — pardon the French, Mrs. Feldman — so there must be some reason why we're still around. You know we got lobster now at every Gas Station's happy hour."

Georgie made a small fortune as a crooked commodities lawyer, then a large one as a restaurateur. First, he amassed the Gas Station restaurant chain in converted service stations across the western provinces. Then came the Nanaimo Bar, pubs that served the custard/graham cracker/chocolate dessert gratis with every drink. That was followed by the Chocolate Bar, western saloons with long bars serving fifty-four chocolate drinks, from milkshakes to egg creams. The Chocolate Bar also offers chocolate by the slab, the box, the solitary hedgehog, or the two-foot-tall rabbit. This Bar is a surrogate 1950s TV mother, providing a glass of milk and plate of chocolate chip cookies for those nostalgic for the nuclear family.

"Jake, knowing your political persuasion, let me ask you about a sign I saw the other day, painted in big letters on a concrete wall near my place in Shaughnessy," says Georgie. "Said Eat The Rich. What does it mean?"

"Feed the poor," Daniel says, swallowing a bite of the vegetarian Hank Greenburger. "After we eat the rich, we'll appropriate your chocolate. Dessert."

Georgie gives Daniel a quizzical look. "This kid of yours sure don't sound like much of a go-getter, Jake," says Georgie. "Chip off the old block, I suppose. But he's young. They say if you are not on the left when you're young you got no heart, but if you are on the left when you're old you got no brain."

"How come it's always old right-wingers who say that?" I say.

"Brain-dead old right-wingers," adds Molly.

Daniel and Molly burst out laughing.

Georgie glances haughtily at the two laughing together unstoppably. "Gotta go. You snooze, you lose," he says. "Let's do lunch, Jake. We got lobster tails at the Gas Stations now."

"By the way, Georgie," I say, pointing to a Benny Goodman record sleeve on the wall, "if you're done listening to my records, I'd like to get them back."

As Georgie makes a hasty getaway, Molly turns to me. "Why are you thinking of leaving Fort Harold?"

"I belong here more than I belong there," I say, and tell them about my day at the beach and the old neighbourhood, meeting another Mac-Pap, learning about the reunion in Spain. And then I say it again.

"I'm going to Spain."

There is a fear on my mother's face that I've seen once before. "Just for the reunion, Mom," I say, erasing her worry for now.

"Jakie and his Spain," she says. "Loyf un freyen zikh."

When Molly called, I knew I would come to Vancouver this time, but it wasn't without trepidation. *Daniel is judgmental*, and even if I'd stayed in the city and become a crusading journalist or radical lawyer he would have thought it was small compared to what I did at twenty-one. When I met him at the Fort Harold Hotel, he wanted to know what kept his father in that town. A hidden life? Depression? Am I Fort Harold's answer to Wells's Ancient Maritimer and its other mystery men of the 1930s? When I told Daniel I didn't do much, it may not have sounded like much of an answer but it was true. *Molly is less judgmental.* She knows that city life is not necessarily better than living in a small town. She has long accepted that there is little mystery to my existence in Fort Harold — I watch too much television, work long days at the store, read in bed until my eyes burn, walk the wilderness trail down by the river, and drive Around the Hoop listening to Artie Shaw's "Frenesi" and Sinatra's "These Foolish Things." These activities, Molly figures, might be as good as it gets in Fort Harold. *Frieda isn't judgmental at all.* She is going to love me no matter what. At the Gas Station, I was struck by how much I share my mother's uncritical way of loving the others at this dinner table. No doubt Molly and Daniel do too. It's just that our uncritical love isn't as uncritical as my mother's was. Soon after the family convenes in the city, my mother dies. Not long after that, practically all of her contemporaries are gone too. And we are on our own. My generation. My family. Vancouver never seems quite the same place without my mother's kindness.

I move to Vancouver in the fall of 1983. When Polly and I left the city in the 1940s, any affection I had for it seemed pretty unrequited. Lately, though, I've been thinking back earlier to the Vancouver I liked growing up in — the bustle of Strathcona, the lively street politics, the picnics in Stanley Park. More importantly, though, returning to Vancouver is a late attempt to be closer to family and to mend relationships. My children either live in Vancouver or are just one flight away.

There is a loose organization of B.C. Mac-Paps and friends that followed up with me after my meeting with Henry Simmons at the Strathcona red light. They sent an invite to my Fort Harold address to the opening of a musical, *Wobblies in Love*, which had been written by retired newspaperman Bob Fucillo, a former Vancouver Wobbly and Mac-Pap. I have just moved to Vancouver, with plans to contact the local Mac-Paps, when I receive the forwarded invite just in time to go to the play's opening and sing the old Wobbly songs with everyone else. After the show, I meet other Mac-Paps. I know hardly any of these veterans but I do, too, and by end of the evening have signed on to help out with their Mackenzie-Papineau newsletter. The next day, I march in the Mac-Pap contingent at a demonstration against a landslide of right-wing legislation that's being enacted by B.C.'s Socred provincial government. It's modelled on the Ronald Reagan-Margaret Thatcher austerity theology. The rally is my first street protest since the Spanish Civil War.

Molly has moved to Vancouver, too, working full-time in the city's film industry. In 1986, she again calls our family together. Early morning, I stop at the Granville Island market where I'm meeting Daniel to shop for a family picnic, but first I climb to a second-floor window table, above a coffee bar called Rick's Place, where I read a newspaper and sip my drink and watch the waterfront. Through the window a small girl is wading carefree into a carpet of pigeons on the market's brick plaza. The pigeons relax the hunched feathers wrapped around them like blankets as they slowly, grudgingly, part for the girl, who looks around in wonder at what she has done. The very young and the very old are less self-conscious than the rest. As the girl, my granddaughter Joanne, draws away from the courtyard, the pigeons instantly take her place, some peck-fighting for her discarded bag of peanut shells.

While Daniel and I watch Joanne, he tells me about his first conversation with her mother, Grace. Daniel met Grace in Flint, Michigan, at a "War Conference" of radical New Left groups. Over breakfast at a pancake house, Grace and Daniel talked about their lives, their families. He told her what I did in the 1930s. She was impressed with that. Said her father was in the Republican Party.

"But not," Grace said, "like the Goldwater Republicans back home in Arizona. He's like the more liberal Republicans in New York — Jacob Javits, John Lindsay." Daniel was unimpressed with this distinction among Republicans.

"I haven't liked a Republican since the Spanish Civil War," he told her.

She laughed. Came up to Toronto with Daniel. "Joined the Vandals too." Eventually, they moved to the West Coast. They're separated now but both dote on Joanne.

The girl runs into her father's arms. We meet the rest of the family at Molly's apartment and load into my car for the drive to Stanley Park. Barbara has come this time too. I'm pleased that Daniel has brought Joanne. "What do you call a country full of pink cars?" Joanne says. "A pink car-nation," she answers when we can't. "When I picked up Joanne this morning," says Daniel, "Grace told me she can live in Vancouver for months without meeting one new person she would care to go for coffee with, but on a one-week vacation in Mexico she and Joanne were meeting interesting people all day."

"I guess socializing is the point of travelling as much as anything else," Barbara says.

At the park, we begin with the tree. A cement curb now prevents motorists from backing into the hollow cedar, the result of a miscreant drinker who almost toppled it. We walk inside the cool rotting wood. "What did the hippie say to the wall?" Joanne wants to know. "How come you're so straight?" she answers.

"She made that up," Daniel smiles.

"Shayna meydelah," Molly says. "Beautiful girl."

At the park's Brockton Oval, an expansive always-mowed, ever-green field, Molly unfurls the blanket from Lithuania and we sit in the sun eating our Sunday lox. Then I say, "I'm going away for a while, to Spain." Daniel and Barbara look up curiously from the Sunday *New York Times* sections spread on the blanket, and I tell them that the fiftieth-anniversary reunion is three weeks away.

"Daniel, that argument we had when you visited Fort Harold years ago — you know, the 1930s versus the 1970s — was the first time in so long that I'd gotten excited over politics. You made me realize I hadn't changed, at least not in any fundamental way. That conversation was really important to me. I went out the next day and walked with the forestry workers on their picket line."

"I had no idea," Daniel says.

"It was you that got me thinking about Spain again," I say. "Something you said about it. And that got me thinking about Vancouver. Everything."

"It's really great that you've reconnected with other volunteers," Molly says.

"Sometimes you have to be on your own for a while," I say, looking to Molly. "It takes time to rekindle self-esteem. Your mother told me that. And without self-esteem it's hard to do the right thing. You care too much about what everybody else thinks."

"You should think highly of yourself," Molly says, facing me. "Your mother told me that."

"You never talked about Spain," Daniel says quietly to me. "I mean, of course I knew you went, but that's all I knew. In my own political circles, Spain would occasionally be brought up. People still talked about what happened there in the 1930s, and sometimes I'd say my father fought in Spain and they would want to know more, but I didn't have anything else to say. I guess I didn't show any feelings about it because you didn't show any. Sometimes I would say, 'My Dad was unemployed, sitting on a park bench, and someone came along and asked if he'd go to Spain. He was broke and it was a way out of the Depression's poverty.'"

"But you knew that wasn't true," Barbara says. "In the 1970s, I was busy having kids, so my brain certainly wasn't focused on the political scene, but I still knew that Spain was more to Dad than that."

Daniel lowers his head, then turns to me. "I'm proud you went to Spain. I'm really proud of you."

"There's not many of us left," I say. "It might be the last get-together like this. And not a lot of Mac-Paps are going."

"Do you know Pac-Man?" Joanne asks me.

"Your grandfather is a Mac-Pap, Joanne," Daniel says. "That means he's a good man who wants to help people."

Before we leave the oval, Barbara, Molly, Joanne, and Daniel play catch. They share Daniel's old glove and my older one. As I sit back on the blanket and watch, Daniel swings the bat, sending the ball bouncing, then rolling towards the picnic spread. My hand instinctively snatches it. He places the bat down. It's beginning to rain. We squeeze into the car and curl out of the park, drive past Sylvia Goldstein, and make our way home through the city.

One week later, Polly is in Vancouver to see the kids. I have not seen Polly since I visited Disneyland and her sister's place two decades ago. Molly and Daniel debate whether to invite me to brunch with Polly, and once they decide to do that, I debate with myself whether to go. So that's how I wound up at Molly's apartment this morning.

I pull Polly aside and tell her something I've wanted to say for years.

"Even in our last few months together, you and I got along eighty percent of the time. I realize now that our conflicts at the end weren't your fault. Or mine. It was both of us. It takes two to tangle."

"It's tango," says Polly. "It takes two to tango. That's the expression."

"I know," I say. "It was a play on words. A joke. I know it's tango.... Why is everything always about dance with you?"

She laughs, and the rest of the family, who've been eyeing the two of us warily from across the room, look relieved.

TWENTY-EIGHT

JOHN GARFIELD
KILLED WARD CLEAVER

Barcelona, fall 1986

"I USED TO THINK ABOUT WHAT IT WOULD BE LIKE TO be on an island," Rebecca says over dessert, "and in a way I've found little islands. Janice's place in Seattle, Susan's in L.A."

Rebecca and I, along with Simon Berman and Pauline Blum, are finishing a long seafood lunch at a cozy Barcelona restaurant. "I'm glad we had this chance to talk," Si tells me. "My good friend Richard Lillard told me yesterday, 'I have something to give Jake Feldman before this reunion is over.' A letter's been passed on to him that belongs to you." Pauline and Si want to go for a post-meal walk. "I want to go back to the hotel," says Rebecca. "freshen up before speaking at the meeting tonight." As Pauline begins her walk with Si, she stops, says, "I always figured, Rebecca, that Manhattan was your island."

Rebecca and I taxi to our hotels, speeding past sidewalks swarming with pickets and other protest that has spread since the troopers stormed the factory. "What does that say?" I ask when we pass a banner which soccer players have stretched around the building that houses their team's offices. "Football belongs to the people. Prepare the general strike," says Rebecca. The cab swings onto the Ramblas.

"Rebecca," I say, as the cab door opens at her hotel, "am I coming with you?"

Ward Cleaver murdered Lincoln John Garfield's friend Louie Lepetino. *Fallen Sparrow* is on television again, and while Rebecca showers I settle into an armchair and watch. Ward "does pretty well what he is told," a German agent tells John Garfield. "You dirty sadistic swine," Garfield says, drawing a revolver on the *Leave it to Beaver* patriarch. "I shot him," Garfield says after Ward dies. "Maybe it was self-defence, maybe it wasn't. I wanted to kill him." Garfield, off-screen, would be blacklisted, harassed to death at thirty-nine, but this evening in a hotel room in Spain he is a New York volunteer for Spain who speaks movingly of his Lincoln comrades and their banner. "A symbol of three thousand guys who were my friends," he says, "a symbol of everything in the world people are fighting for.... There'll be brigades forming again."

"I've seen this movie before," Rebecca says, nodding at the screen as she sits on the bed to dry her hair.

"So you knew that in the end John Garfield would kill Ward Cleaver," I say.

"Yes, I've known that all along," she says.

Rebecca and I go to a small, hot union office where she is among a half-dozen nurses welcomed by a Spanish hospital worker standing at a microphone. When Rebecca is called to the microphone, it is the first time I've heard her speak in public and I'm taken by her eloquence and her manner. Talking with her hands as much as her voice, in Spanish as much as in English, she tells of the urgent need for medical supplies in Nicaragua, likening its conditions, under bombs and bullets, to Spain. The applause for her fades, and hospital workers mill with their guests in the crowded steamy room, doors and windows open wide to the evening rains. I sip wine and chat with an assistant to the Australian prime minister, at the reunion to research a book on volunteers from her country. Rebecca stands beside me talking with Sonny Abrams.

"Ever since Spain, whenever I see a nurse I think of you nurses," Sonny tells her. "There's this hospital I drive by on my way to work. The nurses there are on strike and they hold up a sign that says Honk If You Love Nurses. I honk all the time."

The Toronto reporter interviews the Spanish hospital worker who introduced Rebecca. A Spanish reporter interviews Kate Quigley and Sarah Weintraub. Sweat beads my face, soaks my shirt as the Australian tells me: "Barcelona is fascinating. I'm curious whether the syndicalists are still —"

Before she can complete the sentence the song begins and the conversational din stops. At first, voices are hesitant, then they swell. "The Internationale," mostly in Spanish, some English, but other languages too. Sonny Abrams sings "The Yiddish Internationale." The woman I've been speaking with sings "The Australian Internationale." Through the lyrical blizzard I see Rebecca across the room singing, and I step forward. "They're playing our song," I say when I reach her. I hold out my hand and we embrace.

The next afternoon, our penultimate day in Spain, I bus up the slopes of Montjuïc, a hill imposingly set between city and sea. The Spanish receiving committee for the volunteers has arranged for a tinny facsimile of a big band to play at Montjuïc's plaza overlooking Barcelona's harbour. With the end of the reunion about to begin, Bob Mitchell is pacing the entrance to the plaza. "Where's Irene? What's with Henry?" he says, approaching Rebecca and me as we make our way onto the plaza, where tables and chairs have been set up for us. The band is finishing "New York, New York." Rebecca takes my hand and leads me down five steps onto the expansive plaza floor. Sonny Abrams, usually in polyester slacks, vinyl windbreaker, and New York Mets cap, so you wouldn't mistake him for anything but a tourist out to capture Barcelona with the camera slung over his shoulder, is wearing a dark suit, tie, and fedora as he grips the microphone and sings "A cigarette that bears a lipstick's traces."

And we dance. Ballroom dance on stone. Pirouettes, Rebecca does, spinning under my outstretched arm as I stand my stiff body on its toes and reach. Others step onto the floor. The Toronto reporter with Susan Barkley. Hildy and Mel Fox. Simon Berman with Pauline Blum and Bob Mitchell. David Zinn with a nurse from Norway. Sadie and Barney Savransky. So many others. But Rebecca and I are centre stage. "A tinkling piano in the next apartment, Those stumbling words that told you what my heart meant," sings Sonny. "These foolish things remind me of you." As the piano fades, the other dancers shuffle aside, Rebecca performs an elegant curtsy and I bow. Our hands drop to a ripple of applause and we return to our table as the band plays on and Sonny starts another song. "I've flown around the world in a plane, I've settled revolutions in Spain..."

"Susan, where's Tom?" says Bob, finding a chair alongside Susan Barkley.

"Oh, he's visiting that Spanish family he was looking for. He'll be back soon."

"They're marching on the capital," shouts Josh Beren. "All hell's breaking loose, again."

As my fellow travellers and I watch the musicians play and each other dance, the mood is jocular, spirits bolstered by Spain's escalating strike and tomorrow's return home. "The students have taken the Autonomous University in Madrid," the Toronto reporter says. "They've seized the docks in Valencia," adds Beren.

"Yeah," Mel Fox bellows, "but who the hell's won the World Series?"

"Boston," a voice answers.

"Barcelona," says another.

"Brooklyn."

I walk over to Sal Scarsone's table, "Do you know," I say quietly, "who *has* won the Series?"

"The Mets did," Sal tells me with conviction. "Went to a seventh game. Something to do with Buckner. Mets won it 8 to 5. Today."

"Good," I say. "I like what I've been reading about the Mets. Scrappy. New York... You remember Rosey Goodman?"

"Sure I do," Sal says. "Why do you ask?"

"I knew Rosey. He hit .325 and made the National League all-star team in 1938. It was his last good year."

Sal smiles. "Probably my last good year too."

As I return to my table, Richard Lillard hands me an envelope. "Jake," he says, "take a look at this."

"Sure could use some coffee," Bob Mitchell says, dropping into a chair across from me. Such cravings will have to wait because our server breezes past us and darts around tables until he reaches the front and hands Sonny Abrams a note.

I watch Sonny pull back from the microphone, read to himself, then say in an impassioned tone that silences the clamour: "I have an announcement!…Today, explosives tore apart a statue of Franco that was standing in a square in Valencia." The reunion is silent for a few seconds, then there is a steady applause, which grows louder and into a crescendo. Now, a part of Franco's Spain has left Spain before the volunteers in this plaza leave.

Sonny begins another song, "The way you wear your hat," and the plaza fills with dancers. I turn my chair and sit with my back to our table to better watch the revelry, knowing it is the last time I will be in Spain with so many of the others who had to be here too. My eyes lock on Rebecca. She's at Sarah Weintraub's table, leaning close to her friend, both laughing. Rebecca stops laughing. She is facing me, looking past me, and then she is up from the table racing towards me. There is a wail behind me. I have been watching Rebecca, but now turn to see Bob slumped, face down. Others rush to him. The din stops, the area clears, Rebecca resuscitates. Ambulance attendants arrive. Rebecca and I leave with them. As we exit, the hush in the plaza leaves too.

"We'll bury my father in Spain," says Bob's daughter when I get through to her in San Francisco. "He always thought he would die there."

Departures are postponed a day for a hastily organized memorial for Bob at Plaça Reial, a plaza off the Ramblas, and the busloads travel the bittersweet streets one more time. The Lincoln banner is unfurled again. But every kind of volunteer for Spain is here. From Canada, Peter Krawchuk has come.

Susan Barkley, too. Andy Tompkins. The Toronto reporter is here without his tape recorder. Bob's daughter and grand-daughter caught the next flight out and have just arrived. Mel Fox has agreed to speak. At the plaza, he approaches me.

"Someone from the Mac-Paps should talk about him too," Mel says.

"A lot of the battalion seems to have disappeared," I say.

"You speak."

Mel is warmly received when he talks about Bob and the everlasting bond between Mac-Paps and Lincolns. When he finishes, I place the flower pouch I'm holding on the plaza floor and step up to the microphone. As I start to speak, a van driven by Sofia Peiro stops at the edge of the plaza. The van's side panel opens, and out comes a young Spanish man. Then Aaro, Irene, Tom, Henry.

"I only met Bob Mitchell two weeks ago, as this reunion was getting underway in Madrid, but I feel like I've known him a very long time," I begin. "Sharing hotels, tour buses, and Spain's Civil War for two weeks is a sure way to fast-track new friend-ships. The more I got to know Bob, the more I learned about all of us. He cared deeply for his fellow volunteers and before he died was in a rush to make sure we'd be remembered. Not for any vain personal glory, but because we were among the first to understand fascism. And our international solidarity with Spain was an act of basic human decency that should live on in some way."

As I speak, I see the Spaniards give the Canadians good-bye embraces and get back into their van. Sofia and the young man were the twenty-something Spaniards at the hotel bar the other day with Henry and Tom. Now, they drive off and the Canadians straggle towards the sound of my voice.

"Bob told me he thought he would die in Spain back then. And pretty much all of the volunteers here today have friends who would be with us at this reunion but for a random bullet at Gandesa or Belchite. Bob could have died, I could have died in Spain and been a young face in an aging photograph in some family album for the past fifty years.

"To Bob's family and others who love him, his name and this country are synonymous. Spain *was* Bob, and the goodness of its fight is one thing he never doubted. The eyes of the world were on this country when he arrived in 1937. What Bob found here — what we all found — was a moment of truth in a time of advancing madness. Spain showed the world what it was up against in the 1930s. There can be a moment of truth between two people. The Spanish Civil War was a moment of truth for the world."

Henry, in heavy grey overcoat dangling open, is the first to reach the memorial. He's immediately joined by Irene, Aaro, and Tom, and the four stand attentively in back of the reunion crowd.

"Yesterday, Richard Lillard handed me this letter I had never seen before," I say, holding it up for the crowd to see. "It's from my best friend, Art Posner, who did die here then. It says as much about Bob as it does Art.

"'Dear Jake,'" I read out. "'I'm going to die in Spain....My mother told me how death was everywhere when the pogrom came to her neighbourhood in Odessa. The mob gouged one man's eyes with a stick. A woman was pushed under a streetcar and crushed to death, a baby was strangled and her arms torn off. Other mutilations, murders. They ransacked homes, threw our broken personal belongings into the streets. From her second-floor window, my mother, who was just a child, saw the most extraordinary sight. Streets of snow in July. But it wasn't snow. The streets were covered in white feathers. From torn pillows, duvets. Clouds of feathers rising from the street. Everywhere.'

"'In the bed next to me there's a Lincoln comrade, Dick Lillard, descended from slavery. His grandmother was beaten unconscious, died in her torched house when the pogrom came to her neighbourhood in Memphis. It's all got to end somehow, some place. I'm thinking that maybe way down the road some kid will find a tattered book about Spain on a grandparent's bookshelf and take heart that once upon a time there were people who travelled across this world to try to end it. I won't live to see it end, but maybe, if you and I didn't do this that kid wouldn't do whatever he or she will do. Who knows? Maybe our deaths—and our lives—will give other generations the will to live. Your Friend and Comrade, Arthur.'

"Being in Spain in the 1930s taught us that we have the potential to do enormous good. Being in Spain at this reunion with Bob and the rest of you taught me that living a life of purpose means you hold on to some of the idealism, the attitude you had at twenty. Bob did that. May his memory be an inspiration. *He fought in Spain* is his epitaph."

The crowd walks slowly through the plaza to the waiting buses. Henry, Aaro, Irene, and Tom tread against the flow until they reach me. We embrace, then begin the walk to the bus that will take us to our hotels.

"I guess," I say to no one in particular, "you heard that a statue of Franco was blown up."

"We heard it," says Tom, stepping arm in arm with Susan.

"That demonstration the other day," I say, "it was something."

"Agreed," says Henry.

"It was," the reporter adds.

"I found out the name of the concoction I drank in Spain," Tom says, closing the fingers on his outstretched hand as if holding a small glass of liqueur. "It's called queimada. Boy, is it hot. Beautiful drink."

"I learned something new about an old box of feathers," I say.

"Jesus, it's a grand country," Henry says. "When we get home, I might pack up everything and move here for the rest of my life."

"It never dawned on me that Spain would mean this much," Tom says.

"Me too," says Susan.

"It's funny how some things stick with you," Peter says.

"I'm going to stay around Barcelona for awhile," Irene says, "then Ireland."

"I have things to get back to in New York," says Rebecca.

"I've a newsletter to produce in Vancouver," I say, "and I might try writing about all of this."

"What do your children think of you?" Irene says.

"Proud," Rebecca says.

"Really proud," I say.

"Hey, Tom," Henry grins. "That was something, you telling that guy. RCMP...or FBI."

They push off each other lovingly, playful, and laugh.

Aaro thumps his chest.

I hand Rebecca a black rose.

TWENTY-NINE

ISLANDS OF LIGHT

Hornby Island, fall 1986

W E LOOK BELOW ON ISLANDS OF LIGHT AS THE plane from Madrid via Toronto descends into Vancouver. At night, the city from the sky above, black with scattered white lights, looks like the sky from the city below. The next day we awake early and Rebecca and I motor through the narrow Stanley Park causeway, then along the West Vancouver ocean drive, seeing in the morning night the lighted porches and streetlamps and luminous signs that go unnoticed in daylight. We drive onto the ferry vibrating in the calm harbour where mauve and white lights dance on the black ripple. Soon after the boat pulls away from the lights at the terminal, the window beside my seat in the lounge turns blinding black. On board, there is an ethereal quiet, somnolent passengers curled up in chairs or queued for coffee. As the inky darkness breaks, Rebecca and I stand at a railing on deck, salty wind slapping back our hair, the cold freezing crisp our hands and faces. Below us, gulls glide close to the water that is churned by the coursing ferry then breaks like cloudbursts beneath the surface of the ocean and turns to suds.

"Is that it?" Rebecca says as we approach the silhouette of an island.

"No."

"What's that one called?"

"I don't know. We pass a lot of islands on the way to the island."

We will return to the city, but for now the key to Irene Blair's cottage is with Rebecca and me, her island ours for a month. As the ferry reaches its destination, a fiery red burns through the grey in a distant sky, and for as far as we can see there are islands wrapped in transparent cloud.

"Oh my God, this is gorgeous, absolutely gorgeous," Rebecca says.

We're almost blown over making our way around the bow to get inside and join the awakening passengers eating eggs in hollandaise sauce, tabulating hockey pools from a morning paper, playing bridge and solitaire.

Exit the ferry and we're in autumn rust and scarlet. We drive up Vancouver Island's coastal highway through towns with waterfront motels and blackbirds wading on pebbly beaches. At every pit stop along the highway, there are signs — large ones that say Coffee Shop or Store and larger cutouts of strawberry ice cream cones. We don't stop before reaching a bay with a ferry terminal. As we park to wait for the ferry, smaller than the last, that will take us on a trip, shorter than the last, Rebecca points at an island facing us. Flat with Douglas fir trees and wild ferns, it looks like a multi-coloured head of spiky hair.

"Is that our island?" she says.

"No. Not yet."

There is a burst of rain at the bay, then sun as we float to this nearby island and drive across it to an even smaller ferry for the short voyage to Irene's island. "That's it," I say, sighting

a mountain of greens and browns, yellows and oranges rising from the sea. From the ferry, we enter Hornby Island and
drive along its winding country roadway streaked with fall
foliage and shadow and light, past cottages and farms and
campgrounds, a ballpark, community hall, bakery, little rainbow schoolhouse. At the island's rustic shopping centre, Tofu
Town, there is a spacious food co-op, which sells everything,
and diminutive wooden shops with books and bicycles and
iced espresso. Rebecca and I find a split-log bench and sit in
the soft autumn sun, munching the island's chewy bagels.

A child crawls beside us onto her older sister's lap, ice cream
dripping from her hands, smeared across her face. "I've found
paradise," their father is sputtering into the public telephone
on the co-op's porch. In sand-soaked running shoes and faded
jeans, his stomach protruding from a worn orange T-shirt with
LEN stencilled on its back, he talks to his suburban law office
in California. "I can't explain it, really," he says. "We discovered
this place by accident, just driving up the coast. But I don't
want to leave. My daughter Sheri hasn't watched television for
four days. She told me, 'It's the first time in my life that I hav-
en't been around a TV. And I don't miss it at all.'"

Rebecca and I walk to the beach and along the shore, the
water washing against pockmarked rocks and smooth slabs
piled onto one another as mysteriously as Stonehenge. We
skirt walls of stone, some cave-shaped, one a giant Halloween
mask with Sasquatch beak and black boulder eyes. The greyish-
brown stone and the sand have taken on a resemblance like
some long-cohabited couples do, unclear where one ends and
the other begins. When we turn back, tidal water is seeping
through this stone garden, so we take shoes and socks off and
our feet sink slightly into the wet sand on the walk to the car.

We drive to a more deserted beach. Rebecca and I have the ocean to ourselves and roll up our pants and play, splashing each other, doing pirouettes in shallow water. Then we sit on beach thick with tangled seaweed, facing distant whitecaps and watching the crystalline bay turn translucent turquoise, then indigo, then darker. Near this second beach there is a park with a trail, a matting of pine cones and needles and leaves, through dense sprouting forest that catches most of the light rain before it can touch us. We follow the trail to a clearing, then step inside an Emily Carr painting, bunched trees now spaced, omnipresent firs, reddish butts rising branchless into aged ashen fingers reaching at the sky. Forest turns to tall brown grass, the trail to a coastal pathway rolling on hills above the beach. As we walk, slopes between the path and the shoreline become cliffs of compacted rocks, and the wind blows hard. We stop at a bench overlooking a smaller island with crystal-green water lapping its shore.

I say the first words between us since reaching Hornby Island.

"This is a nice place to sit."

Rebecca takes a deep breath.

"The Cliffs of Dover have nothing on this," she says.

"I'd like to savour this moment for awhile," I say.

"You talked about moments of truth," she says. "The key, I think, is to use those moments as openings to the rest of your life."

"Like Spain," I say.

"We did what we did and it made sense then," she says, "and it does now too."

The wind stops. Rebecca looks away from me. I lean forward to follow her eyes to a deer standing in grass and trees behind the bench. In the seconds it takes for Rebecca to glance back at me and reach out her hand, the deer is gone. I take her hand and we return along the rolling path and through the woods to the car. Rebecca and I are quiet again, driving, watching, holding hands. There is a fine rain and the sun shrouds the island like a coat of paint. We pass a corner and a dip in the road, and below, through a blaze of amber maple leaves rising from the hillside, there is a deep green pasture reaching to the breaking sea and to islands on the horizon.

Rebecca and I turn onto a dirt road to a cottage on the water, set in a garden of fern, bramble, violet.

And we rest.

AUTHOR'S NOTES

Thank you to my gifted colleagues at Ronsdale Press: Wendy Atkinson, Robyn So, and Kevin Welsh. Thanks, too, to my old friend David Lester for his striking cover art and design.

ABOUT THE AUTHOR

David Spaner has been a feature writer, movie critic, reporter, and editor for numerous newspapers and magazines. Born in Toronto and raised in B.C, David is a graduate of Simon Fraser University and Langara College. He's also been a cultural/political organizer (Yippie and manager of the legendary punk band The Subhumans). David is the author of *Dreaming in the Rain: How Vancouver Became Hollywood North by Northwest* and *Shoot It! Hollywood Inc. and the Rising of Independent Film.* His most recent book, *Solidarity: Canada's Unknown Revolution of 1983*, was nominated for the George Ryga Prize for Social Awareness in Literature.